GALLOWGLASS

GALLOWGLASS #1

JENNIFER ALLIS PROVOST

CONTENTS

EVERYTHING IS NOT OVER

"**T**his can't be happening."

Chris paced back and forth across my living room, doing his best to wear a hole in the carpet. We usually hung out in his larger Manhattan apartment, but the paparazzi camped out in the lobby had ruined that idea. Actually, all of this was happening because Chris's ex-fiancée had gone on every talk show that would book her, and spilled her guts about their relationship. That meant Olivia had ruined things.

"I just..." Chris stopped and scrubbed his face with his hands. "I can't lose my job too. I just can't. God, Rina, what am I going to do?"

"I don't know," I whispered. Not the best response, but my mind was reeling with my own drama. I hadn't even told Chris about my alcohol-fueled late night hookup with Jared, and how I was terrified he would tell my advisor and somehow get me kicked out of my program. I didn't even know if Jared could get me kicked out of my program, but he was a teacher's assistant, and I was just a student. Based on how the school viewed things between Chris and his ex, they didn't like those enrolled dating any members of the student body, much less a faculty member.

No matter what Jared pulled on me, Chris was much worse off than I was. I was still a student at Carson University, but Chris worked there. He had graduated years ago—with a doctorate in Shakespeare, of all things—and currently taught Elizabethan literature. He was also a bestselling author, which, until recently, had been a great side job.

Olivia had been one of Chris's students. He admitted being attracted to her as soon as they met, but he'd waited until the last day of class before asking her out for coffee. Fast forward three years and one lawsuit later, and they were having a very public breakup, one that the university was not at all pleased with.

My stomach growled, and I remembered the coffee and bagels I'd picked up earlier, and left on the floor outside Jared's door. "Come on, let's go to the diner," I said. "Everything is always better on a full stomach."

"Fine," Chris grumbled. "I just hope no one recognizes me."

"The only people that will recognize you are the cooks." I almost said that he wasn't that famous of an author, but that wasn't what people were recognizing him for these days. I grabbed my wallet, looked inside and swore; I'd used the last of my cash earlier that morning, and my stipend wouldn't be in my account for another two days.

"I'm broke," I said. "Can you pay this time?"

"No idea," Chris replied. "Olivia's lawyers threatened to freeze my accounts."

"Can they even do that?"

Chris shrugged. "Does it matter? It's over. Everything is just... over."

I took a deep breath and assessed the situation. It wasn't good. "Okay, I'll just make us some coffee here," I said, then I heard a clang at the door.

"Don't open it," Chris shouted.

"It's just the mail slot," I said. I scooped up the mail, and noticed a large blue envelope. The return address read Spiritual Research Organisation of the United Kingdom. I'd never heard of them, but then again, I was only familiar with the US-based organizations. Intrigued, I ripped it open.

"I mean, plagiarism?" Chris wailed. "She's suing me for plagiarism? I teach this crap, of course I didn't plagiarize anything!"

"Did you mention that to your lawyer?" I asked as scanned the contents of the mailer.

"Yeah. About a minute after that, the school put me on administrative leave."

I should have said something then, or at least gasped or grunted in his direction. Instead, I stared at the paperwork from this Spiritual Research place. The cover letter explained that the board of directors had come across my master's thesis on ley lines, and were offering me a grant to continue my doctoral work in the UK, primarily Scotland. The grant would cover all of my transportation and living expenses, and included a stipend for food and other necessities...and a traveling companion. Best of all, I could book my flight as soon as the board received my signed paperwork.

I could get away—far away—from Jared, and the mistake I'd made. Chris could go someplace where no one thought he was a criminal. We could get our lives back, if only for a little while.

"Chris," I said, "Do you want to go to Scotland? Like, now?"

DOON HILL

"**I** can't believe you're dragging me to another old rock."

I glared at Chris. Why had I brought him along, again?

"It's not an old rock. It's a church. And since we're in Scotland, it's called a kirk." I would have said more, but I needed to concentrate. This driving on the wrong side of the road business was for the birds.

"Kirk," Chris repeated, rolling the word around in his mouth. "And, what are 'kirks' made of?"

I scowled at him, almost veered into a ditch, and jerked the car back onto the road. I'd grown up in northern New Jersey just over the water from New York, which was the Mecca of public transportation. I'd done more driving during these last two weeks in the United Kingdom than I'd done in my entire life. "Chris, do you have to be such a jerk all the time?"

"Rina, do you have to be such a bad driver?"

"Stop drinking all that complimentary Scotch, and you can do the driving."

"When in Rome."

He had a point. Nearly every place we'd visited in Scotland had either presented us with a few samples of the local whisky, or boasted a friendly proprietor with a flask at the ready. Add these samples to all the pubs we'd visited, and the many pints we'd downed, and my liver was starting to ache.

"Besides," Chris continued, "if I was driving, you wouldn't get to drag me to every known fairy sighting in the UK."

"You liked Stirling," I reminded him. During our tour of Stirling Castle's grounds, Chris had made full use of that Shakespeare degree by randomly quoting the Scottish play, despite the guide's many reminders that *MacBeth* was a work of fiction. After the third time he shouted, "Out, out, damn spot!" I was worried she'd deck him.

As for me, I was working toward a Ph D in geology at Carson, just a few buildings over from where Chris lectured about dead Elizabethans. Since I was technically in the UK to research my thesis, I was mostly interested in Stirling Castle's location on the Stirling Sill, a quartz-rich expanse of bedrock that ranged throughout the countryside. Though the ghost stories were cool, too.

I'd always been interested in supernatural occurrences, which was the main reason I'd applied to Carson. It was one of the few North American schools that studied mystical subjects as well as the mundane. I'd ended up majoring in geology and minoring in alchemy; both subjects concerned the earth and how its elements worked together, though it was hard to do any real alchemical work in the states since the transmutation regulations had gone into effect over one hundred years ago. Back when railroad barons had still been a thing, some politician had gotten the idea that alchemists would go around transmuting all the base metals into gold, thus using up all the iron and subsequently bankrupt the industry. My advisor speculated that the politician had tried transmuting metals into gold himself and failed, and had a case of sour grapes. All I knew was that if it really was that easy to create gold from things like iron filings and aluminum foil, instant noodles wouldn't be my go-to dinner.

When the packet about the research grant had arrived in my mail slot, I knew it was the perfect opportunity to learn more about my minor, and fine-tune my thesis. That, and putting an ocean between mine and Chris's problems was about the only thing keeping us sane.

My brother didn't believe in anything that he couldn't see and touch and smell, never mind that his department chair was a scholar so old he'd studied under Aristotle. That was the rumor, anyway. I'd always found it ironic that the least magical guy in the world taught at the most renowned magical university on the east coast. Chris was of the opinion that all magic had died out centuries ago, and magical creatures along with it. Most shared that viewpoint, even those en-rolled in alchemy and other metaphysical courses, which is why I kept most of my ideas to myself. I didn't need some nonbeliever casting a critical eye on my work. My work just needed to get done.

"At least real people lived at Stirling," Chris said as we pulled into the car park. "What sort of imaginary creatures inhabit this kirk?"

"No imaginary creatures." Not letting yourself be baited is a crucial survival tool for younger sisters. I pulled up the emergency brake, pocketed the keys, and jammed my water bottle into my daypack. "There was a reverend here in the seventeenth century called Robert Kirk, and he had dealings with the local fairies and elves. I guess this place is something of a *nemeton*," I said as we got out of the rental.

"*Nemeton?*"

"You know, a magical place alongside a church," I explained. Chris gave me a look over the roof of the car, raising a single eyebrow. That had always irritated me, since my own eyebrows refused to act independently. Chris must have some mutant extra muscle on one side of his head. My brother is a freak. "Anyway, the reverend wrote a book telling everyone their secrets, and it angered the fairies so they imprisoned him in the tree at the top of Doon Hill, just past the kirk. They still call the tree the Minister's Pine."

"Anyone can write a book," Chris grumbled. "I've written several."

I bit my lip; Chris had just enough midgrade liquor in him to be itching for a fight, and anything I said about his crumbling literary career, good or bad, would add fuel to the fire. After a few moments of silence, I said, "The walk starts with that bridge."

Chris and I started walking toward the stone bridge that spanned the River Forth. "Did you get a pamphlet about this place?" he asked.

"Yeah." I rooted around in my daypack, and pulled out the wad of information supplied by Spiritual Sights of the UK, the tour group my research grant had booked on my behalf. I was glad that I'd opted for the cheaper, self-guided package, and hadn't saddled a hapless tour guide with my brother's foul attitude for the duration of the tour. That sort of torment was reserved for family.

I pulled out the slightly rumpled pamphlet and handed it over. Chris opened it, scanning the paragraphs with an English professor's ease. "The reverend wasn't taken by fairies," Chris said. "He had a stroke while he was walking around the hill."

"You know where the term stroke comes from?" Without waiting for his smart-ass reply, I continued, "It was thought that a fairy stroked your cheek. That's why only one side was paralyzed."

"Thank God for modern medicine," Chris muttered. We reached the remains of the kirk, and headed toward the cemetery. Chris might think I was a loon, but he readily agreed that gravestones were cool. After we poked around for a few minutes, he announced, "Look, your man's buried right here. Case closed."

I walked over to where Chris was standing, and gazed at the minister's grave. It was a headstone coupled with a long rectangular slab that was set flush to the earth. The slab was engraved with a shield, and the inscription, *Hic Pultis Ill Evangeli Promulgator Accuratus et Linguae Hiberniae Lumen M. Robertus Kirk Aberfoile Pastor Obiit 14 Maii 1692 Aetat 48.*

"Can't these people write in English," I muttered. "What is that, French?"

"Latin. It says, 'Here lies the accurate promulgator of the Gospels and light…no, *luminary* of the Hibernian tongue, Robert Kirk, pastor of Aberfoyle, who died May 14, 1692, aged 48'," Chris translated. I guess it hadn't been a waste of his time to take eight years of Latin. "Do you know why they called him a 'luminary'?"

"He was some sort of language expert, and translated things like the Bible and the Book of Psalms from Latin into Gaelic," I replied. "I think he was the first to do so." Chris grunted; while he would never lower himself to read a book about fairies, he maintained a healthy respect for his fellow scholars. After a suitable moment of silence, I suggested we climb the fairy hill.

"We're here, so we might as well," I said when Chris whined. "Besides, the walk will burn off some of that booze."

Chris grumbled as he followed me toward the hill. After a far longer and more difficult climb than I'd anticipated, we stood at the top of Doon Hill, gazing at the Minister's Pine.

The tree was, in a word, magnificent. It was old and stately, like a Scottish version of Yggsdrasil, and wishes, scrawled on white or colored bits of cloth, were tied to the branches and tacked to the wide trunk. More offerings were nestled around the gnarly old roots, and shiny coins and colorful bottle caps were jammed into the bark.

"Some walk," I grumbled, digging in my pack for my water bottle. The water was warm, but it was better than nothing.

"So, they say the preacher's still in here, huh?" Chris leaned close to the trunk, and picked at a coin. "Why hasn't anyone tried to chop it down, set the poor guy loose?"

I shrugged. "To keep from angering the fairies?"

Chris barked a laugh. "Yeah. Or, they don't want to kill this golden goose of a tourist trap." I glanced around at the packed dirt path and discarded crisp packets; Disneyland, this was not. "This stuff is all so lame, Rina. Honestly, I don't know what you see in all these bedtime stories."

I fingered one of the cloth prayers, scrawled in a child's hand on a red strip of cloth; it read 'save my Mum'. "They remind us of where we came from, where we're going. They're comforting."

Another barking laugh. I suspected that Chris had had more complimentary whisky than he'd let on. "Comforting? That's your explanation for all of this nonsense—that it's *comforting*?"

"Of course," I said, trying to keep my voice even. Chris would sober up soon enough, and my normal brother would be returned to me. I hoped. "Why would people keep doing these things," I gestured at the tree, all of the flapping bits of cloth prayers and the offerings scattered about, "if no one ever got anything out of it?"

Chris looked from me to the tree, and back at me. "If all this goddamn magic shit is real, then why is my life over?" he ground out. "You think I didn't pray for an answer? For Olivia to come back to me? I did. Every single day, I did. You know what I got?" His voice cracked, and he looked toward the horizon. "Nothing. Because there's nothing to get."

He stalked down the hill, muttering away about the uselessness of magic and prayers. I watched him until he disappeared around a curve, then I turned back to the tree.

"Don't worry," I said, patting the rough bark. "I believe in you, Reverend Kirk. I know what really happened. And I'd rescue you if I could."

All the Whisky in Scotland

I stalked down the hill toward the rental car, mad at myself for lashing out at Rina, mad that she'd brought me to this God awful tourist trap, mad about so many things.

I was sick of being an angry jerk. My situation was the fault of exactly one person, and one person only: Olivia.

Olivia, whom I'd loved more than I thought I could love someone.

Olivia, who'd filed a lawsuit against me and was slowly, methodically, ruining my life.

I tripped over a rock, and caught myself against a tree. Once I was steady, I grabbed the rock and flung it as far as I could, and watched it drop soundlessly into the brush. Just like my life, the rock went out with a whimper rather than a roar. Shit. I'd do anything for a good roar.

I leaned against the tree, and gave myself a little pity party. In the past month, I'd failed as an author, teacher, and man, and I just couldn't wait to find out what else life had in store for me. All the whisky in Scotland couldn't make me forget how I'd screwed up, nor could it help me fix things.

I heard Rina on the path behind me, and felt like an even bigger jerk. Rina had just had her own bout of life kicking her in the arse, and was she wallowing in her sorrows like a pathetic sot? No, she was out living her life, working hard on her degree and moving forward. Rina was the one person who'd never doubted me, and the only one who had always had my back. If it wasn't for her, I don't know if I would have survived Olivia leaving me, and the rest of the fallout.

I straightened up and ground the heel of my hand against my eyes, not that I'd been crying. I'd moved past tears some weeks ago. I wanted to be strong for Rina, not some loser whose life was crumbling to bits. She's always been there for me, and I would be there for her.

I needed to be there for her, if for no other reason than to not fail again.

"Hey," Rina said, when she saw me after she rounded the bend in the trail. "You all right?"

"Yeah," I replied. "Just catching my breath." Rina eyed me, but said nothing. I hated that she'd been reduced to taking care of me, when I should be the one guiding her. "Would you like to get some lunch? My treat, even though you dragged me to another lame pile of rocks," I added.

Rina's face broke into a smile; she'd never been offended by my teasing, not when we were kids, and not now that we were adults. "I do like lunch. And I saw a really cute pub when we passed through Aberfoyle."

I nodded, then we resumed walking toward the car park. "Cute pub it is."

THE LUCKY QUARTZ

We drove away from the latest lame pile of rocks, as Chris had so eloquently put it, and went straight to the center of the village. Since the pub I'd wanted to go to had a window display of fairies dancing in a ring, I passed it and parked near the next, smaller pub. After how upset Chris had gotten at the kirk, and the last thing I wanted was to get into another argument. Besides, the poor guy had been through enough.

The pub was a seat yourself affair, so we picked a table near the bar. We'd just gotten settled when our waitress arrived.

"Welcome, welcome," she said as she set down menus. "Drinks to start?"

"Beer, a big one," Chris said.

"I'll have tea," I said. "What kind of soup do you have?"

"Today's is a cullen skink."

"Um." I glanced at the menu. "That's fish, right?"

The server smiled. "Aye, 'tis fish. A bowl with some bread and butter then?" I nodded, and she glanced at Chris. "And for you?"

"May I get a sandwich, roast beef or something like that? And a whisky with the beer," he added.

"O' course ye may." She gathered up our menus, and we stared out the window at the car park. When our drinks were delivered, we silently tended them, me stirring my tea and Chris downing his whisky. As I watched my brother wallow in alcohol and despair, my heart cracked a little further. It killed me to see him like this; it killed me even more that there wasn't anything I could do for him, short of turning back time, and I'd watched way too many science fiction movies to think that would end well. I'd probably step on a butterfly and ruin the world.

"What are you going to do when we get back home?" I ventured.

"What can I do?" he countered, staring into his beer. "I've lost my job, I've lost my reputation… Hell, I'm about to lose my home." He uttered one of those short, barking laughs. "Maybe I'll burn all the copies of my books and set up shop in the shipping boxes. Maybe the garbage men will pick me up, throw me in a trash compactor, and put me out of my misery."

"You don't know what's going to happen," I reminded him. "The case is still ongoing. If you get the plagiarism charges dropped, all of this could go away."

Chris narrowed his eyes over the top of his pint. "This will *never* go away," he said. "She's been on talk shows, telling them about how we researched the manuscript together, telling them about us." He slammed his glass onto the table, beer sloshing up and over the edge, and held his head in his hands. "Us. Out of all of this, I wish there was still an us. I miss Olivia so goddamned much."

And now we were on to the waterworks portion of our day. Since Chris had been hit with the plagiarism suit by his ex-fiancée's lawyer, his days have gone thusly:

    1. Wake up, ready to take on the world and prove my innocence!

2. My professional credentials will see me through!

3. I can't believe Olivia would do such a thing. What did I ever see in her?

4. My colleagues hate me. My friends won't speak to me. I am ruined, both professionally and personally.

5. Why can't Olivia just love me again?

Ah, Olivia. While I'd never disliked her, I had always suspected that there was a bit more to her than she let on. She had met Chris while he was in the midst of writing his third novel, *Bones of the Bard*, the New York Times bestseller that had made him a household name. It was a masterpiece of historical fiction, weaving together the known facts of Shakespeare's life along with several other Elizabethan writers, and some rather scandalous court intrigue. Olivia had stood by Chris while he struggled with the first draft of the novel, through rejection slip after rejection slip, while those first few reviews trickled in, and during the book's steep, quick climb up the bestseller list, where it had remained for nearly a year.

The day Chris had received a *two hundred and fifty thousand dollar* advance for his next book, Olivia's agent cum lawyer filed a lawsuit stating that Chris had plagiarized one of her manuscripts. We hadn't even known that she'd written a book. The fact that Olivia had met Chris while she had been a student in Chris's sophomore literature course was not helping matters.

The fact that Chris was actively trying to drown himself in all forms of booze also wasn't helping matters.

"Are ye all right, lad?" the server asked as she placed Chris's plate in front of him. It was filled with his sandwich, and a side order of neeps and tatties, which was what us Americans called mashed turnips and potatoes. I hoped all that protein and starch would sober him up a bit.

"He's fine," I answered. "Just been out in the sun a bit too long." I gave her my brightest smile, the one that had always worked wonders on grumpy professors and misbehaving customers alike. In addition to being a grad student, I'd held my own fair share of waitressing jobs.

My smile still had it, and the server looked sympathetically at Chris, and patted his arm after she set my soup down. Before I started on my soup, I pulled out my field notebook.

"You took notes at the hill?" Chris asked.

"I take notes everywhere," I replied, adjusting my glasses on the bridge of my nose. Sometimes Chris was proud of me working toward my doctorate in geology. Other times, I think he wished I'd chosen a major that didn't involve me being filthy all the time. Shakespearean professors do prefer having presentable siblings.

"Tell me again how you got your benefactors to buy into your hare-brained thesis?"

I ignored the jibe, but answered the question. "Probably because it's never been researched before." My "hare-brained thesis" was about the rock types and layers found in and around ley lines that passed through historically significant spiritual sites. Ley lines had been studied plenty—Carson even offered a dowsing certificate—but no one had ever studied the bedrock beneath the lines.

It is a known fact that certain types of stone, such as limestone and quartz, vibrate on specific frequencies which can be measured with an oscillator, which is why they're used in things like wristwatches. My theory was that areas said to contain spiritual phenomena were constructed of and on a similar type of stone, thus resulting in locations across the globe having accumulated similar magical attributions over the years. Basically, I thought ghosts were an expression of a location's natural vibrational capacity.

Chris snorted. "Why don't you interview some of those archeoastronomy and ley line experts on that television show?" he pressed. "You know, the ones that talk about ancient aliens?"

I glared at him; I knew exactly what show Chris was referring to, and it was atrocious. If you're going to claim to be a scholar, the least you can do is comb your hair. "My work has nothing to do with aliens, ancient or otherwise," I snapped. "There is a scientific foundation for what I'm doing. Telluric currents, for instance." He raised that eyebrow again, so I explained, "Telluric currents are natural energy currents running throughout the earth. Look it up."

"I don't need to look up," he grumbled. Satisfied that I'd won that little bout, I turned my attention back to my notes. No matter what Chris said, this "hare-brained theory" of mine had gotten me this research grant across the pond that we were both enjoying. Therefore, someone other than I thought it held water. That was good.

I penciled in a few notes while I nibbled at my bread, then I glanced at my phone. It was still early afternoon, and I was hoping we could stop by the Trossachs Discovery Center after lunch. If I'd read the map correctly, there was a walking trail that was adjacent to the Highland Boundary Fault. Walking trails with nearby fault lines were just the kinds of things that make geologists happy.

Satisfied with that day's notes, I reached into my pack for my favorite pen. When I couldn't find it, I upended the entire daypack onto the table, and noticed I was missing a few other items as well: a brush, a battered hair clip that had traveled to many dusty sites with me, and a lump of rose quartz.

My heart thudded as I searched for these items. Most—well, all—of them were easily replaceable, but the rose quartz had been a gift from

Jared. I'd carried it around since I was a freshman at Carson University, and even though I'd resolved to cut all ties with Jared, I couldn't bring myself to get rid of the stone. Despite what had happened with Jared and me, the quartz had become my talisman.

I searched my memory, trying to recall the last time I'd held it, when I remembered reaching into my pack at the top of Doon Hill.

"I have to go back to the kirk," I said suddenly, sweeping everything back into my pack. "I think I dropped my lucky quartz."

"Jared's rock?" Chris smirked, and I glared at him. We had an understanding, my brother and I: as long as he didn't mention Jared, I wouldn't mention Olivia. If we didn't keep to the agreement, we were both liable to weep our way across the countryside.

"Yes," I replied. "Will you be all right on your own for half an hour or so?"

Chris drained his pint, and waved to the server for a refill. "I'll manage."

I sped back to the ruined kirk, my knuckles white as I gripped the wheel. The real reason I didn't get on Chris about his constant mooning over Olivia was that at least he and Olivia had had something. I'd had nothing with Jared. No, it hadn't quite been nothing, but it may as well have been. One thing that Chris and I had both learned on this trip is that an ocean is not nearly enough distance to outrun your past.

I parked in the kirk's tourist lot, leapt out of the rental and ran across the bridge and up the fairy hill, startling some of the local wildlife along the way. When I reached the Minister's Pine, I was panting, my heart pounding as sweat poured down my back.

I had to find that quartz. I just had to.

I dropped to my knees and felt around near the base of the tree. I found my brush rather quickly, along with my hair clip and the stupidly expensive Mont Blanc pen that my advisor had given me when I earned my masters degree. But the quartz, the quartz wasn't anywhere. The bits of lunch I'd had turned to lead in my stomach; if the quartz was gone, then it was really, truly over.

"Lookin' for this, are ye now?"

I turned toward the voice, blinked, and pushed my glasses up to my forehead. Yeah, he was really there. Standing in front of me was a tall man in what I assumed was period dress. Instead of a kilt—we American girls tend to think that all Scotsmen run around in kilts, no matter the occasion; sadly, this is not the case—he was wearing a padded brown leather coat topped with chain mail, along with matching brown pants and well-worn leather boots. A helmet was tucked under his arm, and I could see the hilt of a claymore, one of those medieval broadswords that were so heavy you had to swing it with two hands, poking up over his shoulder. A shield rested next to the sword's hilt, its curved edge just visible above the man's shoulder.

I hadn't realized they did reenactments at Doon Hill, and I made a mental note to check the brochure for show times. I also noticed that the actor had his hand extended, with my lump of rose quartz sitting on his open palm.

"Yes!" I got to my feet, and grabbed the stone. "Thank you," I said once I remembered my manners, stroking the stone with my thumb. The man looked at me intently, his expression wavering somewhere between confusion and curiosity. "What made you think it was mine?"

"Saw ye drop it, I did," he replied.

"And you've been waiting here since then?"

"I knew ye would be back for me."

I blinked, since I must have misunderstood his accent. What I'd heard as 'me' must have really been 'it'. Accents do tend to garble words. "I really appreciate you waiting for me. Thank you," I said, extending my hand.

He eyed my hand, dark brows low over his blue eyes. Then he grasped my fingers and brought them toward his mouth.

"What are you doing?" I snapped, snatching my hand away.

"I thought ye wanted me to kiss your hand," he explained.

"I wanted to *shake* your hand!" He looked befuddled rather than offended, so I attributed this to yet another cultural misunderstanding. It was becoming quite the list. "Well, regardless, thank you. I'm Rina."

"Rina," he repeated, that Scottish brogue of his making my nickname sound positively decadent. "'Tis quite an unusual name."

"It's short for Karina," I explained. "Karina Siobhan Stewart," I added, wondering why I'd felt compelled to give him my full name. Historically I'd only been called Karina Siobhan when I was in trouble.

"And I am Robert Kirk," he said, extending his hand. This guy was way deep in character, like method actor deep. I shook his hand, and we both smiled.

"Good to meet you, Mr. Kirk."

"Reverend Kirk," he corrected.

"My apologies, Reverend Kirk." These reenactors sure liked to stick to their roles, though I'd never expected to see a reverend wearing chain mail. We stood there for a moment, holding hands and grinning like a couple of fools, and I took the time to really look at him. He was older than me, probably a bit older than Chris too, with dark, tousled hair, chiseled features, and a roguish glint in his blue eyes. They had obviously picked reenactors that would appeal to the ladies.

"Do no' fash, Karina lass, no offense was taken," he murmured, and my cheeks were suddenly hot. I took back my hand, barely resisting the urge to fan myself.

"I should be going," I said. "My brother's waiting for me." I scanned the area around the Minister's Pine, ascertained that I'd left nothing else of import behind, and turned toward the path. A hand on my arm stopped me.

"Ye canna leave me here," the reenactor said. "Ye must take me with ye."

"What? No!" I faced him, planting my feet before him and whipping out my cell phone. "I don't know what goes on here in Scotland, but I'm an American citizen. Stay back, or I'll call 911." I didn't even know if they had 911 in Scotland. Would I have to call Scotland Yard instead? I hoped my phone had some kind of app for international emergencies. I waved my phone in what I hoped was a menacing manner, and Robert—or whatever his name was—eyed it as if it would bite him.

"Put away your tricks, lass," he said. "It was ye what called me here in the first place."

I shook my head. "This is an act, right? Reverend Kirk, freed at long last from the Minister's Pine?"

"'Tis no act, lass. Would that it were." He stepped closer, and took my hands in both of his. Robert's hands were warm and callused, and, despite all this nonsense, comforting. "I am Robert Kirk himself, and ye have freed me no from just a tree, but from Elphame, and the Seelie Queen herself."

"Elphame?" I asked.

"Aye," he replied. "Some refer to it as the Fairy Realm."

I leaned against the Minister's Pine. He claimed he was from Elphame. Of course he was. How did I always attract the weirdos?

It was generally agreed that when magic left the world, it was because the fairy realm had closed its doors to humans. Some claimed that human industrialization, and its rampant use of iron, had caused the fae to retreat, while others claimed the global shift from pagan to monotheistic faiths was the culprit. No matter which theory you favored, the end result was the same; there was no new magic. For hundreds of years humans had made do with a few crumbling artifacts and enchanted items, but those items were wearing out too. It was as if magic had a half-life, and we'd long since passed the middle point.

"You can't be from Elphame," I said. "It's closed. It's been closed for centuries."

"Has it, now? I will say this, when I was a boy the land was thick with magic. Ye could hardly walk the roads without encountering one o' the Good People."

"When you were a boy," I repeated, then I remembered that Robert Kirk had lived in the seventeenth century. Magic hadn't started disappearing until a century later. "Still, it's closed now."

"Just because a door has been closed, does no' mean it canna be reopened."

I slid down to the ground and Robert sat beside me, both of us leaning against the tree he'd recently emerged from.

Wait, when did I start believing him?

"So, um, you think all of this is real?" I ventured, gesturing around the clearing. "The legend and all?"

Robert smiled wanly. "Ye have heard o' me, then?"

"They say you told the world of the fairies' secrets, so they imprisoned you in a tree."

"That is no the whole of the tale." Robert closed his eyes as he leaned his head back against the trunk. "I did have dealings with the Good People, but it was no them who abducted me."

"Then who did?"

"'Twas Nicnevin, the Seelie Queen herself."

My jaw dropped, and if I hadn't already been on the ground I would have fallen. As it was, my arm went out from under me, and my shoulder bumped into Robert. "Are ye all right, lass?" Robert asked.

"Yes," I lied. There was nothing all right about this. "Why did the queen take you?"

"She fancied me," he replied. "Offered me an apple, ye ken. I said no, it angered her, she cursed me. And here we are today."

I looked up at him. He still had his head tipped back against the tree, his eyes closed. "That sounds like the ridiculously oversimplified version."

At that, he opened his eyes and speared me with his gaze. "Would ye be likin' all the details, then, lass?"

I swallowed. "Um, maybe not just yet." My gaze moved from Robert's face to the quartz in my hand. "What makes you think I freed you?"

"Ye made contact wi' the tree, wishin' to rescue me. Wishes are powerful things, ye ken." Robert leaned over and touched the quartz. "Then ye dropped your stone, and a door opened for me. I ha' been waitin' for ye ever since."

"Wishes are powerful things," I repeated. "Why do you want to leave with me? You don't even know me."

"I know ye freed me, and that is no small thing," Robert replied. "I also know that as soon as Nicneven kens I've left me post, she will send her creatures to retrieve me."

"Creatures?"

"Aye. And I do no' want to be here when they arrive."

I took a deep breath and got to my feet, Robert following suit. Once we were standing I looked into his clear blue eyes, his guileless face, and sighed. He was either telling the truth, or he was the greatest actor in the world. Or I was the world's biggest idiot; the jury was still out on that.

"Well, let's go."

"Go?" he repeated hopefully.

"If you're telling the truth—and I'm not saying that you are—I can't just leave you here. And, if you're not telling the truth, I'll drop you at the nearest police station," I added, trying to act tough in front of the armored man with the sword.

Robert inclined his head, and took both of my hands in his. "Lass, soon enough ye will ken that I only speak what's true." He once again brought my knuckles to his lips; this time, I let him kiss me. It was nice, having one's hand kissed by a dark, handsome man. "Karina Siobhan Stewart, I am now your charge, and I shall follow your every command."

"Okay. Um." I looked him over and issued my first command. "First of all, you can't tromp around Aberfoyle wearing chain mail. You're going to have to take off your armor."

ELVES, FAUNS, AND FAIRIES

"**W**hat do ye mean, take off me armor?"

"I mean just that." Robert and I had walked down Doon Hill and toward kirk's car park, and I still hadn't convinced myself he was lying. So much for me being the smarter sibling.

When we reached the rental I opened the boot and gestured toward the empty space. When Robert eyed it warily, I continued, "Look at what I'm wearing. People dress like me, not you. If you don't want these creatures finding you and dragging you back where you came from, you need to blend in."

Robert frowned, then he handed me his helmet. "Aye, lass, ye have a point."

I accepted the helmet and held out my hand. "Sword and shield, too."

His frown deepened, but Robert relinquished his weapons and set about removing the chain mail, and then the padded leather tunic he wore beneath the mail shirt. Underneath it he was wearing a homespun brown shirt, matching pants, and brown leather boots. He looked more like a farmer than a warrior, or a reverend for that matter.

"We have to meet my brother at the pub," I said after I'd closed the boot. "It's just a short drive there."

"Aye, then," Robert said, and he hopped into the passenger seat as nonchalantly as any modern man would.

"You're familiar with automobiles?" I asked. While history was not my main field of study, I was fairly certain that motorized transportation had not been available in seventeenth century Scotland.

"I have no' spent all this time at Nicnevin's court," he replied. "She frequently used me as a messenger."

"Who was she sending messages to?" I wondered.

"Those whose names should not be spoken in the bright light of day." He settled into the passenger seat, his fingers digging into the arm rest. "Iron is good," he murmured. "They canna reach me beyond the iron."

I didn't tell him that cars were mostly plastic and Styrofoam nowadays. At least he could take comfort in the metal engine. "Reverend—"

"Call me Robert," he said. "I've not seen the inside of a kirk for so long I can hardly claim to be a man o' the cloth."

I ignored the bitterness in his voice; if he really was Robert Kirk, he had every right to be angry. "Do you really think they'll come after you?"

He stared straight ahead when he replied. "Aye. I ken it well."

We drove the rest of the way in silence, but my mind was reeling. Who was this man? Why did I buy his story, and let him into my car? How long would it take the authorities to find my body?

One thought clamored louder than the rest: What if it really is him? What if all, or even some, of the stories I'd read were true? What if magic hadn't really died out? I shuddered; I didn't know which fate was worse, being in a rental car with a delusional Scot, or the knowledge that the things that go bump in the night might be real.

Why did Jared have to give me that stupid rock in the first place?

We got to the pub where I'd left Chris by late afternoon. Despite Robert's claim that he liked being surrounded by metal, he leapt out of the rental before I came to a complete stop. Once we stepped inside his shoulders lost some of their tension, as if he'd let himself breathe again.

"Nothing like a friendly pub, huh?" I asked.

"I find it amazing how some things have no' changed at all across the span o' the years," he replied. "Lass, could a poor old man trouble ye for a hot meal?" Robert's eyes twinkled, as his mouth curled up at the corners.

"I think I can manage that. Come on, I'll introduce you to my brother."

Chris was right where I'd left him, along with four empty pint glasses scattered on the table before him. At least he'd eaten his lunch, along with mine. Hopefully the bread would soak up the worst of it.

"Who's this?" Chris slurred when he spotted Robert.

"Chris, this is Robert." I thought omitting Robert's surname was a wise choice, especially since he was something of a local legend, and his clothes made him look like an extra from *Braveheart*. Good thing he'd ditched the chain mail and assorted weaponry. "Robert, this is my brother, Christopher Stewart."

"Are you an actor?" Chris asked, taking in Robert's clothing.

"O' sorts," Robert replied. "Good to meet you, man."

They nodded to each other, and Chris gestured for Robert to take a seat. I waved to the waitress for menus.

"Find Jared's rock?" Chris asked after Robert and I had ordered. We'd requested shepherd's pie and broiled salmon, respectively, along with a couple pints of beer.

"Yeah," I replied, while Robert asked, "Who is this Jared?"

Chris got a devilish gleam in his eye, but kept his mouth shut. "Jared is the person that gave me the quartz I left behind on the hill," I explained.

"Ah." Robert leaned back, and watched the waitress set down our pints. "That explains a few things."

"Such as?"

"Such as how ye managed to transform a simple stone into a talisman."

"Not you too," Chris grumbled. Robert's eyes swiveled toward Chris, and he elaborated, "You're into all of that stupid woo-woo crap like Rina? Magic and fairies?"

"Only as a matter of scholarly pursuit," Robert replied. That placated Chris, momentarily at least, and Robert turned back to me. "You loved him, eh?"

"Um." I opened and closed my mouth like a fish, then I sipped my beer. And some more. If I was consuming a beverage, I couldn't be expected to answer any questions, now could I? I might accidentally inhale the beer, and that would be bad, very bad indeed.

Our food came before I managed to drink myself into a stupor, but only just. My salmon was excellent, and Robert tucked right into his shepherd's pie.

"Mmm, 'tis perfect," Robert said, his eyes rolling back in his head. "For all that they're known for their revels, their food is ashes on the tongue." He chewed contentedly for a few moments, then he eyed my salmon. "Would ye mind if I had a wee bite o' yours, lass?"

"Help yourself," I murmured, pushing my plate toward him. Robert speared a generous portion of the pink fish, and took a few roasted potatoes and some asparagus for good measure. Truth be told, it was a joy to watch him take such pleasure in something as simple as eating. My brother was not as intrigued by our guest, and had wandered over to the bar. He'd been trying out his "I'm an American professor" pickup routine on the local girls, with little success. As long as Chris was out of earshot, I figured I could ask the good reverend a few questions.

"Elves, fauns and fairies," I began. Robert raised an eyebrow—could everyone do that but me?—but he looked amused rather than offended. "What's the difference between the three?"

"Firstly," Robert replied, dabbing at the corner of his mouth with a napkin, "the wise among us do no' say such names aloud. They can hear ye, ye ken."

"They can hear me whenever I say their names?" My gaze darted about the pub, but I didn't see any sprites or pixies.

"Of course not," he laughed. I glared at him, but it was hard to stay mad at such twinkling eyes. "They hear only as far as any ear can." Suddenly serious, he continued, "However, ye should still be careful. If one was sitting beside ye, he surely would have heard ye clear as a bell."

I nodded, warning taken. "Are any here?"

"Truly, lass, I've no notion." He glanced around the room. "If any o' the Good People are in attendance, they ha' hidden themselves well." Robert took another bite of shepherd's pie, and chewed thoughtfully for a moment. "If ye don't mind me sayin' so, lass, you are readily acceptin' of a notion that most would deny to their dying breath."

"What notion?" I asked, when Robert gestured to himself. Oh, *that* notion. I picked up my pint glass, swirling the beer until it made a tiny amber whirlpool.

"It's hard to explain," I murmured. "I'm usually a good judge of character, and... And you just seem to be telling the truth."

He reached across the table toward my hand, but I pulled away. Robert smiled tightly, and said, "I ne'er tell an untruth, not for any reason."

"And, I know it's crazy," I continued, "more than crazy. But, just because something is new to us doesn't make it any less real. I mean, when scientists first discovered that the earth revolved around the sun the church had them burned at the stake. That didn't negate their findings, just kept their research out of the public eye for a time."

Robert's smile widened, though his brows had peaked when I'd mentioned the earth revolving around the sun. I made a mental note to double check the dates of Copernicus's works. "Are ye comparing me to the sun, lass?" he asked.

"No, I'm not comparing you to a blazing ball of gas," I said. Robert's eyes went wide; we were going to have to play science catch-up at some point. "What I'm saying is that some things just need to be taken on faith."

Just as quickly as it had fled, his smile returned. "Aye, o' that ye are correct. In all me time, as a reverend and afterward, me faith has been what's seen me through both good times and bad."

I nodded, finishing off my pint and signaling for a refill. "Now that you're free, what are you going to do?"

"Truly, lass, I haven't the slightest clue." He shoved a heaping forkful of potatoes in his mouth, his face pensive as he chewed. After a long draught of beer, he continued, "Scotland's still Presbyterian, eh?"

"I think so." That was the sort of detail Chris would be more certain of than me. "You'd want to be a reverend again?"

The waitress arrived with our refills, and Robert took another long draught while he mulled this over. "Nay," he decided, "I only became a reverend in order to study, as me father did afore me. It was the easiest way to attend university in my day. Besides, what if today's kirk now demanded for me to be a priest? I canna rightly do that two wives later, now can I?"

"Two wives?" Chris said as he resumed his seat *sans* girl from the bar. Apparently American professors weren't so exotic around here. "Divorce?"

"Not hardly," Robert scoffed. "I outlived them both."

Chris kicked me under the table, his uber-subtle way of asking if Robert was a serial killer. I shook my head at him, then I turned my attention back to Robert. "That's very sad. I'm sorry."

He smiled wanly. "Thank ye, lass. Time dulls the pain, but it never quite leaves ye, does it?"

"It sure doesn't."

We finished our meal in silence, each of us thinking about the ones we wanted to be with, but couldn't. Once our plates were empty I sent Chris to the bar to get us some whisky. I was in desperate need of something eye-wateringly alcoholic, and I had a feeling that Robert could use a stiff drink too.

"Tomorrow, we're going to have to get you some clothes," I said, while Chris was at the bar. "No offense, but you look like you should be in a play or something."

That eyebrow went up again. "You're keeping me, then?"

"Um, yeah." Robert was my responsibility, since I'd dragged him not only out of the Minister's Pine, but right into the twenty-first century... and that meant that I needed to hide his identity from whoever or whatever he thought was following him. Chris and I had come to Scotland to escape trouble, not find more of it, and whether Robert was con man or a fugitive fairy soldier he was definitely trouble.

I glanced at him beneath my lashes. I really hoped he wasn't a con man.

No matter what he was, I had to help him. In these days of social media, celebrity scandals, and GPS, it's not like a man with no documented history could just blend into modern culture. He would need paperwork, and we'd have to concoct a history, and... And, what if I was overstepping myself here?

"Do you not want to be kept?" I asked.

"Women have changed the most of all," Robert murmured. "In my time, a lass would have blushed something fierce if she even thought o' those words, and ye just spit them out in front o' God and everyone." He shook his head, then he met my eyes. "Aye, lass, I think I'd like it verra much if ye kept me."

At that I did blush, then scowled when I caught Robert smiling. And we were going to discuss him calling me lass.

Chris chose that moment to appear with our drinks, balancing three glasses of whisky without the benefit of a tray. My brother has many faults, but one thing he would never do was spill a drop of good Scotch. Or bad Scotch, for that matter.

"Robert's coming back to the B&B with us," I blurted out, suddenly terrified that Chris would forbid Robert from coming with us and him being left all alone in modern Scotland, a true stranger in a strange land. To my mingled relief and indignation, Chris grinned.

"Go sis," he said, clapping me on the back. "Getting friendly with the locals."

I narrowed my eyes. "Lame talk coming from a Shakespearean scholar."

"Ye are familiar with Shakespeare?" Robert asked. "I once took in a play o' his in London. Fine work, it was."

"Really," Chris said. "Which play? I'm something of an expert," he added.

"*MacBeth*," Robert replied.

I dropped my head into my hands, and massaged my temples. He just had to say *MacBeth*.

A LEARNED MAN

By the time the three of us left the pub, Chris had thoroughly impressed Robert with the depth and breadth of his Shakespearean knowledge, if you take impress to mean that he probably made him hate it. Chris regaled us with a few sonnets, a soliloquy, and compared his life to an hour of sound and fury before collapsing onto the table in a drunken heap.

"Woman?" Robert asked, after we'd wrestled Chris into the back of the rental car.

"Woman," I confirmed.

I slid behind the wheel as Robert claimed the passenger seat, and then I drove carefully and a bit too slowly to the bed and breakfast Chris and I were staying in. Not only had I been drinking—never a wise move before driving—it was pitch dark, I had to remember to stay on the wrong side of the road, and there was either a seventeenth-century priest wanted by the Seelie Queen or a modern day lunatic sitting in the passenger seat. I didn't know which was worse.

Reverend, not priest. Robert had made sure that I understood the distinction between priest and reverend, and that he had outlived both—both!—of his wives. I remembered a snippet of Robert Kirk's story, and that he had died—or, according to him, been abducted—while his second wife was pregnant. To be gone before you ever had the chance to hold your child is a true tragedy.

"Do you know any of your descendants?" I asked Robert. When he gave me a look, I elaborated, "I mean, have you kept in touch with your family over the years?"

"Yes and no," he replied. "I am aware of where they are today, and I do my best to watch o'er them, but I keep me distance. 'Tis no' like I can pop in for Sunday dinner and announce myself as their great grandfather many times over. That would no' go over verra well."

"I bet."

Robert and I fell silent, and we didn't speak again until we arrived at the bed and breakfast. With a sigh, I asked Robert to help me wrestle Chris out of the back seat we'd recently wrestled him into, and prop him against the side of the car. Then, to both my and Robert's amazement, Chris managed to enter the B&B and navigate up the stairs all under his own power, with only a few bumps against the walls. He stumbled through his bedroom door and flopped over, fully clothed, onto his bed. At least he hadn't injured himself.

Being the good sister that I am, I yanked off Chris's sneakers and tossed a blanket over him. As I turned to leave I noticed Robert's decidedly unmodern clothing, and raided my brother's suitcase; it's not like Chris was in any condition to argue. And that's what he gets for passing out drunk on a Sunday. No, make that the last four Sundays.

I grabbed a pair of Chris's sweats and a couple tee shirts, his spare sneakers, and what I hoped were a clean pair of jeans. The, uh, *rest* would just have to wait.

"For you to sleep in, and for tomorrow," I explained, thrusting the wad of clothing at Robert. I turned to enter my room across the hall, realizing a moment too late that Robert was following me. Of course he'd rather room with me than my drunk brother. In fact, I'd rather he roomed with me, too; knowing Chris, come morning he wouldn't remember who Robert was and call the cops. That would entail some mighty explaining, and I was not the storyteller in the family.

So there we were, me and the reverend, standing in my rather small bedroom with its single bed, and trying very, very hard not to look at each other.

"I'm going to the bathroom," I declared. I grabbed my robe, towel and travel kit, and fled to the communal bathroom at the end of the hall.

Luckily, the bathroom was unoccupied; stalking back into the bedroom only a few seconds after stalking out of it would have been almost as awkward as stalking out in the first place. It was a quaint old bathroom, full of interesting old fixtures, such as the claw foot tub that took up most of the room, a white porcelain pedestal sink topped with a fancy oval mirror, and one of those ribcage showers that looked like it belonged in a science fiction movie, restraining aliens or the Abominable Snowman. But the water was hot, and the rose-scented soap lathered nicely, and for ten minutes I pretended that nothing weird had happened that day.

After I'd washed, rinsed, and repeated, I wiped the steam from the mirror and took a good, long look at myself. Between me and Chris, I'd inherited more of our father's Scottish genes. I was short like he was, and had dark brown hair and fair, freckly skin. My blue eyes were the legacy of my beautiful Scandinavian mother, though that and the ghost of her fine bone structure was about all I'd gotten from Mom. Chris, on the other hand, was the perfect masculine copy of our mother, being that he was tall, blond, and had the sort of skin that started out alabaster pale but tanned to an even golden brown. I burnt if I stood next to a microwave too long.

What is wrong with me? The longer I stared at the wide-eyed girl in the mirror, the more my convictions about Robert faded. Was I still so hung up on Jared that I was now picking up weirdos at historical sites? Was I really that pathetic? I sighed; based on what—no, make that *who*— was waiting for me in my room, it seemed that I was.

Maybe I'm not pathetic. Maybe I'm just insane.

I shook my head, and then I combed my hair and twisted it up into a clip. No matter what the answers were to those questions, I wasn't going to learn any of them by hiding in the bathroom. I just needed to take a deep breath, get dressed, and tackle this head-on. Not that I had any idea of how I was going to do that.

After I'd repacked my travel kit and folded my towel, I scanned the bathroom and swore. In my haste to have a few minutes alone with my thoughts, I'd forgotten to bring my pajamas with me. Great. I was about to march into a room I was sharing with a possible crazy man I'd met only hours earlier, wearing nothing but a robe. I suppose I could have put my clothes from earlier back on, but I have a thing about dirty clothes on clean skin, probably because during the course of my fieldwork my clothes ended up filthy more often than not. Yes, I make frequent stops at Laundromats while traveling.

I sighed again, a sure sign of my brain developing a slow leak, and gathered up my things. I really couldn't put off returning to the bedroom for much longer, especially since the bathroom was shared by all of the guests, and the B&B was full. I packed up my shampoo and conditioner, wrapped up my dirty clothes in my still-damp towel, put on my robe, and made the short walk back to my room. After I'd mustered the nerve to push open the door, what I saw nearly made me drop everything at my feet.

First of all, Robert had changed out of his rough, mud brown clothing, and was wearing gray sweats and a threadbare Iron Maiden tee; the thin cotton strained across his muscular shoulders, and struggled to contain his biceps. Unbeknownst to the common observer, that padded leather armor and homespun shirt had been concealing a Mr. Universe-worthy body. Which led to my second observation: who knew that reverends could be muscular? Then again, I suppose that seventeenth century life involved a bit more toil that we deal with today. Farming and such, or churning butter. I mean, a reverend probably had someone who churned his butter for him, but those biceps certainly weren't the result of reading or preaching.

My third observation was that Robert was sitting on the edge of the bed, reading one of my geology texts. Despite those biceps and shoulders, it was the reading part I was most interested in.

"Ye are a scholar, lass?" Robert asked without looking up, once I'd shut the door behind me. I recalled that he had been quite an educated man in his day, well versed in sciences and languages.

"I'm working on my doctorate in geology. It's the study of the earth." I dropped my things on a nearby chair, and sat beside him on the bed so I could have a look at what he was reading. "It's why I'm here, in Scotland. I'm on a research grant."

"Where do ye hail from, then?"

"America," I replied. "It's to the west, across the Atlantic Ocean."

Robert turned a few pages; the text he was reading explored how the geology of the British Isles had changed following the most recent Ice Age. "I remember the first stories I heard about America," he murmured. "A pristine land across the sea, where all were free to worship and live as they wish. Tell me, lass, is that what it's like?"

"It's how it started. We might have gotten a bit confused along the way." I watched him flip a few more pages, stopping on a map of Great Britain. He traced the coastline with his finger; I wonder if he'd ever been to the sea. Then again, Scotland is an island. "Are you interested in geology?"

"I've always wanted to learn about everything I could," he replied. "'Tis why I became a minister in the first place, in order to continue my studies. I never thought they'd lead me where they did, ye ken."

I nodded; I expected that most individuals, scholars of folklore or not, didn't think they'd someday end up as a prisoner, and a prisoner of fairies at that. "I'm sorry," I began, but Robert waved it away.

"Truly, lass, my predicament 'tis not any o' your doing," Robert murmured. "Why did ye come here, to Scotland? Surely there are plenty o' stones and such for ye to study in your America."

"There are," I allowed. "My thesis was originally based on ley lines. Do you know what those are?"

"Aye," he replied. "The Good People occasionally use them as roads." He frowned. "What do ye mean, originally based on?"

Finally, someone who agreed that ley lines still exist in more than just the geometric sense. "Well, I first posited that the stone underneath all ley lines is similar," I began. "You know, since so many spiritual monuments are situated on ley lines. I ended up expanding my theory to include all spiritual places, in an attempt to determine if the bedrock beneath similarly spiritual locations is of like composition. I'd planned on doing the research in the university library at home, but I was offered a grant to come here and do some of the work in person. So, here we are."

Robert rubbed his chin. "Your theory has merit," he announced, after a moment's contemplation.

I blinked; I was so used to people shooting my ideas down, I hardly remembered what it was like to have someone agree with me. "It does?"

"O' course it does," Robert stated. "The natural world is what gave rise to magic, no' the other way 'round. It stands to reason that if magic can be attracted to an oak grove, or a mossy glen, then why no' to a certain sort of stone?"

I grinned; after these past few weeks with Chris, it was nice to talk with someone who thought of magic as more than a fairy tales for children. "Want to see something cool?"

Dark brows furrowed. "Cool? As in cool weather?"

"Um, no. Cool as in interesting." Robert may have traveled in the modern world, but he was a bit behind on slang. I took the text from him, and flipped to the section on the Silurian period, which had been a scant four hundred and forty three million years ago. "Since you were at university, we've learned quite a lot about the earth and natural processes. For instance, the earth's surface is covered in land masses called plates that rub up against each other. Sometimes, they bump into each other and cause earthquakes."

Robert looked skeptical, but nodded. "Go on."

"Well, these land masses weren't always in the same positions as they are now. For instance, Scotland used to belong to a continent called Laurentia, and England was part of a different continent called Avalonia. You know what continents are, right?"

Robert shot me a withering glare. "I am a learned man, ye ken," he stated.

"Right. Sorry." I flashed him an apologetic smile, and continued. "Anyway, Scotland was part of Laurentia, and England was attached to Avalonia. There was an entire ocean in between them." I flipped to a modern map of the UK, and indicated the Iapetus Suture, which ran from Solway Firth right on to Lindisfarne, never straying more than a few miles from the political border that separated Scotland and England.

"See this line? It's where Laurentia and Avalonia fused into each other." Robert's brow furrowed, and he leaned closer to the page, lips moving as he read a few lines of text.

"What ye are tellin' me, lass," Robert began as he scrutinized the map, "is that we Scots have no' always been saddled with our neighbors to the south, orderin' us about in our own homes?"

"That's right," I affirmed. "For most of geologic history, England was hundreds or thousands of miles away." I thought for a moment. "Maybe that's why Scotland and England have never seen eye to eye. They really are from different worlds."

Robert snorted. "That, I do believe."

I laughed, and Robert glanced up, a wry smile twisting his lips. We grinned at each other for a moment, just two scholars sharing in a discovery, when his gaze dropped to where my robe gaped open beneath my neck. I bunched the sides together, my face and neck flaming to what I'm sure was an impressive shade of red; another side effect of my fair skin was that I could never hide a blush.

"I. Um. Sorry," I said as I reached toward my suitcase. "I'll grab something and go get dressed."

"Lass." Robert's hand was on my elbow, stilling me. "Worry not, I've a mind to visit this bath room o' yours. I shall allow ye plenty o' time."

I nodded, unable to look at him or even move until I heard the door click shut. I threw on my pajamas and leapt into bed, pulling the blankets up over my head. The last thing I remembered was listening to the blood pounding in my ears.

THE B&B, THE PRIORY, AND THE FUATH

It was rather awkward waking up with a strange man sleeping on my floor, since the stranger in question was wearing my brother's clothes, and that he claimed to be a man who by all accounts had been found dead on a hill over three hundred years ago.

Worst of all, I kind of believed him.

Before I could dwell on my situation any further, I got out of bed, grabbed some clothes, and headed down the hall toward the bathroom. I went about my morning routine slowly, at first hoping that Robert would be gone when I returned so I could put this whole incident behind me. But if he did sneak out that would mean he was everything Chris had warned me about, nothing but a freeloader looking for a hot meal and a night's lodging from a dumb tourist. I'd done some foolish things in my time, but this would really take the cake.

Still, I didn't want to rush back. If Robert was still there, that would open up a whole host of other concerns; namely, is he really some kind of a con artist? A modern day Bluebeard, with a closet full of his dead wives' bodies? And if he's neither of those things...

Could he really be a man from the seventeenth century? Or was he just another Jared?

I gathered my long hair into a pony tail, and left the bathroom. I wasn't going to stick my head in the sand any longer, and live in my fantasies. Karina in Scotland was New Karina, and she wasn't about to let a man push her around.

Full to bursting with my newfound resolve, I stalked back into my room. I found Robert, awake and dressed in jeans, a blue tee shirt, and the leather boots he'd been wearing yesterday; I looked around and saw Chris's spare sneakers on the floor next to the door. Either they hadn't fit, or Robert was squeamish about wearing shoes that someone else's feet had been in. Robert was standing next to the side table, staring at the electric teakettle.

"The kettle has a tail o' sorts?" he said as he fingered the cord. I smiled; if this guy was acting, he was on track for an Oscar.

"It's a cord." I dropped my things on the bedside table, and approached the counter. While the room didn't boast an actual kitchenette, it had come with an electric kettle, teapot, mugs, and a small refrigerator that I'd stocked with milk, butter, jam, bread, olives, and other basics. After the proprietress had spied my box of teabags, she'd appeared in the doorway with a tin of proper loose tea, muttering on about foolish young Americans the entire time. "You stick the pronged end into the outlet," I explained, indicating said receptacle, "and it heats the water."

Robert's eyes widened. "Where is the fire?"

"It's, ah, internal," I replied. His eyes got even wider when I plugged in the cord and the little red light flicked on. While Robert acquainted himself with modern technology, I packed up my clothes and books. It was our last day in this bed and breakfast, which was too bad. It was the nicest place we'd stayed in during our trip, except for a hotel in

London that Chris had insisted on; that place ended up costing him an arm and a leg. I was going to miss the quaint little B&B, chipped china, lace curtains, and all.

The kettle whistled just as I finished stashing my research notes in my daypack. I thought I heard Robert jump at the high-pitched squeal, but I didn't turn around in time to see it. However, I did make note of his awestruck face as I poured the steaming water into the teapot.

"Would you like some bread?" I offered. He nodded, and I emptied out the fridge onto the small wooden table. While the proprietress was a gracious lady, and an excellent cook, I did not think she would take kindly to me bringing an extra man down to breakfast. A quick bite in our room would just have to do. While I spread butter across the thick slices, Chris stumbled into my room.

"Hey," Chris grumbled. He raised that mutant eyebrow of his at Robert's presence, but didn't comment. "You know what I really miss about the US? Coffee. Fricken' coffee." Chris grabbed my mug of tea and poured in so much milk it spilled over the sides. I grabbed a towel and mopped up Chris's mess. Once that was done, I filled the remaining mug for myself. "Olivia and I would always stop at the café on our way to Carson. She would get a latte, but I always stuck to straight Joe." Chris sipped his way too milky tea. "Sunday mornings were best. We'd stay in bed with a pot of coffee and the paper."

"Olivia was your wife?" Robert asked.

"Almost wife," I said, sliding into the chair beside Chris. "She sucked all the talent out of his brain and left him high and dry." Chris glared at me, but he was too hung over to argue. And it was the truth.

"Sounds like a *leannan sìth*," mused Robert. "They're known for ruinin' a man, stealin' his thoughts and dreams, and leavin' him as nothing more than a husk o' his former self."

"Great. More woo-woo crap," Chris mumbled. Before Robert could point out that he was living proof of the "woo-woo crap", Chris asked, "Where are we off to today? Candy shop run by leprechauns?"

"Leprechauns are cobblers, not candy makers. Everyone knows that." I rifled through my daypack, and checked the itinerary. "Inchmahome Priory," I proclaimed. "It's on an island in Lake Menteith."

"Oh, so there will be mermaids," Chris sneered.

"Nay, lad, mermaids prefer brackish water," Robert said. "However, we may witness a nymph or two."

"By nymph, I assume you are referring to an immature dragonfly," Chris stated.

Robert smiled broadly. "O' course. What else could I be meanin'?"

Chris looked at Robert for a long moment, then turned to me. "Is he coming with us?" he whispered.

"He can hear you," I said. "And, yes. He is." With that, I downed the rest of my tea, and started packing our leftover breakfast in the travel cooler. "We still have some bread. Maybe we can stop at the market, and get some tuna, or turkey and cheese. After that, we can go pick up some clothes for Robert. There's a sporting goods store in town; I think it's called Hamilton's. They should have what we need."

"Hang on." Chris stood, eyeing Robert in his borrowed clothes. "Who is this guy?" I opened my mouth, but Chris kept going, "He shows up out of the blue, you buy him dinner, he sleeps with you—"

"We did *not*—"

"And now you're going to buy him clothes?" Chris glared at Robert, clenching and unclenching his fists. "Just how stupid do you think we are?"

Robert didn't flinch; based on where he'd been for the past few centuries, I imagined that he'd seen a lot scarier things than an indignant literature professor with a hangover. "Truly, I meant no imposition. And, if it's funds ye be wantin', I can pay me own way."

"You can?" I blurted out. Robert nodded, then he rummaged through the tote bag that held the clothes he'd been wearing yesterday; I was forever picking up interesting bits of rocks and such, so packing extra totes had been a must. It would probably cost me a thousand dollars to ship all of my finds back to the States.

As Robert looked through his things, my heart fell. If he really had money on him, that meant he wasn't really Robert Kirk, the man who had been taken by fairies. He would just be a regular man, and a con artist at that. Worse, it would mean that I'd let someone pull the wool over my eyes yet again. I steeled myself for the sight of pounds Sterling or travelers checks or whatever sort of currency Robert had, but what he placed on the table made my jaw drop.

First, Robert laid a gold brooch set with amethysts and pearls on the table. It was round, about three inches across, and the surface was etched with the spirals and winding animorphs that were typical of Celtic artwork. Just as I got up the nerve to touch it, he laid a jeweled dagger beside it.

Now, the brooch was gorgeous, but the dagger was a true work of art. It was long and slender, one of the *sgian dubh's* I'd read about. The scabbard was covered in whorls and knot work, and the knife's handle was studded with rubies and emeralds. I spied tiny flashes of light between the larger stones; upon further inspection, I learned that dozens of tiny diamonds were set between the red and green gems.

"Robert, these must be worth a fortune," I said, grazing a fingertip across the brooch.

"Did you steal these?" Chris demanded. I smacked my jerk brother's arm, but Robert answered him anyway.

"They were fair given to me by the queen herself," Robert replied, omitting the name of the queen in question, "as I now give them to ye, Karina lass. I trust they are worth the price of a few shirts and trews."

My head snapped up. "These are priceless!" I squeaked. "Are... are you sure?" Part of me wanted to bite back the words; while the grant allowed for my travel and accommodations, I'd still had to budget down to the last penny. Chris, who had been rather well off before the lawsuit hit, had been contributing to the trip as well, but Olivia's lawyers had threatened to freeze his bank accounts more than once. Those were the sorts of threats a poor girl like me took very seriously.

"I am," Robert replied as he placed the brooch in my hand and closed my fingers about it. "A man pays his own way. Do not argue wi' me, lass. And," he added, that twinkle having returned to his eyes, "I've a feeling that the brooch will look a fair sight better on ye than it e'er would on me."

I smiled, ignoring the tiny, rational voice in the back of my mind that wondered how in the world I was going to turn the brooch and dagger into actual money. The rest of me couldn't wait to wear those sparkling amethysts. "It's settled, then," I said, rising from the table. "We'll stop at the market for snacks, and then Hamilton's, pick up a few shirts and trews, and then we'll head to the priory. After that, it's on to the cottage in Fife."

"Rina," Chris warned.

"I'll get you a bottle of single malt if you let it go."

Chris weighed his options, and apparently decided that a bottle of hooch was worth betting on his sister's safety. "I'll let it go, for now," he said.

I nodded. "Fair enough."

After a quick stop at the market—where we picked up sandwich fixings, some fruit, and I replenished my olive supply—we hit the local sporting goods store. Well, Robert and I hit it; Chris went off with a handful of my carefully conserved cash to find the single malt he'd been searching for all his life.

"That Olivia drained more than the inspiration from him," Robert commented as Chris stomped away from us.

I shrugged, and pushed open the door to Hamilton's, the town's sporting goods store. "What can I say, he gets cranky."

I don't know if Robert knew what cranky meant, but he accepted my explanation and followed me into Hamilton's; the sign in the window boasted that if they didn't carry it, you didn't need it. We would just see about that.

Our first order of business was securing footwear for Robert, being that his leather boots had already gotten him a few interested glances. As we headed toward the show section I assumed that finding Robert some modern footwear would be a simple task. Yep, wrong again. It seemed that men in the seventeenth century had inordinately large feet, something that greatly intrigued the saleslady.

"O' course his feet are huge, just look at the man," she commented after she'd measured and touched and fondled Robert's feet. "He's a braw one, isn't he, like a warrior of old. What are ye, man, six foot six or thereabouts? And ye have muscles as the day is long... Are ye a professional athlete, then?"

Robert's brow furrowed, though I didn't know if it was due to her calling him an athlete, or because the woman was sizing him up as if he was a leg of mutton. "I... ah..."

"He's shy," I interjected. "Are there, maybe, some work boots in the back that would fit him?"

"Certainly there are. I'll just pop back for a look." She turned to enter the storeroom, then she added, "I hope he is no' so shy when it is just the two o' ye."

My eyes widened, and it took me a moment to find my voice. "We aren't like that."

"Mmm. Perhaps, he and I could be like that," she added with a knowing smile. My mouth dropped open as she sashayed into the store room.

"Lass?" Robert asked. "Is something amiss?"

"No," I said quickly. "Come on, let's pick out some clothes while she finds boots for your giant feet."

After we'd trolled the menswear section of Hamilton's, Robert's arms were laden with jeans, sweaters, knit cotton shirts, and a few packages of socks and underwear. I herded him toward the changing room, though he was protesting the need to try things on; maybe he was like a modern man after all.

We had covered the store in record time, mostly because I wanted Robert to be safe in the changing room before the horny saleslady returned with his boots. Not only did I not know how Robert would react to her advances, I didn't want to go through the hassle of explaining that he was married, and a reverend, and therefore please keep your grubby paws off of him.

Not to mention, one minute she thinks we're a couple, then the next minute she hits on him. Who does that?

No sooner had I shoved Robert into the changing room than the saleslady reappeared, boxed boots in hand. And, she'd brought two other girls along for the show. "Here we are," she trilled, once she spotted me. "Trying things on, is he? I'll just give a quick knock and offer my assistance," she offered as the girls giggled.

Before I could decide between telling her that no way, no how was she getting into that changing room, and asking her why she'd brought along an audience, Robert himself cracked the door. "Karina? Would ye come here, please?"

"Is something wrong?" I asked.

"I... I do no believe these blue trews are fitting me properly."

"Well, then, step on out and show us, so that we may give ye our professional opinion," called the saleslady. I seriously considered decking her and her entourage.

Robert grumbled something under his breath, but he obediently exited the changing room. Being that I was busy glaring at the saleslady, I was fully aware of when her jaw dropped and her eyes got so wide I worried they'd roll right out of her head. When one of the girls squealed and covered her mouth I turned toward Robert, and almost squealed too.

When Robert had been wearing my brother's old sweats and ratty t-shirt, he had looked good; hell, he had even looked good in that thick leather armor and chain mail. But now, clad as he was in a burgundy knit shirt that stretched across his chest and shoulders, along with a pair of jeans that fit exceptionally well, he was downright mouthwatering.

"Around," the saleslady said, making a twirling motion with her hand. "We need to assess the entire fit."

I glared at her; the woman wanted a peek at his butt. Had she no shame? Then Robert turned, and I realized that I had no shame either. Like I said, those jeans fit exceptionally well.

"These trews are somewhat snug," Robert said.

"That is how they are supposed to fit," the saleslady murmured as the girls nodded. Before she could get any more ideas, I grabbed the boots from her hands.

"Here, try on the boots," I said, thrusting the box at Robert and shoving him back into the changing room. "I'll wait here." He nodded, and shut the door behind him. I turned around and leaned on the door, fanning my overheated face.

"No like that, eh?" the saleslady quipped.

"It's complicated," was all I said. She nodded, then she and the other girls—seriously, did those two even work there?—went off in search of other men to harass. Me, I wished for a cold drink to magically appear at my elbow.

Robert made his final selections soon enough, and we hauled his starter wardrobe to the cash register. I even sprung for matching waterproof jackets for him and me; dorky, yes, but also practical. These Scottish nights were awful chilly.

While the cashier rang up our purchases, it occurred to me just how much I'd enjoyed our shopping trip. Not only was I having fun, I was having fun with an attractive man, one that seemed to appreciate both shopping and my company. Scotland suited me, in more ways than one.

Once Robert had been properly outfitted, we met up with Chris and his single malt, and the three of us headed toward Inchmahome. Being that Chris wasn't drunk, not yet anyway, I gladly let him drive.

Not only was he the better driver, mostly because he actually owned a car, it also gave me the opportunity to study Robert in the side view mirror.

I suppose he could be from the seventeenth century. Robert's dark hair, while neatly trimmed, didn't conform to any recent style. And there had been his confusion in Hamilton's about operating common clothing fasteners, such as zippers and Velcro. Nor was his bearing that of a modern man. Robert carried himself more like a warrior than a reverend, his eyes constantly scanning the area with his spine held as straight as an arrow. I wondered if he even knew how to slouch.

Added to that were the odd things he said. Robert's brogue was so thick that at times I hardly understood him, and he used such quintessentially Scots words as fash and ken; as yet, there had been no havering, but one could always hope. Granted, all of those words were still used today, but the way he said them reminded me of a knight from a bygone era, one who had lived and died during the age of chivalry. Yes, Robert had proven that he was a chivalrous man, from the way he held doors for me to the way he'd laid down on the floor at the B&B and hadn't even looked toward my bed. Despite Chris's conclusions, Robert had been no threat to my virtue. If only...

Great. I'm fantasizing about him, and I still don't know if he's legit. Or crazy. Hell, maybe I'm crazy.

As I wrestled with my less than wholesome thoughts, Robert caught me watching him in the mirror. My cheeks heated, but before I could look away he smiled. As I smiled back, red face and all, I realized that I believed in Robert, and not just because I wanted to. With Jared, I'd so desperately wanted him to be the man of my dreams that I had been willing to tell myself all sorts of lies to make him into that man. The truth was that Jared had only ever used me, and I deserved better.

I wasn't lying to myself about Robert. It was plain to see that he was a good, honest man.

Once we reached the lake—Robert snorted and corrected me with "loch", refusing to accept that the advent of English tourism had long ago doomed Menteith to lakehood— it was just a short ferry ride to the island and the ruined priory. As soon as our feet touched the island's shore, Chris started in on me.

"So Rina, why are we here?" he asked. "Ghosts? Vampires? Werewolves?"

"It's just a priory," I bit off.

"But your tour is all about paranormal crap," he pressed. "Isn't the motto 'Find The Magic', or something?"

"It's a spiritual tour," I retorted, forgoing that the grant had arranged the tour and that's why we were on it; it seemed that this tour was the only one that lined up with the housing they'd also set up. "And priories are spiritual places." When he rolled his eyes, I whined, "Can't you just enjoy the scenery?"

Chris harrumphed, then he stalked off toward the tourist signs. I glanced at Robert, and shrugged. "Chris is just irritated. I have taken him to a few haunted spots, and some that claim to have had fairy sightings" I admitted. "You know how some people think magic still exists?" Robert nodded. "Well, Chris doesn't. Not even a little bit."

"Ye will be hard pressed to find a place devoid of magic here in Scotland," Robert said. "The very fabric o' the land is woven with enchantment."

From what I'd seen so far, I agreed. Not being in the mood to follow the tour group, or my brother, I skirted the visitors' center and headed toward the tree line, my mysterious man hot on my heels. Once I was certain that Robert and I were out of earshot of the rest, I asked him what I really wanted to know.

"How did it really happen? When you were taken, I mean," I added when Robert quirked a brow. "The history books all say that you had a stroke while walking on Doon Hill."

"Och. I was as healthy as a horse." He stopped before one of the tourist markers, though I didn't think he was reading about the priory's history. "What else do these books say about me?"

"That you betrayed the Good People, and that they punished you by imprisoning you in the Minister's Pine atop Doon Hill."

Robert smiled, pleased that I'd remembered the euphemism, only to sigh and rub the back of his neck. "I swear to ye, lass, I've ne'er betrayed anyone in me life. Even after she took me, I ne'er did."

"I believe you," I murmured.

"Do ye, now?" He flashed that grin again, and took a few steps toward the trees. "Well, it was like this: I did uncover a fair bit o' their secrets, but I did no' put to paper anything that could have caused them harm. And, I revealed nothing that they did no previously agree to bein' revealed."

"Then why were they mad at you?"

"They were no' mad at all. They allowed me free passage to and from their hollow hills, and ne'er once did I suffer a glarin' eye or a harsh word from my hosts." We reached the tree line, and Robert ran his hand across an oak's rough bark. "I caught her eye, I did."

"Her? Her who?" I asked, then I remembered what Robert had told me at the Minister's Pine. "Oh, you mean Nicnevin?"

"Aye, lass, the Seelie Queen herself," Robert said, as nonchalantly as if he'd been relaying the day's specials at the market. "She was wantin' me to play piper to her maiden, ye ken."

"I thought the Seelie were the good ones," I said.

Robert barked a laugh. "Ne'er mistake one o' them as good, lass. There's blatant evil, and then there are those who would view us as pets, not as living beings with hearts and minds and souls. Personally, I've come to prefer the blatant evil. At least they are honest about their intentions."

I nodded; I myself had never had any patience for insinuations and double-talk. "So, about the queen... You became her, um..." I spread my hands, unable to say the word 'lover' to a minister.

"Consort?" he supplied, to which I nodded. "Nay, I refused her."

"You refused the queen?"

"Aye, that I did."

"What were you thinking?"

"I was thinkin' that I was a married man, and that she was needin' to find her sport elsewhere," Robert replied.

"How did she not kill you?" I wondered.

"Verily, she nearly did. She tried to bribe me, trick me, humiliate me before the whole o' her court." He was silent for a moment. "Once, I found a chink in her armor, if ye will. I assembled the means to contact a relation o' mine, and explained to him the actions that would set me free o' her."

"And?" I pressed. "Did she catch you?"

"Nay, but 'twas no matter. My relation, he did no' do what I'd asked, and he left the ritual incomplete. Afterward, when she learned of my attempt to escape, she was no verra pleased wi' me." Robert was silent for a moment, staring out at the water. "E'en so still she wanted me, always plying me wi' gifts I did no' want nor need, but I refused her. After all manner of indignities, and my countless refusals, she set me in a ring against her gallowglass."

"Gallowglass?"

"Once, in our world, they were warriors for hire," Robert explained. "Mercenaries of a sort. In Elphame, the gallowglass has the dubious honor o' being the royal assassin."

"Oh," I murmured. Robert's words sunk in, and my eyes widened. "Oh! You had to fight against an assassin?"

"Aye. And I won. By right of succession, I then became Nicnevin's gallowglass. And so I have been these last many years, until a lovely lass arrived in Aberfoyle and sought to free me with a talisman o' her own creation." Robert caught my hand, and brushed his lips across my knuckles. "For the gift o' my freedom, Karina, I will e'er be in your debt." I blushed yet again, cursing my glass face while my fingers curled around Robert's hand. If he kissed my hand again, I was going to have to stick my head in the lake-not-loch.

"So, um, what happened after you became her gallowglass?" I prompted. Robert released my hand, and gazed toward the priory.

"She bound me to her with a curse, and occasionally loosed me into the world to carry out her will." He laughed through his nose. "The teind to hell? I collected it every seventh year. The wild hunt? I rode beside her steed, guarding her most glorious person. When e'er she took a lover, I escorted him to her bower." He turned his gaze back to me. "But I ne'er went there meself."

"Not even once?" I squeaked. "Isn't she supposed to be incredibly beautiful?"

"Aye, that she is," Robert agreed. "But she has no soul, nor any heart to speak of. If I am to make love to a woman, I need to be in love wi' her. And I canna love naught but a pretty face. I require a pretty heart, as well."

"Oh." My mouth went dry, and I grabbed my water bottle from my pack. Robert's words rattled me; my brief, blink-and-you'll-miss-it time with Jared had soured my view of relationships, so much so that I doubted that men could feel both love and loyalty. I mean, Chris had been in love with Olivia, but that hadn't stopped him from hitting on the local girls in every pub we'd stopped in across the UK. His behavior had made me wonder if I was the only person left with old fashioned morals. Then again, Robert sure did put a new spin on the term 'old fashioned'.

Robert noticed that I'd gone silent, and grimaced. I wondered if he had bared a bit more of himself than he'd meant to, since he touched my elbow and gently guided me back toward the priory.

"Come along, Karina lass," Robert said, "I would hate for ye to miss a spot on your tour after all ye went through to—"

Robert grabbed my arm like a vise, and dragged me to a halt. "'Tis one o' the *fuath*," he growled.

"The who-ah?" I asked.

"*Foo ah*," Robert repeated, stretching out the syllables. "They are water demons that act as Nicnevin's assassins. Like as no', she has sent this one to collect me."

"I thought you were her assassin."

He ignored my comment, and said, "We must leave, lass. Fetch your brother."

"Leave the tour?" I asked. "Can't we just walk around to the other side of the ruin?"

"No. We must leave this place altogether."

"We're on an island," I reminded him. "We have to wait for the ferry."

"We canna," he hissed. "'Tis no safe."

"Um, okay." I scanned the tour group; it was comprised of a rather harried looking guide, a gaggle of senior citizens armed with cameras and fanny packs, and my brother, the only individual under sixty. None of them looked to be likely candidates for a fairy assassin. "Where exactly is this *fuath*?"

"At the rear o' that gathering." Robert jerked his chin toward a white haired woman leaning on a cane who looked so frail, I worried the breeze would topple her.

"Are you sure?" I pressed.

"'Tis one o' them, o' that ye can be certain," he insisted, his grip on my arm tightening. "The beast is wearing a glamour."

I stared at Robert, the man I'd known for less than twenty-four hours, who had claimed that I'd liberated him from centuries imprisoned within the Seelie Court. The man I had believed, until he started avoiding my questions. "You haven't answered me. I thought you were her assassin?"

"I was but the deadliest of many," he replied, then he spied Chris. "Come, we'll collect Christopher and commandeer a vessel."

"What? No!" I shook my arm free, and glared at him. "That little old lady can't hurt anyone, and we are *not* stealing a boat!"

"The boat? Ye are concerned about a wee boat when a killer's naught but twenty paces from ye?"

"This is insane," I muttered. "Just insane." I turned my back to him, rubbing my temples. Chris had been right; Robert was nothing but a gigolo, one who was now playing his part a bit too intensely, and I was his willing mark. I'd crossed half the world to get away from one man that had used me, only to run smack into another.

The tour group had noticed Robert's and my argument, and a few of the old ladies were whispering about us. I smiled and waved, trying to impress upon them that everything was fine, just in case anyone was of a mind to call for enforcements. The last thing I needed was a headline that read "American Graduate Student Arrested For Making A Scene At Scottish Landmark" making its way back to my grant funders.

One by one, the ladies lost interest in us, and followed the guide to the next location. All of them, except the one Robert had labeled as an assassin. She was standing stock still, leaning on her cane and peering at me.

"Why isn't she moving on?" I wondered. I glanced over my shoulder; Robert had stalked off toward the trees again, muttering to himself. "Robert, could you come here, please?" I called. "I think someone needs help." All I could think of was that something of a medical nature was happening with the woman, maybe a stroke or a heart attack, and Robert—or whatever his name was—was a big guy, and could carry her if necessary. As soon as I called his name he returned to my side.

"Who is needin' help, then?" Robert demanded. He looked past me, the blood draining from his face.

"Gallowglass," a voice hissed. I tore my gaze from Robert and back to the old woman, who wasn't looking so feeble any longer. Her eyes glowed red, and her mouth was packed with long, needlelike teeth, way too many teeth to be in such a small opening. I stood, mesmerized, as she kept opening her mouth, wider and wider until her jaw unhinged, her teeth growing longer and sharper with each passing second.

"Behind me," Robert shouted as the woman sprang at us. She crossed the twenty or more paces in a single leap, landing like a cat on Robert's chest. Then she screamed, a horrible, shrill noise that physically hurt my ears, and reared back to bite Robert's neck.

I shrieked, certain this monster was about to take Robert's head off, when he pitched himself forward, throwing his full weight on top of the much smaller creature and knocking them both to the ground. While the monster was still dazed, Robert leapt to his feet. He extended his arm to the side, and the claymore he'd carried the day before materialized out of thin air. Robert grasped the sword with both hands, and with a single swing he decapitated the creature.

I was shaking like a leaf, staring from the body to Robert. There was blood everywhere, black stinking blood marring the lush grass, some of the foul liquid having sprayed onto Robert's chest. I hated gore, even the fake gore in horror movies and in cheesy Halloween displays. I swayed, certain that I was going to faint, when Robert caught me.

"'Tis all right," he murmured, his arm about my waist. "It canna hurt ye now." I pressed myself against Robert's side, hiding under his arm and trying not to touch the bloody parts of his shirt. All of my doubts about Robert had ceased just as surely as that creature's life had ceased. I would never doubt him again.

"What the holy hell was that?" Chris demanded.

I looked up and saw my brother jogging towards us. Behind him, the tour group was screaming and pointing at the man with the gigantic, bloody sword, and at the body at his feet. "Robert had to," I whispered.

"Had to?" Chris repeated. "He *had* to kill a little old lady?

"Not a lady," I said, shaking my head.

"Old man, whatever—"

"Chris!" I pointed at the creature's head. "Look at the mouth." He did, squatting down to get a better view. I stayed where I was; I already knew more than I wanted to know about that thing.

"Shit," Chris murmured. Being that Chris considered such language beneath a man of his stature, I inferred that he understood the gravity of our situation. He reached toward its teeth, and I looked away. Did he have to touch it? He couldn't tell just by looking at it that it was wrong? As I tried not to lose my breakfast I noticed an official-looking man striding toward us.

"Lose the sword," I muttered. Robert crouched down, and took what I thought was an inordinately long time wiping the blade on the grass. Once it was as shiny as it was going to get, Robert stood and extended his arm to the side. A moment later, the sword was gone. While I stood gaping at the empty space where there had just been a freaking sword, the official-looking man started yelling at us about defiling a holy place, not to mention defacing a registered historical monument. The dead tourist had not made his list of priorities.

"About stealing that boat," I began, then I turned to my brother. "Chris, we are going to steal a boat."

Chris nodded. "Good plan."

Robert grabbed me by the elbow, and the three of us raced toward the dock.

WELCOME TO CRAIL

T he commotion behind the priory had drawn the ferry's crew, so, being that the boat was unoccupied, we hopped onboard and ran toward the dashboard control panel. It was covered in a blinking lights and switches and I had no idea how to work any of them.

"Start the engine or something," I said.

"How exactly am I supposed to do that?" Chris snapped. "I've never operated anything like this."

"You and Olivia used to take vacations at that yacht place!"

"This is a commercial ferry," he shot back, "not a pleasure boat!"

"Shit," I said. "Then how are we going to get away?"

"What about that one?" Robert asked. Chris and I followed his gaze, and we saw a much smaller motorboat docked nearby.

"That, I can handle," Chris said. He moved to leave, then he spied a black binder and grabbed it. A second later we were running off of the ferry, then we were scurrying about the motor boat as Chris jumped into the driver's seat and Robert unwound the rope that secured it to the dock. The engine started up, and Chris guided the boat across the lake not loch.

"What's that?" I asked, nodding at the binder on Chris's lap.

"Passenger log," he replied. "Has our names in it."

"Oh." I had nothing more to say. I was just glad Chris knew how to drive a boat.

Once we reached the opposite shore, Robert docked the boat while Chris wiped down the hard surfaces. After all what had happened on the island, the fact that my brother was a criminal mastermind hadn't even registered on the weird factor.

No, the *fuath* had pretty much heightened the weird up to epic levels.

My brother, the man who'd killed either a tourist or a monster, and I were silent as we drove toward the Kingdom of Fife, where a prepaid rental cottage awaited us in Crail. Chris was driving again, despite the fact that he'd taken a few shots of his single malt before we'd set out. I'd taken a shot myself, hoping it would calm my nerves. Instead, my hands were shaking so hard my wrists ached.

About an hour into our drive we stopped on a deserted stretch of road. Chris put the rental in park and grabbed the passenger log, then he stared at me. I stared back until I realized that he wanted a lighter; I've never smoked, but I carried all manner of oddities in my pack. One never knew what would be needed during field work. I dug it out and handed it over, then Robert passed forward his bloody flannel button down.

Robert and I stayed in the car while Chris started the fire, me trying not to think about what he was burning while Robert dug out a fresh shirt from the Hamilton's bags. After the fire had reduced the passenger log and Robert's shirt to ash, Chris poured water on the smoldering mess and returned to the car. He passed around his single malt, and once we had each gulped some liquid courage, we were off.

We reached Crail, a fishing village situated right on the Firth of Forth, about an hour later. We found the rental cottage, then there was the small matter of dealing with the landlord, one Dougal MacKay, and the collecting of keys. If Mr. MacKay had been surprised to greet a party of three, rather than just the two who were expected, he hid it well. Then again, the cottage had been well paid for, and in advance.

Mr. MacKay gave us a quick tour of the one floor cottage, and we were sure to *ohh* and *ahh* over the two bedrooms and spacious common room, complete with a kitchen, television, and a stocked bookcase and video library. After he'd shown us every detail, including the brand new laundry basket nestled under the kitchen counter, he left us with two sets of keys, a map of Fife, and a list of restaurants and other local amenities. As soon as the door had closed behind Mr. MacKay, Chris looked at me for the second time since we'd left the priory.

"What happened back there?" he asked.

I didn't ask for clarification. I cleared my throat, and replied, "It wasn't an old woman."

"I get that."

"It was one of Nicnevin's creatures, sent to either kill Robert, or take him back to the Seelie Court."

Chris leaned on the kitchen table and crossed his arms over his chest. "Seelie Court?"

"The fairy court."

Chris pinched the bridge of his nose. "What does that nonsense have to do with anything?"

I swallowed, and replied, "This is Robert Kirk, Chris. The *real* Robert Kirk. He escaped from the fairy queen, and she sent that monster to take him back."

"Maybe you should have let it have him." Chris glared from me to Robert, his fists clenched so tight the veins bulged in his forearms. "Maybe you never should have hooked up with this freak in the first place."

"He's not a freak! And we did not hook up," I added. "Why are you being such an ass?"

"Why is he going around with a sword? Is that even legal?" Chris countered.

"It's his sword," I shrieked. "Chris, Robert's been a prisoner in Faerie for hundreds of years!"

"Magic is gone, Rina," Chris said. "It was already dying out long before that preacher in Aberfoyle was born, long before Shakespeare, even. No matter how much you want things to be different, magic is gone."

"Then how do you explain the creature at the priory?" I demanded. "Dental work gone bad?"

"Genetic aberration," Chris replied. "If regular human DNA can make Lobster Boy, it can make a toothy old woman." Robert opened his mouth, but Chris held up a hand. "No. A world of no. I do not want to hear anything you have to say." Chris grabbed his jacket and the car keys, and headed toward the door.

"Where are you going?" I demanded.

"Someplace without freaks or monsters," he grumbled.

After the door slammed shut behind Chris, I stared at it for a small eternity. For the second time in as many days I found myself alone with this strange man, his strangeness not only due to the fact that we'd just met. After what happened at the priory, I knew that Robert wasn't a hustler, nor was I his mark. But what did that make him? What did that make me?

If I ever see a monster like the *fuath* again, I may actually die of fright.

Eventually, I took a deep breath and turned around, folding my arms across my chest as I did so. Robert stood perfectly still, his eyes wary as if he was watching a predator stalking him through tall grass.

With a start, I recognized the emotion glazing his eyes: fear. I was all that he had in this modern Scotland, and if I stopped believing in him, he truly would be lost.

I wanted to believe him, so badly I could taste it. He just needed to give me something I could hold on to.

I unfolded my arms, letting my hands hang loose at my sides. "I thought regular people couldn't see them. The Good People," I added, as if he didn't know what I was talking about.

"Typically, ye canna," Robert replied. "The *fuath* at the priory had taken over a mortal's form, which is why ye could detect it."

"A mortal's form? You mean—" I doubled over as my stomach churned; that really had been a human body. Robert had beheaded a little old tourist wearing a fanny pack. Then Robert's arms were around me and he was guiding me to the couch, pressing a wet dish-cloth to my forehead as he set my glasses on the coffee table.

"Forgive me, lass, I wish I could say otherwise," Robert said, "but 'tis true. The *fuath*, terrible beasts that they are, will take over a mortal's body, and twist it around to do their bidding."

"You killed a woman," I whispered.

"The *fuath* had already killed her, long afore we set eyes on her," Robert corrected. "I merely dispatched a monster."

"How did you do that with your sword? Not the swinging part," I clarified. "How did it just appear out of thin air?"

Robert shrugged. "'Tis but a *fath-fidh*, a simple charm to keep things close yet hidden."

"Yeah. Simple." I snuffled, and wiped my nose with the dishcloth. There was nothing even remotely simple about this. While I under-stood that Robert had had to kill the *fuath*, that didn't mean I had to like it. Especially not when that poor woman's headless corpse was permanently imprinted on the backs of my eyelids. And those teeth;

just thinking about them made me shiver. "Did…it…use a similar charm?"

"Nay, lass. Ye could see the beast because it was already inhabiting her body."

"So, I could see it because it was inside a mortal?"

"Aye." Robert took the cloth from my hands, and threw it across the room and into the kitchen sink. "Most mortals have no idea that the Good People walk among them."

"But you can see them?" I ventured. "You can see what they really look like. Even before she took you, you could interact with them." Robert pursed his lips, and nodded. "They say that you were born with the second sight."

"Aye, that I was, but second sight allows one a glimpse o' the future, no' the Good People." When I blinked expectantly, he continued, "When I was a wee lad, I made up a wort to see them."

"A wort? You mean like fairy ointment?"

"One and the same," he replied. "With its application, anyone may see them as they truly are, glamour or no."

I searched his face, but I could find no evidence of falsehoods. Fairy ointment! I remembered those tales, which mostly involved midwives who were given the ointment to help laboring fairy women. The ointment allowed regular people to see the truth beyond glamour and spells, and often led to those who'd received it being blinded or imprisoned. Of all the things to be real… "Do you remember how to make it?" I asked.

"Och, no, lass! That's what started this whole mess in the first place." Robert sat beside me on the couch, supporting his head in his hands. "The wort, it does no wear off. Once ye can see them, you're cursed to see them until your dying day."

I leaned toward him, trying to peek through his fingers at his eyes. "But if I can't see them, how will I be able to protect you?"

I said protect, but I meant believe. Robert frowned, and said, "It should no' be ye protecting me, lass. Ye should be the one what's protected."

I reached for him, then thought the better of it and dropped my hands. "I set you free. You're my charge."

He raised his head at that. "That I am," he murmured, his icy blue eyes searching mine. Robert cupped my chin, and grazed his thumb across my cheek. "Karina lass, ye do no ken what you're asking," he murmured. "The Good People, they aren't all lovely, like the storybooks would have ye believe. Some are right terrible, both in appearance and in deed."

I shivered, only partially due to the prospect of coming nose to nose with a real live fairy. "Sounds like people," I said with more conviction than I felt. I took his big, warm, callused hand, and held it between mine. "Robert, please. Let me help you."

He sighed, then stood and pulled me to my feet. "All right. Do no' say I did no' warn ye." Robert strode toward the door while I grabbed my daypack. "Firstly, we'll be needin' to visit the apothecary."

SORCHA

I plodded down the cobblestone streets, so furious I hardly saw the people or shops I passed by. I was shocked—no, make that appalled—that Rina had taken in that guy from the kirk, bought him things... And no matter what she said, that freak had killed something at Inchmahome. Maybe it hadn't been a little old lady, but Robert had killed something. All that blood didn't appear out of nowhere. And those teeth...

No. This was not about the teeth. This was about Rina taking some random freeloader's word over mine.

A cold gust of wind chilled me, so I pulled up my collar. I turned a corner, and saw a slender woman with a long, dark braid cross the road and disappear down a cross street. Even though I was half-drunk and in an unfamiliar environment, I'd know that braid anywhere.

"Olivia," I called, and ran after her. If she was here, it meant that she'd come looking for me, probably to make whatever amends she could. We weren't too far gone, this could all be fixed. I just had to catch up, and we would talk, and we would fix this.

If Olivia was here, it meant that she still loved me.

I wound up at a crossroads, unsure of which direction she'd gone. I checked one street after the next, frantic to find her; after I'd run the length of the third street calling her name, I admitted defeat. It was a feeling I'd become all too accustomed to these last few months.

At the end of the street was a pub, the sign promising cold ale and strong whisky. I could do with both. I slipped inside the darkened pub, and claimed the booth in the far corner. It was quiet save for the clink of glasses and the dull crackles and pops from the fire, and the other patrons ignored me. I hoped fate had finally thrown me a bone, and given me a place to rest and get my thoughts in order.

A waitress came by. "You'll be having a pint?"

"Yes, please."

The waitress walked toward the bar, and I leaned back against the worn leather seat. As much as I was not willing to believe that Robert had spent time in a fairy court, or was anything other than a freeloader and a murderer, I had seen the dead woman's head. Those teeth, rows and rows of them, thin and sharp like needles, so many packed into that mouth that they protruded outward from the too-wide maw...

I shook my head. Those hadn't been human teeth, of that I was certain. But the body had been human, with human skin and hair and clothes. And, whatever it was, Robert had killed it, chopped off its head and set loose a river of dark blood. I didn't know if he should thank Robert for ridding the world of whatever that *thing* was, or run back to the cottage and rescue Rina from a killer.

"Long face, eh?"

I looked up, and saw the waitress standing at the end of the table. On her tray was two pints and a shot of golden liquid. "I only ordered one pint."

"With a face like that, ye will be needin' a wee dram of something a fair sight stronger than ale," she said as she plunked first the pint, and then the whisky in front of me. When I hesitated, she added, "Come, now. On the house."

I glanced from the whisky to the waitress; I guessed she was on the younger side of middle-age, with the beginnings of laugh lines creasing the skin around her eyes and mouth. Her coarse dark hair was messily secured on the top of her head with one of those plastic clips you could find in the drugstore. Rina always put her hair up with clips like that. Olivia had thought they were tacky.

Since I didn't want to offend her, or waste free whisky, I muttered a thank you and drank the shot. It burned more than most, and I grabbed my pint.

"There's a lad," the waitress murmured, setting down her tray with its remaining pint on the table. "I'm called Sorcha."

"Christopher Stewart." I set down the pint, and shook Sorcha's hand.

"Mind if I join you, Christopher?" Sorcha asked. "My shift's just ended."

I gestured toward the opposite side of the booth. "Be my guest."

Sorcha slid into the booth, and clinked her pint against mine. After a moment, she pulled the clip from her hair, letting her long, dark curls tumble around her shoulders; when she set the clip on the table, I noticed it was gray metal—pewter, maybe—not plastic. Elegant. And how could I have thought her hair was coarse? It slid around her neck and shoulders like silk, a Stygian waterfall of softness. I wondered if those curls felt as silky as they looked. "Pleasure to meet you, Christopher."

I nodded, noting how her dark eyes gleamed in the low light, and how her smooth, pale skin was like that of a porcelain doll. I had been wrong about her age; the lighting must have been to blame, for she looked to be no older than Rina. She could have been as young as Olivia.

"Chris," I said, as I raised my pint. "My friends call me Chris."

FAIRY OINTMENT

Despite his insistence that making fairy ointment was a bad idea, Robert and I were soon out the door, with the map and an ingredient list in hand. Now that he'd told me there was a way I could actually see the magical creatures he claimed existed, no way was I letting him off the hook.

"There are some things you should know," I began as we walked toward the center of the village. "The places you knew as apothecaries are now called pharmacies. And we probably won't find all of the ingredients there."

"In my day a body could acquire anything needed at one," Robert muttered. "Why should that be different today?"

"Really? You got everything there?" I teased. "You could just wander into any old apothecary and purchase a loaf of bread or jar of jam?"

"O' course not. Those were made at home."

"Well, today you can buy those things," I said. "I'll have to teach you about these modern conveniences. After we make the ointment."

Robert grunted. "Be careful what ye wish for, lass."

I glanced up at him and grinned. "Why start now?"

Much to Robert's chagrin, the pharmacy only stocked one of our ingredients, and that was beeswax. We ended up going to the adjoining florist for roses and marigolds, pesticide-free versions of course. Our next stop was the grocer, where we purchased a double boiler, small glass canning jars, lavender oil, dried thyme and St. John's wort, and assorted other supplies necessary for ointment preparation. Robert had been disappointed that all of our plants weren't fresh—"'Tis the life force what makes it potent, lass," he'd said—but had been quite pleased to come across the lavender oil.

"What's the lavender for?" I asked. "To make the Good People appear more attractive?"

There was that twinkle in Robert's eyes. "To make it smell nice, o' course."

We laughed at that; for not the first time, I thought this reverend was a bit of a rake. I supposed that three centuries in Elphame would have had that effect on anyone. Once we'd left the grocer I'd assumed that we had all of our ingredients, but Robert informed me that we were still missing the most vital portion.

"But we got everything on the list," I said.

"What we're missing is no' something you can purchase," he explained. "Our last ingredient is something that one o' them has touched."

"Couldn't we use you?"

That earned me a withering glare. "Enough o' that. Let us look for a fairy ring."

With that, we walked away from the store and into the grassy plains beyond the village proper. Since I had no idea of what I was looking for, and doubted I'd even be able to know when I'd found something a fairy had touched, I let Robert hunt through the grass while I admired the view. The grass in Scotland was just so much greener than American grass. Maybe it had something to do with all the sheep droppings.

"Ah," Robert said at last. He beckoned me to his side and indicated a circle of mushrooms.

"Oh," I murmured. "The mushrooms?"

"Nay, lass, the grass within." He got down on his knees, and brushed his palm across the tips of the blades. "This, Karina me lass, is what's known as a fairy ring."

I dropped to my knees beside him, gazing at the circle in mingled awe and confusion. I'd heard of fairy rings, the spots that marked where fairies cavorted under the moon and stars, the place of their revels being temporarily marked by a ring of mushrooms. Only, the circle before us was less than a meter in diameter.

"Isn't it a little small?" I asked. Maybe only one fairy had been dancing.

"They can appear large or small at will, solid or insubstantial," Robert replied. "The rules of our world mean little to them." He plucked a few blades of grass, and dropped them into one of the zip-top snack bags we'd picked up at the grocer. Once the final ingredient was secured, Robert stood, dusted off his jeans, and helped me to my feet.

"All right, Karina me lass, let's be off. It's time to make ye see things ye will most surely regret."

The late afternoon sun was warm, and we had a nice walk back to the cottage. As soon as we were inside, we got to work on the ointment.

Robert took care of washing and chopping the plants, and I heated the beeswax in a double boiler. Once the wax had melted into a clear liquid, Robert added the plants and a touch of lavender oil, then he removed the pot from the heat and set in on the counter, so the wort could steep. While we waited, I made tea.

"I feel that I am needin' something a wee bit stronger than tea," Robert grumbled when I set his cup before him.

"I'll take you to the pub after the wort's finished," I said, omitting the fact that Chris had a stash of whisky in his suitcase. Unless he'd finished it off, that is. "How much longer until the stuff's ready?"

Robert glanced at the clock. "No' much longer, now."

We sat in silence, sipping our tea and avoiding each other's eyes. I understood why Robert didn't want me having the ability to see supernatural beasts, but I couldn't think of any other way to prove to myself that he genuinely was a man from the seventeenth century, cursed by the Seelie Queen herself. Even the *fuath* from the priory wasn't a definitive answer; what if it had just been a human with a severe dental deformity? And superhuman leaping abilities? While Robert exuded nothing but honesty, the fact remained that until I could see the creatures that he claimed were hunting him with my own eyes, I couldn't believe or help him.

And there was the possibility that he was an escapee from an insane asylum. That still needed to be ruled out.

After a time, Robert got up, gave the mixture a final stir, and unfolded, then refolded, a square of cheesecloth. I stood by his shoulder as he strained the mixture through the fine mesh and into one of the canning jars.

"It really does smell nice," I said. "Like spring."

"That it does." Having finished straining the wort, Robert put the cheesecloth aside and took my hands. "Lass, I'll ask ye one last time, then ne'er again. Must ye do this?"

His hands, which were always warm and comforting, were now hot. "I must," I replied. "I need to see them."

Robert sighed, and smiled wanly. "I wish to God ye didn't, but I do understand. I needed to see them, too." He squeezed my hands. "Close your eyes, Karina lass."

I did, and a moment later felt Robert dab the strange mixture on my eyelids. "It's warm," I mumbled.

"O' course it is," he said. "We just boiled it." Robert's words were light, his fingers gentle. After the first application of the wort had, I don't know, absorbed, he dabbed a bit more on the corners of my eyes, then dotted it across my cheekbones. Lastly, he swept his thumbs across my brows.

"That feels nice," I murmured.

Robert grunted. "Open, lass."

I opened my eyes, sweeping my gaze across the cottage. At first, I was disappointed that everything appeared the same, though I had no idea what I'd been expecting. Brighter, richer colors, perhaps, or a brownie sweeping out the hearth? Then I realized how clear everything was, even though my glasses were sitting on the table.

"That's weird," I mumbled. I put on my glasses, and the world was blurry again.

"What's weird?" Robert demanded. "Are ye pained?"

"Nothing like that," I said. "I can see better without my glasses than with them. Is better vision a side effect? Seeing things clearly, and all?"

"I suppose so," Robert said.

"Is it permanent?"

He shrugged. "We will know, in time."

I set my glasses down on the table and turned toward Robert, my gaze catching on something around his neck. He wore a wide silver collar, one that hadn't been visible to my pre-ointment eyes. "Does that hurt?"

"Never has." Before I could ask, he continued, "Now ye ken how Nicnevin bound me."

"Wow." I'd assumed that "bound to a fairy queen" was a figure of speech, but the evidence was plain before me.

Robert spun the collar around on his neck, and showed me a short silver chain. The last link was broken, clinging to its neighbor for dear life. "And, thanks to ye I am bound no more. Ye broke me free, ye did."

I touched the dangling links. "Can the whole collar be removed?"

"Aye, but that's another discussion entirely. Now, about that pint ye promised me?"

Before we left the cottage, Robert had given me a set of instructions on walking amongst the Good People:

1. Never acknowledge them

2. Never look directly at them

3. If they touch you, do your best not to scream

It was strangely similar to the lecture Chris had given me before the first time I rode the subway by myself. Unlike my overprotective and slightly paranoid older brother, Robert's instructions were spot on.

I saw the first member of the Good People as soon as Robert and I stepped outside the cottage. She was in a tree, wound about an upper branch as lithe and supple as any snake. Fun fact about me: I despise snakes with every fiber of my being. After hearing all those adages about 'no snakes in Ireland' I'd felt sorely betrayed to learn that there were snakes slithering about in the rest of the UK.

However, the fairy above me was no slimy, slithery beast. Her skin was a vibrant pink, and I caught a glimpse of bright eyes and even brighter teeth as Robert and I passed underneath, her long, leafy hair dragging across my shoulder. It took every ounce of will power I possessed not to crane my neck around for a better look at such a beautiful yet terrifying creature.

By contrast, the next fairy we came across was so ugly I assumed that a wild boar had wandered into the village. I started to ask if we should call animal control, but Robert shook his head slightly; when I was too dense to take the hint he squeezed my hand. Realization dawning, I squeezed back, and I studied the creature out of the corner of my eye. It was short and squat, its pink hide covered with brown, wiry hair. Tusks framed its slobbering jaws, but strangely, it had eyes as clear and blue as sapphires, eyes that betrayed an intelligent mind. Just as I finished my assessment, the boar fairy stood up on its hind legs and ambled off, its cloven hooves clicking against the cobblestones.

Robert and I encountered a few other members of the Good People as we strolled down the lane, each of them obviously inhuman. I was impressed with my ability to ignore that which was right in front of my nose. This little walk amongst beasts and monsters was going better than I'd anticipated; I mean, some were beautiful, and some were ugly, but as long as I kept my cool they would have no idea that I knew what they really were. Then we turned a corner, and I confronted the stuff of nightmares.

It—he?—was tall, like seven or eight feet tall, with a thick gray hide that was peppered with putrefied lesions. Its arms were so long that its blood-crusted knuckles dragged on the cobblestones. Its feet, also too long for its form, and had extra joint or two, with toes that sported long, cracked nails. Above the feet sagged a belly that was taut and distended, as though it had just eaten a huge meal. Crap. What does a thing like that even eat?

I have no idea what its head or face looked like. Nothing in heaven or earth could have made me look up. As it was, I was gulping down so many screams I thought I might hyperventilate.

Robert slipped his hand inside mine, and gave it a squeeze. "The pub is just up ahead," he said, pointing away from the gray creature. "Almost there, now." I tore my gaze away from the monster and nodded.

Somehow, we made it past the beast and into the welcome dimness of the pub. We slid into a corner booth, my heart hammering against my breast. How had Robert managed to walk by those creatures every single day? I could hardly breathe when I saw that gray... *thing*, never mind act as if it wasn't there. I wondered if time made it easier to ignore them, or if Robert had been born with nerves of steel.

I looked down, and saw that our hands were still joined across the table. "I hope you realize I'm never letting go of your hand."

Robert's brows raised a fraction, but he said nothing. Instead, he lifted my hand and brushed his lips across my knuckles. That made what, three, maybe four times that he'd kissed my hand? Each time, I minded it a bit less.

"Reverend Kirk," I admonished, ignoring how hot my face had gotten, "you're a married man."

He released my hand. "My wife has been gone a long, long time." The waitress appeared at that moment, bearing dinner menus and an indignant scowl. "I am a widower," Robert explained.

"Och, ye poor dear," the waitress soothed, patting Robert's shoulder. "Be sure ye take good care o' your man, lassie," she added with a wink. And my face got even hotter.

Since my blush had also dried out my throat Robert ordered for both of us, and the waitress bustled off. "Amazing. I ha' no' been a part o' this world for so long, yet I can still manage a decent meal in a pub," he murmured, shaking his head.

"What was she like?" I asked. "Your wife, I mean."

"Wives," he corrected. He was silent for a few moments, his dark head bent, and I wondered if I'd overstepped myself. Just as I opened my mouth to apologize, he continued. "My Isobel, me first wife, she was like a ray o' sunshine. Ye could no' help but laugh when ye were near her, she was always so gay."

"She sounds like a wonderful person."

"Aye, that she was. She had this dark hair, soft like a fall of silk, so soft you could lose yourself in it. Her eyes were deep and knowing, her skin pale as milk." Robert glanced up. "Ye look a fair bit like her, Karina."

"I do?"

He nodded. "That ye do." The waitress arrived with our pints, and we drank in silence for a while.

"After she died, I was lost," Robert continued. "I blamed every-thing, and everyone, for her death. Myself. The Good People, e'en. I loved her with every ounce of my being. My last act o' lovin' Isobel was when I carved her gravestone with me own hands." He took a long draught of his pint. "I'd been able to see them for a good while, but after her death I began consorting with 'em in earnest. I was certain that if I could learn just a few more o' their secrets, I could find my way to the Summer Land and back to my Isobel."

By the despair in his voice, I knew he'd never found her. "Could she see them too?"

"Aye. We shared everything, my Isobel and I did." He reached across the table, this time grabbing both of my hands. "Have ye ever shared in such a connection? The feeling that the two of ye are in your own world, somehow separate from the rest? That ye be two halves of the same whole?"

"I thought I did, once," I replied. "Turned out, he didn't feel that way."

"The boy what gave ye the stone?"

I nodded, and changed the subject. "Could your second wife see, too?"

Robert grunted and released my hands. "Margaret was a different woman altogether," he said. "She had no time for anything other than the basics of life; why waste time speakin' o' the Good People when there is bread to be baked, she'd say. She was a good woman, and a fine wife, but practical, ye ken."

"You didn't love her?" I asked.

"Aye, love her I did," he said. "I just loved her differently that I'd loved my Isobel."

The waitress arrived with our food, a meat pie for Robert and grilled salmon for me. I'd been so shaken up by the gray monster, I hadn't realized what he'd ordered.

Robert noticed me staring at my plate, and asked, "Is your meal no' to your liking? I thought ye enjoyed salmon."

"I do. I like all seafood. I'm just surprised you remembered." I stuffed a forkful of fish in my mouth, hardly tasting it. "Are we safe here?"

"Look for yourself."

Taking the gallowglass's advice, I stood, and walked to the coat rack to by the door and hung up my jacket, sweeping my gaze across the other patrons as I did so. There were none of the unhuman sort in attendance, and there was absolutely nothing in the pub like the gray monster, thank all the gods ever.

"Well?" Robert asked, once I'd returned. "Report, please."

"All clear," I proclaimed. Now I could enjoy my salmon.

"Did ye happen to glance behind the bar?"

I looked toward the bar, and almost dropped my fork. There was a woman—a *fairy* woman—pulling pints. Her long, yellow hair—not blonde, but a bright, glaring yellow like a buttercup—had pink blossoms woven into it, and her skin was a bluish white, like the crag of an iceberg. She smiled at one of the customers, revealing dozens of tiny, gemlike teeth.

She caught me staring, and a cold sweat bloomed across my shoulder blades. I lifted my pint in the universally acknowledged gesture for a refill; somehow, I kept my hand from trembling. She jerked her chin toward Robert, and I nodded. While she filled the pint glasses, I drained what was left in mine.

"Good job, lass," Robert said, when I lowered my glass. "Ye need to be quick o' mind, and able to out think—"

He stopped abruptly as the Ice Princess approached. She set down our new pints and collected the empty glasses.

"Everything to your liking?" she asked.

"The food is excellent," Robert replied. "Thank you."

"Good. Yell if ye be needin' anything," she said, and the fey woman disappeared through a swinging door into the kitchen.

"Why work in a pub?" I wondered. "Why work at all?"

Robert shrugged. "Amusement, most likely." With that, he tucked into his meat pie, and we passed the time speaking about non-fairy subjects.

By the time our food was gone, and we'd switched from beer to whisky, the prospect of seeing the inhuman among us seemed downright dandy to me. If the Ice Princess hadn't been so attentive to our needs I'd have interrogated Robert about them something good. Since we were limited in subject matter, I settled on his love life.

"So why'd you marry Margaret?" He raised an eyebrow, so I elaborated, "I mean, you loved Isobel so much."

"That I did." He swirled the liquid in his glass; he was drinking his whisky straight, but I had ice in mine. I liked the clinky sounds. "Still, 'tis unnatural for a man to be alone. We are meant to take mates, ye ken? If the Good Lord had no' meant for us to pair off, he would no' have given us bodies that fit so well together."

Despite my mateless life, I nodded. "Have you married again?"

"And who would I have married?" he countered. "I became the gallowglass to avoid bein' Nicnevin's consort. 'Tis no like anyone wi' half a brain would risk steppin' on her toes."

"Wait." I placed my hands flat on the table, bracing myself. "Are you saying that you've been, um, *alone* since then?"

Ice blue eyes met mine. "That is the truth, lass."

I flopped back against the booth. "Wow." I mean, I'd heard of, and experienced, some rather epic dry spells, but this was unreal. "You might as well be a priest, huh?"

Robert scowled, and tossed back the rest of his whisky. "Come along, lass," he grumbled. "'Tis long past time I should ha' gotten ye home."

We walked toward the door, but unfortunately for Robert I'd gone into full on babble mode. "Do you want me to help you find a girl? Chris has lots of pick-up lines. Although, most of them don't work, so you probably shouldn't use them." We stepped out into the cool evening air, and I shivered. "My jacket!"

I reentered the pub and grabbed my jacket, waving a final goodbye at the Ice Princess. Maybe all fairies weren't so bad. Maybe I could even make a few fairy friends, and go out for a gambol on the grassy knoll with them. That would be fun, and I bet they'd bring the beer or mead or whatever fairies drink. As I stepped out onto the street as I slipped on my jacket, I bumped right into it.

The gray monster.

Since I'd already made contact with it, and there was no way I could pretend I hadn't. I fought the urge to look up, to see its face, meet its eyes. They eyes were probably the worst, dark and burning like vortexes to hell. I trembled, certain that it was going to kill me, and pick its teeth with my bones.

"Karina!"

I looked to the left; there was Robert, feet planted and his arms crossed over his chest, scowling at me. "You're drunk, lass. Get a move on."

I nodded, and sidestepped the beast as I made a beeline toward Robert. He took my elbow, all the while complaining loudly about how I was so inebriated I could hardly navigate an empty street. Me, I kept my mouth shut. If I opened it, I would scream.

Once we were safely inside the cottage, Robert pulled me into his arms. I was shaking so hard I couldn't speak, tears streaming down my face.

"There, there, Karina lass," he murmured. "'Twas no' your fault. Beastie snuck right up on ye, he did."

I burrowed into his safe, warm arms, seeking a haven from what I'd seen. "When can I stop seeing them?" Robert stiffened, so I elaborated, "I mean, I know you said that the ointment's permanent, but there must be an antidote, right? A counter-spell or something?"

He was silent for a time, then he tightened his arms around me. "No, lass," he murmured. "There isn't."

THE PROMISE

After the pub closed down Sorcha and I stumbled out to the sidewalk, our arms wound tight around each other. I don't know how we'd gotten so utterly, smashingly drunk; we hadn't gone up to the bar, and no server came by after Sorcha sat across from me. Maybe one had, a server that brought fresh whisky and refilled our pints, and I'd forgotten. All I remembered was Sorcha, sitting across from me and smiling. I pulled her close, and kissed her.

I blinked at the early morning light. When had the sun risen? Had we been standing here, kissing in the street, for half the night? Did we really have to stop? I could have kissed her forever.

A passerby yelled for us to get a room. I broke free from Sorcha to offer my own witty, if somewhat late, comeback, but the street was empty. I turned back around, the air thick like a dream, and was nearly blinded by golden glow.

Was that the sun?

No. The glow was coming from her.

Sorcha.

At that moment her back was to me, her dark hair a river of night against the rising sun. I was certain that I'd never see a more beautiful sight as long as I lived.

"Have we really been talking all night?" I wondered aloud.

"We have," Sorcha replied, leaning her back against my chest.

I caught her in my arms, and spun her about. "Spend the day with me," I murmured, kissing a path from her cheek to her neck.

"I cannot," she said.

"Why?" I asked. Sorcha placed her hand on my chest, looked up through her thick, dark lashes.

"I have many obligations," she purred. "Do you not have matters that require your attention?"

"I can't think of a single thing I have to do that's more important than this," I replied, my lips against hers. "Sorcha," I breathed, tasting, experiencing her name. I backed her against the brick wall of the pub, trapping her between my arms. "Tell me that I'll see you again."

"You're seeing me now," she purred.

"I need more of you," I insisted.

"Then meet me here tonight," Sorcha said.

"In the pub?"

"No, right here. This very spot." Sorcha took my hands, holding them against her breast. "Promise me that, no matter what, you will come to me."

"I promise."

Sorcha tilted her head up and pressed her lips to mine; I noticed that her mouth was sweet, like nectar. Sweeter than anything I'd ever tasted. I forgot that we were standing in the street, that my careers as both a professor and an author were ruined, that Olivia was gone. All I knew was Sorcha.

BRAVERY

I shifted, awake but not yet ready to open my eyes. Slowly, I became aware of a crick in my neck, and a corresponding ache in my side. My toes wiggled, and I realized I was still wearing my boots, which was just weird. I only slept in my boots during field work in areas where snakes were common, and I did not make a habit of working in snake-prone areas.

I shifted again, and realized that my head was resting on something that felt like denim, or maybe it was flannel; it was firm, far firmer than a pillow or a cushion, but welcoming to my tear-swollen head. Comfortable. And, whatever my face was against smelled...nice. No, nice was an understatement. This pillow smelled downright decadent.

I blinked my eyes open, and saw that Robert and I were on the couch, him sitting up and me snuggled into the crook of his arm. That soft pillow was nothing more than his flannel-clad shoulder, which was also the source of the amazing, earthy scent. For a few moments I was content. Then I spied a drool mark on his shirt, and was completely and totally mortified.

"Are ye awake, then?" Robert murmured, thus confirming that he was also awake, and removing all chances of me sneaking away to my room.

"Good morning," I said, placing my hand against his chest and covering the wet mark. No need to reveal all of my secrets before coffee.

"'Tis barely light," Robert said, then he grazed his thumb across my cheek. "Your tears have stopped."

"Um, yeah." Good. He thought I'd been crying, not drooling. Crying was light years better than drooling. "Why are we on the couch?"

"We took a moment to sit, and ye collapsed against me," he explained. "I would ha' carried ye to your bed, but I did no' wish to wake ye."

All at once I remembered the wort, the Ice Princess in the pub, the gray monster. I could still feel the monster's flesh where I'd bumped into it, cold and clammy and covered with the nastiest scabs I'd ever imagined; no, I had never imagined anything like that nightmare. It had been disgusting, like the contents of a walking biohazard container. Thank God I hadn't been stupid enough to look up and see its face; its eyes must have been truly terrifying.

"I don't think I can do this," I whispered. "They're horrifying. I... You were right. I'm sorry I made you put the wort on me."

"Lass," Robert murmured, tightening his arms around me. It was then that I realized that I hadn't moved away from him once I'd woken. I was holding him as if he were my lifeline. "Karina lass. Ye are a brave one, that's for certain. Can ye just continue to be brave when ye are around them?"

"I... I don't know."

Robert frowned a bit, then he sighed. "I believe ye can," he murmured.

As I watched his face, his impossibly pale blue eyes and his tousled dark hair, I wanted to believe him. I wanted to do anything for him, just to make him proud of me. Knowing that I needed to put some distance between us before something unplanned and irrevocable happened, I unwound myself from his body and stretched. I shivered, having lost the heat of him.

"I'm going to bed," I declared. "Thank you, for sitting with me."

He nodded, those blue eyes searching mine. Being that I'd given all I could, at least for the time being, I retreated to my room and closed the door. Maybe Robert was wrong, and the wort would wear off. Maybe I'd wake up tomorrow morning, and realize that all this fairy nonsense had been nothing more than a dream.

I've never been good at lying to myself.

TEA, TOAST, NO COFFEE

The morning after the gray monster incident, I hid under the blankets until my stupid bladder forced me to get out of bed. Robert let me pass in silence on my way to the bathroom, but he pounced on me once I emerged.

"Here, lass," he said, thrusting a mug of tea under my nose. I guess he'd conquered the many nuances of the electric kettle. I looked past him to the table, and saw a pile of slightly burnt toast resting on a chipped earthenware plate. Two appliances in one day, then. Not bad. "Something hot in your belly will do ye a world o' good."

I took the mug, and let the warmth seep into my fingers. After a few sips, I asked, "How do you do it?"

Robert's brow furrowed. "Do what, now?"

"Walk among them like it's nothing. How can you ignore it all?" My voice cracked at the end, and I sat on one of the kitchen chairs and leaned my elbows on the table. "You were right, they're terrible, horrible beasts. I don't know why I wanted to see them. I wish we'd never made that ointment."

Robert claimed the chair across from me. "There, now, most are no' so bad," he soothed. "The one in the pub, the one ye called Ice

Princess? She treated us right well, did she not?" I nodded, and snuffled a bit. Robert snatched a tea towel, and placed it before me.

"Now lass, I will no' lie to you," he said, while I wiped my cheeks. "Most o' the Good People are nothing like that gray monster, though some are a fair bit worse. However, most are just creatures like you and I, living their lives and going on about their business, no more of a threat to ye than a squirrel or a rabbit."

I peeked at him over the tea towel. "Really?"

"Really. And," he added, as he poured himself some tea, "that gray beast gave me a sound fright, o' that ye can be sure. While I have seen such creatures many times o'er the years, I do no' believe I shall ever be 'used to' those sort o' monsters, as ye say."

That admission was more comforting than the tea. "You were at the Seelie Court for what, over three hundred years?" I asked, and he nodded. Wow. If Robert hadn't gotten used to them after such a long time, I had no hope of doing so in the fifty or so years I had left. "How are you even still alive?"

Robert shrugged. "'Tis a combination o' factors. First, time moves differently there, in Elphame. As such, none o' the Good People age as regularly as we do. Then there is Nicnevin's elixir to consider."

"Elixir?" I repeated. I'd studied elixirs as part of my alchemy coursework. "Is that like the *elixir vitae*?"

Robert smiled, skin crinkling at the corners of his eyes. "Aye, 'tis that exactly. The elixir burns away one's mortality, and, if one is no' careful, their will as well."

"Is that how she tried to get you to be her, um, piper?"

"It is." Robert fell silent for a moment, as one of his long fingers traced the edge of his mug. "If I had been a lesser man, I do no' ken what would have happened to me. As it were, she offered me a glass o' what I thought was wine; 'twas the sweetest drink I'd e'er tasted. No one was more surprised than I when she tried leading me to her bower, and I declined the invitation." Robert grinned. "Actually, Nicnevin might ha' been a fair bit more surprised than me."

"You said no to the Seelie Queen, even after she'd used magic on you?" I murmured, and he nodded. When Robert had told me how he refused to break his marriage vows, I'd been impressed, but resisting actual magic was nothing short of amazing.

"That I did." Robert sipped his tea, then he scraped a generous lump of butter across his toast. "One thing I do no ken is if the elixir e'er wears off. Once I had attained the lofty status of bein' the queen's gallowglass, rarely again did I have the opportunity to taste its sweetness. Yet here I am, not a day older than when she captured me."

"Do you think you'll age at all now that you've escaped?" I asked. I didn't learn the answer to that, since Chris picked that moment to walk through the front door. "Are you just getting in?" I demanded.

"I had a good night," he replied. I shuddered and looked at my tea; some things you just did not want to hear the details of, especially when they were your brother's details. "Is there breakfast?"

"Tea, toast, no coffee," I rattled off. "Where were you?"

"The pub." Chris sat between Robert and me and poured himself a mug of tea.

"Robert and I were at the pub," I said. "We didn't see you."

"Rina, we're in Scotland," Chris said, rather unnecessarily. It was stamped on my passport. "There are pubs every ten feet, or so."

"Point taken," I murmured. Still, I did not like the idea of Chris out at night among the Good People, dangling himself like fresh meat in front of gray monsters and Ice Princesses and who knows what else. Then again, since he couldn't see them, he was probably a lot safer than either me or Robert.

Speaking of Robert, he was eying my brother warily, his jaw tense. Chris seemed to have forgotten all about his distrust of Robert, or maybe he was just really drunk. Or tired, or hung over. I don't know which explanation I'd have preferred.

"I'm going to go down to St. Andrew's today," Chris announced, shoving his chair back from the table. "To visit Ethan and David," he added, naming two of his former classmates from Carson. Both had secured teaching positions at the prestigious university, one in English, and the other in Divinity. Their presence in Scotland was how Chris had officially justified accompanying me on this trip.

"They don't have classes?" I asked, being that it was a weekday.

"I'm not sure," Chris replied. "Even if they do, we can catch up after class ends. May I take the rental?"

"Of course," I replied. With that, Chris rose, clapped me on the shoulder, and retreated to his room.

"I guess he's decided you're not a serial killer," I said, after Chris had shut the door.

"'T'would appear so." Robert shook his head, and left the subject of my brother behind. "Now, then, Karina lass, have ye more research to do? This old scholar would love to lend ye a hand."

"I have some notes to organize," I said in a rush. "I-I might not have any time for field work today."

Robert nodded, his narrowed eyes telling me that he was well aware of my ruse. "As ye wish, lass. If I may be o' any help, you've but to ask."

I smiled—okay, it was probably more of a grimace—and rose from the table. After refilling my mug, I hauled out a few sheaves of field notes, and spread them across the coffee table. If I was going to pretend to work, I needed to at least look like I was working.

THE CHASE

I blinked myself awake, then I rolled over and steeled myself for the inevitable hacking fit that came after a night of drinking... But it didn't come. In fact, I felt great. Amazing, even, better than I had in weeks, maybe years. I felt like I could take on the world, and win. And from now on, I would have Sorcha beside me.

Before I could dwell on her too much, I took a shower and shaved. While I took care of that, I wondered why I hadn't told Rina about Sorcha. We had always been close, despite our seven-year age gap. I remembered when Mom and Dad had brought Rina home from the hospital, a tiny little being wrapped in pink that smiled and cooed at me, and how I'd resolved to protect my perfect baby sibling from anything that could hurt her.

Eventually I'd transitioned from Rina's defender against the neighborhood bullies—though I'd really lost that title when she delivered one Jonathan Morris a black eye, even though he had been a year older and thirty pounds heavier than her—to her best friend and confidant, just as she was mine. I'd told Rina about Olivia the first day she sat through one of my classes, and Rina had yelled at me to leave my students alone. When it was apparent that Olivia and I would be together regardless, Rina had counseled discretion, but that was all.

Rina had always supported me, no matter the situation. Ever since our parents' death Rina was the one constant good thing in my life.

"I'm going to tell Rina about Sorcha," I said, as I put on my shoes. "She'll be happy for me." Filled with resolve, I opened the bedroom door and saw Rina sitting at the kitchen table with her field notes scattered around her. Next to her, Robert was flipping through one of her books; only my sister would take all of her textbooks with her on vacation.

What does she see in that freeloader? Rina was a smart girl, too smart to fall for the nonsense this guy was peddling. I had half a mind to call the police and have Robert removed, maybe even file a restraining order against him... Then Robert pointed out a passage in the book to Rina. She read the lines in question, then she looked up at Robert and smiled. As I watched the scene before me, I realized where I'd seen the expression on my sister's face.

Rina was looking at Robert the way Olivia had once looked at me.

I would give anything—no, *everything*—to have Olivia look at me that way, just one more time.

Maybe Robert was just what Rina needed after that whole mess with Jared. What's more, I was certain that Sorcha was exactly what I needed.

"Morning," I said as I entered the common room. I withdrew my phone from my back pocket, and saw the time. "Afternoon," I amended. "I'm going to St. Andrews now. Would you like me to pick up anything on the way back?"

"I think we're good," Rina replied. "Have fun."

"Aye, man," Robert said. "Enjoy yourself."

I nodded, then I grabbed the keys and left. It was only after I'd pulled onto the road that I felt a twinge of guilt; not only had I lied to my sister, I hadn't said anything to her about Sorcha.

I parked the rental car and rushed through the narrow streets and alleys, not wanting to be late for my meeting with Sorcha. I'd never felt so strongly for a person after knowing them for so short a time, not Olivia, not anyone. After Sorcha and I had parted earlier that morning, I'd missed her so much I felt near-physical pain, as if I'd lost far more than just her company.

And how did I know that I was to meet her precisely at three? I shrugged off the question like a duck sheds water; I didn't care how I knew, so long as I knew it about her.

I reached the pub and placed my hand on the door, having arrived with a scant five minutes to spare, when I remembered Sorcha's exact words: *meet me in this very spot*. Unsure why she would prefer to meet in the street rather than in the warmth of the pub, I released the polished brass knob and moved a few feet to the left, and leaned against the brick wall I'd pinned Sorcha to only a few hours prior. And so I waited. And waited.

Just when I decided that I'd been stood up, I felt a hand on my arm. "You're early," Sorcha breathed into my ear.

I turned around, my bewilderment over how Sorcha had seemingly appeared out of thin air quickly replaced by desire. "Actually, you're late," I countered, taking a good long look at her. Sorcha was wearing tight faded jeans and a fitted tan leather jacket with a cream sweater and tan boots, her dark curls loose and tumbling across her shoulders.

Sorcha stood on her toes, and kissed my cheek. "I do hope you will allow me to make reparations for my tardiness."

I draped my arms around her shoulders. "Of course I will." I tugged her toward the pub's door, but she slipped out of my arms and away from me. "You don't want to go inside?"

"I want you to chase me," Sorcha replied, dancing away. I laughed and lunged at her, but she was too quick. Before long it was a full-on chase through the streets of Crail, heedless of the fact that I was running around like a loon after a woman I hardly knew in broad daylight. Others going about their days paid us no mind, and we cavorted like children, darting around people and objects alike.

"Caught you," I said at last, Sorcha squealing as I grabbed and held her upper arms. She twisted around to face me, and I kept my hands on her the entire time. After the mad chase she had led me on, I wasn't risking her flight.

"What do you demand?" Sorcha asked. When I cocked my head, she elaborated, "Your prize, for capturing me."

Instead of replying, I kissed her hard. When we parted, she gazed at me from under her lashes, her lips red and swollen.

"Follow," Sorcha said, sliding out of my arms.

"I'm not letting go of you," I said as I gripped her hand.

"I wouldn't dream of it."

Sorcha led me down a darkened causeway, until we were standing before a stately old home set far back from the road, the entry flanked by stone gateposts and a pair of apple trees laden with fruit. The entrance was a set of stone steps, topped by a pair of massive oak doors. I imagined that it had at one time been a grand manor, the home of one of the area's elite families. I wondered if Sorcha was descended from one of those grand genteel names of old.

"Where are we?" I asked.

"This is my home," Sorcha replied. "Will you come inside with me, Christopher?"

"I'd love to come inside with you," I said, then I cringed. That was the lamest thing I'd ever said, and I'd been using lame pickup lines all across Scotland. Sorcha laughed and fluttered her lashes, unoffended by my sudden lack of wit.

"I am glad." Suddenly, she pulled me against her, her breasts flush against my chest. "You make me so very, very glad. Never leave me, Christopher."

In that moment, I realized several things about Sorcha: her utter lack of a Scottish accent, her unusual and quick declaration of feelings, that she'd brazenly demanded a commitment from me. Most importantly, I realized that I didn't want to leave her, either.

"I won't," I promised. "I'll stay as long as you want me."

Her gaze heavy, Sorcha led me through the dark oak doors of the manor, down a marble hall, and into her chambers. I hoped she would never let me go.

JEWELRY, WINE, COOKIES, FLOWERS

Morning came, and I was no more eager to venture out into the world of gods and monsters than I had been the day before.

One of my chief discoveries the day before was that the coffeemaker came equipped with an automatic timer. Eager to try out my new toy, I'd prepared the grounds before going to bed, and woke up bright and early to the greatest aroma in the world. Once I'd had a cup or three, I made Robert and me some scrambled eggs, bacon, and toast for breakfast, then I moved on the living area.

After we'd eaten I settled on the couch while Robert claimed the kitchen table. He spent the morning reading one of my geology books, while I alternated between flipping through channels and forcing my way through a four hundred page text all about the wonders of bedrock composition in Britain, which, unfortunately, was directly related to my other great discovery.

Some of the places I'd visited on my Spiritual Sights tour had been reporting supernatural phenomenon for hundreds of years, which made me wonder how long certain rocks, like quartz, could retain vibrations. I was cross referencing this text with another, much slimmer tome, that detailed the various ways igneous rock eroded, and how long they retained their unique characteristics once they'd broken down to the size of gravel and eventually grains of sand. If I could establish a correlation between bedrock composition and reported spiritual activity, and prove that certain vibrations can remain accessible even after said rock had substantially eroded, my thesis would practically write itself.

Of course, these two facets of my theory did not account for the fact that, in most cases, the erosion of igneous rocks takes place over thousands or millions of years, and the bedrock I was researching hadn't had humans tromping around on it until the end of the Upper Paleolithic period, which was around eleven thousand years ago. Let's face it, no one had ever, not even once, claimed to see the ghost of a dinosaur or dire wolf. This meant that I was barking up the wrong tree, the really *really* wrong tree. Which was why I was letting the television distract me. Sherlock Holmes, you know.

Still, I would rather read about erosion and bedrock that leave the cottage and risk another encounter with the gray monster. Robert was determined to keep me company in my misery, and he amused himself for the better part of the morning by reorganizing the bookshelf. Good thing we had the books since he wasn't interested in watching the local programming with me; he kept shooting the television these furtive glances as if the moving pictures were the results of tiny demons, and not radio waves transmitted through air and space. Then again, based on my recent experiences the former just might be more likely.

"Why don't you go for a walk?" I suggested, after Robert had alphabetized the bookshelf in ascending and then descending order. "Get some air."

Robert perked up at that. "Will ye come along with me, lass? 'Tis a lovely day."

"No," I said a bit too quickly. When his brow quirked, I added, "I really do need to get through these books."

Robert pursed his lips and nodded, obviously not buying my excuse, especially since I'd already told him that I didn't think this avenue was going to work out. I got up and opened my daypack, and grabbed some money from my wallet. "Here, why don't you pick us up some lunch? Hopefully, I'll power through this book and be done before dinner."

Robert eyed my too-eager smile, the fistful of cash I held out to him, and decided to let me get away with my little white lies. For now, at least. "As ye wish, Karina lass," he said. "Now, then, what would ye be likin' for lunch?"

"Fish and chips?" I suggested, glancing toward Chris's still-closed door. I'd heard him stumble in shortly before dawn, which was typical Chris and Ethan behavior. I sure hoped Ethan didn't have any early classes to teach. "Get three orders, in case Sleeping Beauty decides to join us."

"That I will."

With that, Robert took the money and set out to the fish and chip shop that was a few blocks over. As for me, I threw myself back into my research, deliberately ignoring the bright sunshine streaming through the windows, and the birds chirping away in the trees.

A little more than an hour later, Robert returned bearing three brown paper bags. My first instinct was to ask him what had taken so long, being that one could walk to and back from the fish and chips stand in under ten minutes, but I held my tongue. There could have been a line, after all. Then I saw the dark smear behind Robert's ear, and I knew what had really happened.

"You saw one of the *fuath*," I accused. He opened his mouth, but I countered whatever excuse he was concocting by grabbing a towel and wiping away the blood. "If it wasn't a fairy monster, then explain this."

Robert eyed the bloody towel in my hand, then he blew out a breath. "Aye, lass, I did encounter one," he admitted. "Rest assured, that beastie will trouble no one else from here on out."

I looked at him for a long moment, then I decided to concentrate on that which I had a hope of influencing. "Are you all right?" I asked, swabbing at his neck.

"That I am," he replied. "No wounds to speak of, no' e'en a scratch."

Robert took the towel from my hands, then we tore into our lunch. As predicted, the scent of hot food roused Chris from whatever stupor he and Ethan had drunk themselves into. By the time Robert and I had unpacked the food, my brother stumbled out of his room, growling like a bear emerging from hibernation.

"What's going on?" he croaked, staring at the takeout packages as if he'd never seen a white paper carton before.

"Lunch is what's going on," I replied. "Robert went out for fish and chips." I'd set out all three orders, but there were still two full bags. "What's in there?"

"Oh, I thought we were needin' a few special items, as well," Robert replied. He proceeded to unpack a newspaper, then a bag of apples and jar of marmalade. Before I could ask what was so special about these things, from the second bag he produced a loaf of bread, a bottle of wine, a brown cardboard box filled with cookies, and a potted African violet.

"Why the plant?" I asked, examining the terracotta pot.

Robert looked a bit sheepish. "Truly lass, I wanted to get ye somethin' that would brighten your day. I considered a bouquet, but the plant will last a fair sight longer than cut flowers."

"You got this for me?" I asked, both surprised and pleased. "What about the wine and the cookies?"

Dark red dusted Robert's cheeks. Had I just made a gallowglass blush? "Well, I reckoned that if the plant was no' to your liking, then the sweets or the wine may be." He cleared his throat, and added, "The apples and jam are for a snack later on, ye ken."

I brought the African violet to my nose and sniffed, even though I knew they didn't have any fragrance to speak of. It was just what one did when one was given flowers.

"Are you courting my sister?" Chris demanded, shattering my warm fuzzy feelings.

"Courting?" I snapped. "What are we, in a Jane Austen novel or something?"

"So far, he's given you jewelry, wine, cookies, and flowers," Chris ticked off. "Sounds like courting to me."

"You're an idiot," I grumbled. I put down the plant and grabbed my container of fish and chips, and stalked over to the couch. I heard Robert and Chris exchange a few remarkably civil words, but I ignored them. Then Robert sat on the other end of the couch, his lunch balanced on his knee. Chris had elected to eat at the kitchen table, which was just fine with me.

"I was just tellin' your brother that I meant no offense," Robert said quietly. "I truly do appreciate ye takin' me in, and I only wished to show ye me sincere appreciation. If ye do no' care for the plant, I shall put it out in the garden."

"Oh, the plant's staying," I said. "If anything's getting put out back, it'll be Chris."

Robert smiled at that, and a few of my warm fuzzies came back. True to form, Chris wrecked it again, this time by uttering an expletive he normally reserved for students who got Milton confused with Spenser.

"Bone in your fish?" I asked.

"No." Chris came over and dropped the newspaper on the coffee table. A headline below the fold read: *Authorities Still Baffled Over Incident At Inchmahome Priory.*

"Oh, crap," I mumbled. The story went on to detail that *twenty-seven* eyewitness accounts reported seeing a man with a sword decapitate an American tourist, yet no trace of the body could be found, and the same could be said of the supposed swordsman. Although, being that a local resident's pleasure boat had been stolen and left at the mainland at around the same time as the murder, it was being assumed that the killer had gotten away on the boat, possibly with the body in tow. Also impeding the investigation was the fact that all twenty-seven witnesses were a part of the same tour group, and that all members were accounted for; as yet, no one could explain the twenty-eighth, and apparently dead, individual. The story closed by stating that the investigation was ongoing.

"Crap," I repeated. I handed Robert the paper, and watched his eyes widen.

"This is not good," Chris hissed. "What if they figure out we were there?"

"You burned the passenger log," I said. "And they must not have cameras there. If they did, the footage would be all over the news."

Chris grunted. "Twenty-seven witnesses," he grumbled. He retreated to the kitchen table, and wolfed down his fish and chips. "I'm going back to Ethan's," he announced when he was done.

"When does Ethan teach?" I snapped. "With all this boozing, you're going to get him placed on administrative leave."

Chris scowled; administrative leave was exactly what he'd been placed on once Carson University had gotten wind of Olivia's plagiarism suit. "By the time I get there, class will be over," Chris said. "Don't concern yourself over the health of Ethan's career."

"Chris, I—"

He held up a hand. "It's fine. I get it." Chris grabbed the car keys, and then his jacket. "Are you going to be okay here?" he asked with a pointed glance toward Robert.

"Yeah," I said. Unlike whatever my brother was thinking, Robert was the one protecting me. "Tell Ethan I said hi."

"I'll do that." With that, Chris disappeared out the front door. I dropped my gaze and stared at my fish and chips, devoid of an appetite.

"Ye and your brother are quite similar," Robert commented.

"How's that?" I dipped a chip in some curry sauce and stuffed it in my mouth. Even though I wasn't hungry, I was loath to waste good curry.

"When e'er a topic arises that ye would rather no' speak of, ye completely change the subject," Robert replied. "Both of ye exhibit this particular trait."

"I... We do not."

"Truly, lass, keepin' such things bottled up is no' verra good for either o' ye."

"Chris is just uncomfortable," I said. "He just met you, you know."

"Of that, I was aware."

I glanced at Robert; he was staring at me, his blue eyes daring me to explain myself. "Want to help me with my research?" I asked, thus confirming everything Robert had just said.

Robert gracefully accepted his victory. "O' course, Karina me lass," he replied. "Just tell me what ye are needin' help with."

I smiled, and grabbed my notes. "Well, I'm worried that the direction my theory is moving in doesn't make sense," I began.

HOPELESS ROMANTIC

I wandered through the streets of Crail, taking almost the same path I'd walked down two days prior. I was furious with that freeloader for taking advantage of Rina, furious with Rina for not using even part of her brain to figure out his scheme, furious for myself for not being man enough to handle the situation.

Crap. I'd left Rina alone in the cottage with Robert. Again.

Granted, Rina seemed to enjoy Robert's company, and I'd had no indication that the guy had laid a finger on her. Still, those facts didn't make Robert respectable, only patient. Patient to rob us, to do God knows what with my sister...

"Christopher."

I looked down and saw a hand on my elbow; I'd know that alabaster skin anywhere. I turned around, and found Sorcha standing behind me.

"Why are you here?" I blurted out, then amended, "Not that I'm not glad to see you. You surprised me."

Sorcha arched a delicate brow. "Are you pleased, then? Pleased enough to tell me what's troubling you?"

I sighed, and scrubbed my face. "It's my sister."

"I didn't know you had a sister," Sorcha murmured. "Bit of a hellion, is she?"

"No, not at all," I replied, "Rina's a good kid. She's my best friend, the only one who really understands…" I straightened, unwilling to let Sorcha know how far I'd fallen. Not yet, at least. "She met this guy in Aberfoyle, and he's been taking advantage of her ever since, but she refuses to see it." I glanced at Sorcha, and added, "She's a hopeless romantic, you know."

"Hopeless," Sorcha repeated. "She met him in Aberfoyle, you say?"

"Yes, at the tourist trap behind the old kirk. He's even calling himself Robert Kirk, after that preacher who was supposedly taken by fairies."

Sorcha pursed her lips. "Might you be able to capture an image of this Robert Kirk for me? On your device?" Her arm snaked around my waist, and she slowly withdrew my phone from the back pocket of my jeans.

"Sure," I replied, then I grabbed her hips and pulled her against me. "Why? Do you have friends in law enforcement?"

"Enforcers," Sorcha murmured, tilting her face upward to mine. "I have enforcers aplenty."

PLANS OF HIS OWN

Thursday dawned bright and cheerful, just as Wednesday had, though I myself didn't share the sentiment. If it was Thursday, that meant it was the second day we were holed up in the cottage; well, only I'd been holed up. Chris had made his obligatory appearance at breakfast, though that was probably just to assure me that he was still alive. And, when he got back on Wednesday night—also known as early Thursday morning—the weirdo had spent twenty minutes snapping pictures of the cottage with his phone. I mean, it was a cute place and all, but I didn't think we needed to preserve it for posterity.

Since Chris had been meeting up with Ethan at St. Andrews, I'd hardly seen him, and today their mutual friend David would be joining in the festivities. That was all well and good, but as for me, I still didn't know if I would ever go outside again.

They were out there.

I was still terrified, if anything even more terrified than I'd been yesterday or the day before, and I was handling it badly. Robert coming home with fey blood smeared across his neck had not helped matters.

So instead of acting like a normal, non-fairy seeing person, I hid behind my varied texts and research notebooks. I lobbed excuse after excuse at Robert as he attempted to get me out of the cottage. Luckily, we'd never gotten around to opening the wine, since that might have just been my undoing. In the end, Robert took a liking to my geology texts. He mentioned again how much had been learned about the natural world since his day, and wondered how many more things we had yet to discover.

When I first staggered out of my room that morning, it had only been to grab a cup of coffee and head back to my room. The second and final time I woke, it had been well after noon. I'd been up until just before dawn, finishing off the driest book ever written about bedrock composition. Granted, not many would refer to geology texts as riveting material, but this book was worse than most. It had taken me all of Wednesday afternoon and most of the night to force my way through the heavy volume, and all I wanted was coffee. However, it seemed that Robert had a few plans of his own.

"What's all this?" I asked. Now that I was in the common room, I realized what had roused me: Robert had gone out for fish and chips again, waking me the same way we'd woken Chris the day before. He had already unpacked and plated the food, and gestured to the seat across from him. I approached the table, then I grabbed a chip, dunked it in curry sauce and popped it in my mouth. Divine.

"I believe you Americans call it lunch," he said, with a wink, then he popped open a beer and pushed it toward me.

"I just woke up," I said, eyeing the bottle warily. Drinking at breakfast was something Chris would do, not his far more responsible sister. You know, the one who had insisted on the application of fairy ointment, thus making it possible for her to see monsters every waking moment. "Is there coffee? Or tea?"

"There was, at breakfast time. Do ye no' recall?" Robert closed the distance between us, and took my hands. It was the first time he'd touched me since the gray beast had terrified me, when I'd bawled on his shoulder and fallen asleep against him. "Karina lass, ye canna hide forever. What must your brother think of ye, cloistered inside this cottage like a nun in her abbey?"

"He won't care," I said. "He's probably off drunk with his friends, anyway."

"And when ye tell him that ye be hidin' from the Good People, what then?" Robert pressed. "Will he send ye to a lunatic asylum? Do they still have those, or is there a more pleasant way for those who ha' been touched to spend their days?"

I dropped into the kitchen chair; yeah, Chris probably would have me committed, and for my own good at that. If that happened, and I broke and told the staff about all the creatures walking among us, they'd lock the door and throw away the key. "What about the *fuath* that attacked you yesterday?"

"It shall ne'er attack another again," Robert proclaimed.

I shuddered. "I... I just wish you'd never seen it."

"I do as well." Robert squeezed my fingers, then took the seat opposite me. "Eat your food, drink your ale. Ye will need your strength."

"Um, what for?"

"You and I are going for a walk."

THE WEE BAIRNS

And walk we did.

I lingered over my lunch for as long as possible, but once your plate of fried fish and potatoes cool off, there's really nothing left to do but chuck it. So into the trash it went, and once I'd washed up and dressed, I did what I'd sworn I'd never do again: I left the cottage.

With a firm hand on my elbow, Robert guided me out into the world, his grip tightening a fraction when I hesitated on the threshold. "I'm not going to run off," I said, though I didn't mention how I'd considered shoving him out the door, and locking it behind him.

"Ye are no runner, 'tis for certain," Robert said. "Here, I've some friends for ye to meet," he added, leading me around to the back of the cottage.

"Friends?" I repeated. I couldn't imagine what he meant, since everyone Robert knew had died centuries ago. Then I realized that he meant fairy friends.

"Did these friends follow you to the cottage?" I asked.

"Not at all," he replied. "Near as I can tell, they have always resided here." We rounded the rear corner of the house, and found ourselves in a lovingly tended garden. Late summer roses bloomed in a riot of color, along with bluebells and buttercups and stately thistles, just in case we forgot we were in Scotland. On closer inspection, I saw a bed of delicate primroses in shades ranging from pale pink to lavender. The lush profusion of blooms, many of which were out of season and should have long since withered away, told me that this garden was tended by magic.

A flutter from the far corner of the garden caught my eye. That portion of the garden was dominated by a large marble birdbath, its many terraces covered with birds gossiping in little chirps and squawks as they stopped by for a drink. Robert tugged me closer, and I realized that those weren't birds, but something akin to pixies or sprites. My legs stopped working, and my entire body shook; he couldn't be expecting me to get closer to those... those *things*.

"Come, Karina lass," Robert said. "I swear to ye upon me verra life, they will do ye no harm."

I nodded, unable to tear my gaze away from their colorful wings. "When did you meet them?"

"Only yestreen," he replied. "When I stepped out for the ale."

"Oh." When I remained rooted in place, Robert altered his tactics and beckoned the creatures toward us. I shrank back, but only for a moment, my dread having been quickly overtaken by wonder.

"They're beautiful," I breathed. They were elegant little creatures, none of them larger than my hand, with slight, pinkish bodies, wings in jewel shades of red and green and blue, and glittering black eyes.

"Thank you, thank you," they chirped in unison.

I laughed, spreading my hands so two could set down on my palms while others settled on my shoulders. A headstrong critter with electric blue wings landed on Robert's head. "What are you called?" I asked the herd at large.

When they giggled instead of answering me, Robert said, "Wights, they are. Keepers o' secrets, tenders o' blooms."

"Is this your garden?" I asked, and they nodded furiously. "It's lovely."

Perhaps it was a trick of the light, but the wights appeared to blush. "Lovely lass, lovely lass," they sang. "Lovely lass with the gallowglass."

My gaze flew to Robert, but he only shrugged. I suppose I shouldn't have been surprised that the wights knew who he was, being that they were fairies and all.

"We must tend our blossoms," the wights announced, the lot of them taking flight as one. "Take care of your lass, gallowglass."

Robert and I watched the wights circle overhead and then swoop toward the birdbath, scooping up handfuls of water and delivering it to each flower in turn. "They are adorable," I said. "So happy and carefree."

"Aye, that they are," Robert agreed. "Now that I've proven to ye that not all o' the Good People are monsters, let's be off."

I smiled at him, and tucked my hand in his elbow. "Okay. But if we see the gray monster again, I'm running. When he's not looking, of course."

"O' course."

With that, we left the garden and its wights, and made our way toward the center of the fishing village. Maybe it was Robert's reassuring presence, or maybe it had more to do with the two beers I'd gulped down with lunch, but I was beginning to think I could do this. After all, most fairies weren't so bad. Some, like the tiny pixies that flitted around the cottage's garden, were uncannily beautiful, and most of the ugly ones seemed harmless. Maybe I wouldn't have to live my life in a bubble.

After a time, we rounded a corner and I saw one of the monstrous ones. It was huge, ten or more feet tall, and it had a thick, rough hide that reminded me of red clay that had been baked dry in the sun. Its shape was vaguely human, with short, squat legs, a round gut, and long spindly arms that flailed on either side. I had no idea how we would pass by without touching one of those flapping appendages.

Robert draped his arm across my shoulders while his other hand reached across my body and grasped mine. To the casual observer, we looked like we were on a date, just a regular man and a woman taking an afternoon stroll, not like a nearly four-hundred-year-old minister and an aspiring geologist avoiding a monster.

"Easy, lass," he murmured when I stumbled.

"Must be the beers," I quipped, flashing him a smile. He laughed, and we passed by the creature with it none the wiser.

"'Tis difficult to not stare," he murmured, once we were out of the monster's earshot. If monsters even have ears, who fricken' knew. "Curiosity, and all."

"You really think I'll get used to them?"

"After a time, ye surely will. Make no mistake, they will still be terrifying as e'er, but it will be a familiar sort of scare."

"Oh." My lack of confidence must have been plain, since Robert fixed me in his sly gaze.

"This way," he murmured, and we walked toward the outskirts of the village. After we'd walked for almost half an hour, and had left the buildings and cobbled roads behind, Robert led me toward a wooded glen. When I asked for the umpteenth time where we were going, he finally answered, "While I canna make them appear any less terrible to ye, I can make ye feel a wee bit safer."

"Feel?" I repeated, picking my way across the uneven ground. "As in, I won't actually be safer? Like a placebo effect?"

Robert's brow wrinkled; I bet there hadn't been much talk about placebos in the seventeenth century. "Well, they can still grab a hold of ye and take a bite out of ye, if they like."

"Great." I followed him through the trees, and we walked until we reached the far edge of the glen.

"Ah." Robert halted in front of a smallish tree covered with red berries; in the US, we called it mountain ash, but in the UK it was referred to as a rowan tree. Robert plucked a spray of berries and handed them to me. "Rowan berries, these are. Now, bind these wi' a length o' red thread, and ye will be safe from all sorts o' beasties, ye ken."

I stared at the berries in my hand, for once understanding how Chris felt when I told him something about sprites or elves. "What if they dry out?"

"No matter. The charm will still hold fast." Robert eyed the hem of my sweater, which just happened to be red. Understanding that the application of thread was a crucial part of the process, I handed him the berries, then I worried a length of yarn free from my sweater's hem. Once I'd bound the yarn around the stem of the berries, Robert smiled.

"See? Ye have a bit o' protection now. Once we ha' returned to the village, we shall ask about purchasing a few amber beads. Amber strung upon red thread is a strong charm against the Good People, indeed." Even though we were standing in the woods, surrounded by monsters that we had to ignore on peril of death, and the "bit o' protection" I was holding was nothing more than a bit of glorified trash, I smiled back at him. Maybe there was something to this placebo theory, after all.

"What about running water?" I asked. "Is it true that evil can't cross it?"

"So they say," he replied. "But what o' the evil that might be trapped on the other side, just waitin' for ye to cross over?"

I shuddered, then came to a realization. "You know what? I'm glad you made me the ointment. As horrible as the monsters can be, I'd rather see things as they are. I'd rather see the truth of the matter."

Robert shook his head. "That attitude is exactly what got me in this predicament."

I laughed, since I'd always been a troublemaker. Apparently, so was Robert. "Tell me about a few more of these charms."

By the end of the afternoon, my pockets were stuffed full with rowan berries and red thread, iron nails, plastic lighters—I still wasn't sure about that one, but Robert was confident—and other such wards against fairies. Robert had also advised me to turn my clothing inside out in order to further confound the Good People, but I wasn't yet ready to sacrifice fashion for safety. I mean, not that I was much of a fashion plate in my hiking boots and chunky sweater, but at least I knew how to properly dress myself.

We had just exited the local bakery when a decidedly new piece of odd happened; we had just purchased a few loaves of bread, which was yet another ward against the Good People. I'd said "who knew" so many times that afternoon, it was rapidly becoming my mantra.

Anyway, Robert and I had just exited the bakery when we saw it in the distance: a fairy, and a rather terrible looking one at that, was eyeing a young girl as if she was a nice juicy pork chop. I looked away, careful to keep the beast in my peripheral vision, but the creep just wasn't moving on.

"Robert," I whispered, "what sort of creature is that one?"

Robert glanced over his shoulder, then he turned around to fully face it. Since Robert was already staring at it, I decided to take a good look at the creature as well. It was vaguely humanoid in shape, and wasn't nearly as large as the other monstrous things I'd seen of late, maybe only three or four feet tall. Its flesh was a pale, putrid pink, and it had black eyes and a few tufts of weed-like hair scattered across its head and back. Its mouth was wide, with its upper teeth protruding outward in the king of overbites. Despite the teeth and nasty skin, the aspect of its appearance that most disturbed me was the battered brown cloth slung about its hips, and the protrusion beneath it.

"Robert," I hissed, "do they ever hurt children?"

"They hurt anyone they damn well please," Robert stated, loud enough to get the creature's attention. "Do no' fash, lass, this beast will not be hurtin' anyone today."

The creature turned toward Robert, and got an eyeful of a tall, muscular man with his feet planted and shoulders squared, staring back at it without the slightest indication of fear. As any sensible person, fey or otherwise, would do when being stared down by a man with murder in his eyes, the creature turned tail and ran. Without a word to me, Robert ran after it.

For a moment, I just stood there in the street, staring as Robert gave chase to the creature. *What the hell*, I thought as I ran after them. Normally, I would have completely and totally avoided getting involved in any sort of pursuit, but my pocket full of anti-fairy charms had made me extra brave. Not to mention, pretty fricken' foolish.

I ran for a few minutes, then I stopped short; Robert had caught the creature, and was holding it aloft by the scruff of the neck. "Are there more o' ye?" Robert demanded, shaking the critter for good measure. "Answer me!"

"More...more what?" I panted, leaning on my knees while I caught my breath.

"More children," Robert ground out. The creature's face was turning a sickly shade of green, so I touched Robert's arm.

"Hey. You're killing it." Robert turned his wild blue eyes to mine, so I added, "If you kill it, it can't answer your questions."

Robert grunted, apparently unpleased by this bit of logic I'd brought up. He dropped the creature, its hide smacking against the cobblestones, its throat making wet, slurping noises as it struggled for breath.

"What did you mean, children?" I demanded.

Robert didn't take his eyes off of the creature as he replied, "In me time as gallowglass I have uncovered—and eliminated—a fair few of these beasties. They lure human children away from their mums, and replace them with changelings."

"We serve our master," the creature hissed. Robert hit it with his sword's hilt, dazing it.

"Changelings?" I repeated. "You mean they're kidnappers?"

"Aye." Hard blue eyes regarded me. "That they are."

"Oh. Well. Kill it!"

"I canna kill it until I know if there are more," Robert explained, reiterating my earlier argument. "I canna leave the wee bairns to suffer."

"Suffer?" I repeated. "I thought those switched children were sent to fairy, to play and eat candy. That's what all the stories say."

Robert shook his head. "They're little more than slaves. Most don't survive the first year after their capture."

"Oh," I said, cold dread in the pit of my stomach. We had to find those babies. "Can you follow its trail back to wherever it lives?"

A shake of his head. "No, but I ken a few ways to make it speak." I must have turned green, or worse, because Robert added, "Ye do no' need to observe this. Stand away from me, Karina lass."

I opened my mouth to argue, but my rapidly rising gorge told me that was a bad idea. Trying not to lose what was left of my lunch, I wandered into a nearby restaurant. I ordered two black coffees and three fruit pastries, then I claimed a corner table, and waited.

After an almost unbearably long time, Robert appeared, standing over my table. He was smeared with dirt, and something resembling grease was streaked across his chest and arms. I was pretty sure that those dark streaks weren't really grease, and that I was never, ever going to inquire as to their origin.

"Is everything..." My hands trembled, so I drank some coffee and started over. "Are there more?"

"Yes." He didn't elaborate, and his grim face didn't change.

"Sit." I gestured to the chair across from me. After a brief hesitation, he did, and I shoved the coffee and two of the pastries toward him.

"What's all this, then?" he asked.

"When I'm upset, the only things that help are something hot to drink, and something sweet to eat," I explained. "I'm not like my brother. I don't think whisky solves all the world's ills," I added, with a smile that was more of a grimace.

Robert looked from the coffee to the pastries. "Ye purchased these for me, because ye worried I'd be upset after all o' that?"

"Well, aren't you?" I countered.

A slow, sad smile curled his lips. "I suppose I am. But I am used to such occurrences. There was no need for ye to go out o' your way, love."

"You brought me cookies and flowers and wine yesterday to cheer me up," I reminded him. "Consider this me returning the favor."

Robert's sad smile got a bit wider. "Aye, that I shall."

After Robert had taken a few sips of coffee, and demolished the pastries in a few bites, I ventured, "Well? It told you about the kids?"

His eyes went cold again. "Aye, and I ken exactly where the bairns are bein' held."

I tossed back the last of my coffee, and stood. "All right. Let's go get them."

Twenty minutes later, Robert and I stood outside of what looked like an abandoned cottage. It was eerily similar to the cottage my grant providers had rented for me in Crail, if you overlooked the untrimmed garden hedges and the elderly shingles that looked about to give way at any moment. When I mentioned as much to Robert, he only shrugged.

"'T'would no' be a verra good hiding spot if it stood out," Robert said. "The Good People, they prefer to go about unseen."

Yeah, I'd figured that out after he'd slathered an ointment across my eyes that made me see monsters. "Exactly what is good about them?" I asked.

"I have always struggled with that term meself," Robert murmured, then he grabbed my wrist. "Karina, you do no' need to enter along wi' me. I can handle them well enough on me own."

"But, what about the children?" I asked. "Won't they be scared?"

"Aye, that they may be." Robert extended his arm to the side, and his claymore appeared. "Verra well. Ye shall see to the wee ones, while I deal with their captors. Be safe, Karina me lass."

"And you, Robert lad," I replied, unsure about the proper platitudes one must utter prior to a battle. I must have done well, since Robert flashed that grin of his. He brought my hand to his mouth and kissed my knuckles, then he kicked down the front door.

Three creatures burst out of the doorway. I dropped to the ground and covered my head with my hands. Robert engaged two of the creatures, but a third ran past me as if I wasn't there. Maybe those anti-fairy charms did work.

I watched the creature run across the yard and to a small shed. I had no idea what was in there, maybe weapons or even more beasts. I stood, grabbed a rock the size of a softball, and threw it at the creature. It hit in the center of its back, and he went down hard.

"Good work," Robert said, his hand outstretched. As he pulled me upright I saw the other creatures' bodies lying across the threshold.

"You too. Let's get inside before more show up."

The interior of the cottage was anything but what I'd expected. I'd been prepared for chaos, all-out war even, but things inside were calm, almost nursery-like. There were several more of the putrid pink creatures wandering along the walls like ducks in a carnival shooting game, along with a nest of children. And when I say nest, I mean it in the purest sense of the word. In the center of the room there were six children snuggled in a circular wad of blankets, sleeping away as if all was right in their worlds. If only that were the truth.

"They look so peaceful," I murmured, taking in their innocent faces.

"They will be a fair sight more peaceful once they ha' been returned to their parents," Robert growled.

One of the creatures noticed Robert and I, and said something to the rest. "Robert," I began.

Robert raised his sword and jerked his head toward the children. "I will take care o' them. See to the bairns."

I rushed to the side of the nest and set about rousing the sleeping children. One by one they opened their eyes, none seeming any the worse for wear. In a somewhat but not really orderly fashion, I herded them all out of the house and into the garden. All the while, I tried not to look at what Robert was doing, but I kept catching glimpses of him in my peripheral vision.

Robert was like a scourge, his arcing blade flashing silver as he destroyed the monsters that had captured these children.

A short while after I had gotten all the children into the garden, a slightly battered Robert joined us. At least the blood splattered across his chest and arms wasn't his.

"Are they all gone?" I asked, unwilling to expand upon who 'they' were and how they'd gone while in the company of children.

"Aye." Robert's gaze swept over the children. "They are all well and hale?"

"They are." I stood, intending to ask him what we were supposed to do with all of these well and hale kids, when Robert crouched in front of a tiny girl who couldn't have been more than three years old.

"Tell me," he crooned, "where is your mum?"

She blushed—I guessed he had the same effect on females of all ages—then she leaned forward and whispered in Robert's ear. A moment later, Robert stood and hoisted her onto his shoulder.

"Where are you going?" I asked.

"Why, to return the wee lass to her mother," Robert replied. "Karina, bring along the rest."

Just as I was about to ask Robert how I was supposed to wrangle all these kids without a rope or a net, the wee ones queued up behind me, each holding the hand of the one behind. With a shrug I accepted this small bit of fortune, and the remaining five children and I followed Robert out into the neighborhood.

Our first stop was at a nondescript apartment building, containing ten or maybe even twenty flats. Robert held the young girl in his arms as he strode toward the entrance, murmuring in her ear the entire time. After a few moments, he brazenly opened the third door to the left. A rather distraught woman opened the door, took the girl from Robert and brought her inside. What the woman failed to notice was the form that exited the door, which resembled a bundle of sticks vaguely in the shape of a child.

"What was that?" I demanded, as I moved to Robert's side.

"When the true child returns, the changeling is forced to leave," Robert murmured, gazing upon the mother and child's reunion with tender eyes. "When the bairn is first taken, an enchantment is laid across it, making it docile and open to suggestion. The enchantment carries o'er to the parent, in most cases, and holds e'en when the bairn is returned to its rightful home. It works out quite well, for mother and bairn alike." Robert's eyes were a clear, shining blue, the happiest I'd ever seen him.

"This is what you did while you were a gallowglass," I said, as certain of that statement as I'd ever been. "Even though you were bound to her, you returned the children she'd ordered taken. You always did the right thing, even though it did nothing to help you."

Robert's gaze settled on me, and he smiled. "Aye. Ye have discovered the truth o' the matter, Karina me lass."

I watched him for a moment, my preacher-warrior who'd just proven to have the kindest heart of anyone I'd ever met. "Since I know the truth of it, may I help you return the rest?"

Robert glanced behind me at the rest of the children. "Aye, that I can allow."

DINNER AND A STORY

When Robert and I returned to the cottage, my feet ached and I was happier than I'd been in days, all because we'd returned the children to their homes. As for the changelings... well, I wasn't really sure what happened to changelings when they got sent back to wherever they had come from. I was just happy that they were gone, and the children with their families where they belonged. My elation deflated a bit when I read the note Chris had left on the kitchen table:

Rina,

I am going to stay with Ethan at St. Andrews for a few days. There are a few conferences he wants me to attend along with him, and, since they begin early in the morning, it will be easier if I stay over. I have taken the rental, but I've left my credit card in case you need transport. Hopefully, the account hasn't been frozen yet.

Love, Chris

I stared at the note for a moment, half angry with my brother for abandoning me in an as yet unfamiliar Scotland, and with someone he thought was a serial killer, at that; half thrilled at the prospect of honing my newfound fairy seeing talent without his skeptical gaze bearing down upon me. In the end I sighed, and crumpled the note in my palm.

"What is it, lass?" Robert asked. "Bad news?"

"My brother," I began, "he's going to be staying at St. Andrews for a few days. It looks like it's just you and me."

Robert's brows shot halfway up his head. I imagined that in his day, unmarried women did not share cottages with older men, at least not without a chaperone. "Is he, now?"

"Yeah." I tossed the note into the hearth, which was rather pointless since there was no fire currently burning in it. I raked a hand through my hair, turned around, and faced Robert.

"If you'd like, we can go to the pub for dinner," I offered. "Tomorrow morning, we can rent another car. There's a natural rock formation I'd like to have a look at, and an abandoned castle that's sort of nearby. They say a white lady haunts it. The castle, that is, not the formation."

Robert smiled, the twinkle having returned to his eyes. "A white lady? Any idea o' who she is?"

"None at all," I said, returning his smile. "But I'd love to find out."

Since Chris had been good enough to leave me his credit card, Robert and I went to a local Italian restaurant for dinner instead of the pub we'd been frequenting; I hoped that the Ice Princess wouldn't miss us too much. After the day we'd had, cavorting with wights and returning lost children and banishing changelings and such, we certainly deserved a good dinner. While it wasn't exactly five-star dining—which was fine, since neither Robert nor I had clothing appropriate for such a place—it was very nice, and the food was excellent. Well, I thought it was excellent; being that there hadn't been much Italian food prepared in seventeenth century Scotland, Robert had never seen pasta before. And the look on his face when my pizza arrived was priceless.

"And ye are certain ye are supposed to eat it that way?" he asked, as I bit into a slice of pizza. It was a traditional Margherita, with marinara sauce, sliced mozzarella, and a scattering of basil leaves, all on a thin, crispy crust. Since I'd been raised on New York pizza it was far from the best I'd ever had, but it was delicious nonetheless.

"Where I come from, this is required eating," I said, once I'd swallowed. "If it hadn't been for late-night pizza deliveries, I might have starved to death during college." I pushed my plate toward him. "Go on. Try it."

Robert narrowed his eyes, then tentatively picked up a slice. He bit into it, chewed, and set it down. "Tastes much as it looks," he grumbled, returning his attention to his plate of roast chicken. "I believe I prefer meat for me dinner."

"More for me," I said, snatching the slice from his plate. We ate in silence for a time, Robert concentrating on his chicken and potatoes and ignoring his steamed asparagus, while my eyes darted around the restaurant.

"None are here," Robert said without looking up from his plate. "Ye are quite safe, lass."

I glanced at him, my gaze drawn by the silver collar just visible beneath the open collar of his dark red button-down shirt. "I know. It's just hard to not keep checking."

"Aye. That it is."

We finished our meal, talking about such boring topics as the weather and how much a rental car might cost us; we needed to acquire one, since without one we would be stuck walking around Crail. And since Chris was footing the bill for our replacement rental, I was definitely upgrading from the subcompact we'd been squeezed into since we'd arrived in the UK three weeks ago.

After the server had cleared our dinner plates, and taken our dessert order, our conversation turned, naturally, to the Good People.

"You never did tell me why you first made the ointment," I said.

"Didn't I?" Robert topped off my wineglass, then finished off the bottle into his. "Och, I made me first batch long ago, long before I attended university. I was a wee lad at the time, constantly terrorized by me brothers. I am the youngest o' seven boys, ye ken."

"You have six older brothers?" I gaped at him, unwilling to imagine what my life would have been like with five additional Christophers dogging my every move. Before I could ask him how he'd maintained his sanity, the server arrived bearing steaming cups of coffee, and our desserts. After we'd murmured our thanks, Robert set to work on his chocolate cake.

"Heavenly," he murmured, eyes rolling back in his head.

"Was their food really so awful?" I asked, sampling my tiramisu.

"Ashes and rot was what it was." Robert enjoyed a few more bites before speaking again. "What was I saying? Ah, yes. How I came to brew up that first batch o' wort. As I said, we were a large family, and poor at that. Me mum and her maid were always up to their elbows what with the cleaning and mending."

"I bet." I imagined seven unruly boys, and all the torn shirts and filthy messes they must have generated.

"So it came as some surprise when one day, all o' that mending and washing was suddenly done," Robert said. I blinked; did he mean that the fairies had been helpful? After my run-ins with the gray monster and the kidnappers, I'd decided that all fairies were evil. Well, all of them except the wights. "Have ye e'er heard of a *habetrot*, lass?"

When I shook my head, he continued, "'Tis a wee thing, terrible to look upon, but with a heart o' gold. When one comes across a family rich in love, and little else, they tend to stop in, and help out for a bit." Robert pursed his lips, and stabbed at his cake.

"And you just had to have a look at it," I ventured. Robert glanced up, and smiled.

"Aye, that I did," he confirmed. "'Twas enough for me mum that the tasks were done, and me brothers had no interest in such things. But me, the little one, just had to know what manner o' creature was invading me home. So, I hied meself off to the local wise woman, had her teach me a thing or two, and," he waved his fork in a circle, "here we are today."

"No wonder you're so calm around them," I grumbled. "You grew up seeing them all around you."

"Do no' mistake me putting on a brave face as calm," Robert warned. "Plenty o' times, I am near to passin' out from fright."

I smiled, and sipped my coffee. "I don't know," I said. "You seemed pretty brave to me when you were fighting those kidnappers, and when we returned the children."

His blue eyes twinkled. I liked it when they did that. "Did I, now? Perhaps I'll embark upon a new career as an actor, then."

We laughed at that, then we finished our desserts and settled our bill. Once we stepped out of the restaurant, I grabbed Robert's hands, walking backwards as I led him along.

"Walk me home, brave man," I declared; all the wine had made my head a bit fuzzy. "Keep all the creatures of the night at bay!"

Robert laughed as he pulled me around to his side. "That, I shall happily do," he said, linking his arm with mine.

Our walk back to the cottage wasn't overly long, though Robert did manage to regale me with the many ways he would defend me from all manner of beasts. Once we crossed over the cottage's threshold, our laughter was replaced by an awkward silence.

"Karina," Robert said at last, "truly, lass, thank ye for such a wonderful meal. I do no ken how I will e'er repay all o' your kindnesses."

"It was just dinner," I demurred.

"I'm no' thanking ye just for dinner," he clarified. His blue eyes searched mine, and he took both of my hands in his. "If not for ye, I might have lived out eternity under Nicnevin's curse. You, Karina lass, have given me my life back." He raised my hands and kissed each of my knuckles in turn, eight sweet, slow kisses. "Anything I can e'er do for ye, ye have but to ask."

"Oh, um." I was trembling again, for once not from fear. "You're welcome. I'm glad I could help. I like helping."

Robert squeezed my fingers. "I know ye do."

I squeezed back. "Is there anything I can help with now?"

Robert chuckled. "And what sort o' help are ye offerin'?"

I bit the inside of my mouth so hard I tasted blood. "In the morning. I meant in the morning. I'm going to go to bed now. Good night!"

I slipped free of Robert's grasp, and fled to my bedroom. I shut the door and leaned against it, my heart hammering away in my breast.

That was the second time I'd resisted asking Robert into my room. I didn't know if I could resist a third time.

PROSPECTING AND A PUB

Robert and I obtained a replacement rental car the following morning, which turned out to be pretty easy; the clerk in the rental office assumed that Robert was my husband and therefore the Christopher Stewart named on the credit card, and swiped away with abandon. Good thing that Olivia's evil lawyers hadn't made good on their threats to freeze Chris's assets just yet.

Rental car thus secured, Robert and I celebrated with one of the best breakfasts I've ever had. Hot, creamy oatmeal, crispy bacon, potato scones, and fried mushrooms and tomatoes all made an appearance at our meal. Thankfully, Robert refrained from mentioning how he had pledged himself to me the prior evening, or any of the other associated awkwardness that followed. As for me, I was pretending that the whole exchange had never happened, even though I'd thought about it all night, and dreamt about a stalwart knight with dark hair and blue eyes galloping around on a white horse. And the epic dry spell continued.

"Where are we off to this morning, then, Karina me lass?" Robert asked as he finished off his bacon.

"I'd like to go to the formation first," I said, at once becoming that geeky middle school girl who had been more into dinosaurs than pop music. "It's called Dob's Linn."

"Oh?" Robert quirked a dark eyebrow. "And where might this Dob's Linn be located?"

"Moffat." I dug out my much-abused ordnance survey map, and pointed to the area in question. "It should only take us about an hour to get there in the car."

Robert looked at the map for a moment, dark brows lowered across his eyes, and it hit me that this was probably the first time he'd seen a map of modern Scotland. I felt a wave of guilt, being that I might have just opened up a few old memories that he'd have rather left buried. Then my rakish reverend flashed me that grin of his, the one that always speared my heart like a hot knife through butter.

"Well, then," he said, "let's be off."

I tossed some money on the table, and we rose to leave. Robert held the door for me, and led me to the car park with a firm hand on the small of my back, which was making my stomach threaten to expel all of my delicious breakfast. Not to mention, there was no reason he should be affecting me this way. Robert was always chivalrous, but after my behavior during our walk home last evening, and the subsequent knuckle kissing incident, I was rather confused.

Robert held open the car door as I slid behind the wheel, and that was the end of our physical contact. If I'd been honest with myself, I would have admitted how I missed his touch, but I'd already decided that being confused was better than being attracted to him. As far as I was concerned, being friends, and nothing but friends, was the only sensible thing to do.

I glanced at him as I put the key in the ignition. Being sensible really was a drag, sometimes.

We stopped at the cottage so I could collect my field kit and my duffel bag, and grab our jackets. Once we'd locked the door and said goodbye to the wights, we were on our way to Moffat.

Apparently, some of the rude comments Chris had made about my map reading skills were spot on, since it took closer to two hours to reach Dob's Linn than the one I had estimated. Okay, maybe two and a half. Or perhaps our extended journey was due to the fact that I had a seventeenth century man riding in the passenger seat, who clutched the armrests as if they were life preservers and swore, rather impressively for a reverend, every time I accelerated.

Whatever the true reason for the long drive, we eventually made the turn off toward the site and entered the car park. "No' that far," Robert grumbled as I parked the car.

"Oh, hush. You liked the trip." When he wasn't concerned that we would careen into a ditch, Robert had enjoyed looking out at the countryside.

I exited the rental, I popped the trunk, and started assembling my kit.

"What's all this, then?" Robert asked as I grabbed a few picks, three sturdy canvas totes, a small hammer and chisel, and my goggles. Since Robert would be prospecting with me, I also grabbed my spare goggles, the ones that were way too big for my head and made me look like an anthropomorphic fly.

"This is my field kit. Well, my travel field kit," I amended, indicating the diminutive size of the tools. "My kit at home has larger and better tools, but these will do for today." I opened a hard plastic case, and retrieved a tape measure and magnifying glass.

"I thought we were looking for rocks?" Robert asked when he saw the magnifying glass. "We canna see them with our own eyes?"

"This place is supposed to be one of the best sites for fossils in the UK," I replied. Robert looked dumbfounded, so I explained, "Fossils are the remnants of creatures that died out a long time ago. Usually, only the bones are left, but sometimes we find imprints of skin or, if we're super lucky, internal organs."

Robert nodded, looking vaguely disgusted by my description. "And we are searching out these beasties for what reason?"

"To learn more about the earth, of course." I unzipped my duffel, and grabbed two granola bars and a package of beef jerky. We hadn't stopped during our journey, mostly because I had held firm to my belief that we were almost there from the fifty-minute mark onward, and my belly was rumbling. "Would you like a something to eat?"

Robert eyed the small green rectangle in my hand. "What sort o' food are ye offering me?"

"It's granola. Nuts and dried fruit and such." I unwrapped one of the bars and took a bite, then I held out the beef jerky. "This is dried beef."

Robert shook his head. "I am no' that hungry."

"Suit yourself." I jammed the unopened bar and jerky in my pocket, grabbed my site map, and oriented it to our location. "It's about a thirty-minute walk to the gorge from here. You up for it?"

"I am a warrior and a scholar," Robert declared. "O' course I am up for a wee walk." He made a face and added, "I will take that strange meat o' yours, lass."

I smiled, and handed him the packet of jerky and a bottle of water. "Let's be off, then."

The hike to the gorge wasn't one of the easiest hikes I'd ever been on, but it was far from the worst. Once we arrived at the gorge proper, Dob's Linn lived up to all the marketing materials I'd read. It was carpeted in lush grass, with dozens of fallen shale blocks and greywackes littering the landscape. Yet again, Scotland's beauty had not disappointed.

Robert, true to his scholarly roots, nodded attentively as I explained the site's significance as a boundary between the Ordovician and Silurian periods—geologic time periods which had occurred four hundred eighty-five million and four hundred forty-three million years ago, respectively—and had the decency to be impressed when I pointed out a volcanic ash layer that streaked across the side of the gorge.

"Ye truly are in your element," Robert said when I pulled out my hammer and chisel. "Ye remind me o' the young lads I studied with at university."

"Well, I am a young woman studying at a university," I pointed out. I picked out a promising looking slab of shale, and ran my fingers along the edge. "I've always been fascinated by the earth, how everything ended up the way it did. For every bit of information we learn, the earth has a thousand more secrets buried within her." I dragged the wedge of shale around, and balanced it on its side. "Can you hold this upright for me?"

"I surely can," Robert said. "Why am I holding it?"

Instead of responding, I set my chisel along the side of the shale, and gave it a few taps. Once I found the cleavage point, I gave the shale a good whack. Robert cursed as the stone broke apart in his hands, but I ignored his mutterings.

"Wow, I never get this lucky with my first strikes," I mumbled, grazing my fingertips across the rock.

"Luck?" Robert repeated, ignoring my charmed comment. "What does luck have to do with the breaking o' rocks?"

I took a swig from my water bottle, then I poured some across the newly cleaved shale. "These are graptolites," I said, the water having defined the fossils embedded within the shale.

"Written in rock," Robert said, translating the fossils' Greek name as he grazed his fingers across the small creatures. "They look more like plants than beasts."

"Yeah, they have a distinct dendritic form," I said, poking at a larger one. "For centuries, they were mistaken for fossilized plants, but they're definitely critters."

"Beasts like trees," Robert murmured. "Ne'er have I heard o' such a thing, no here on God's earth, nor in Elphame."

"I'm not surprised. They went extinct around four hundred million years ago."

Robert's eyes widened, then he shook his head. "I do no ken how ye can refer to these vast expanses of time with such ease."

"Says the almost four hundred-year-old man," I said with a smirk.

Robert threw back his head and laughed. "Ye have me there, Karina me lass." He tilted the shale toward the sun, tracing his fingers across the surface. "Actually, I think I have seen beasties such as these."

"Really?" I leaned in for a closer look. "Where?"

"The cottage's garden. Do these beasties no' resemble the wight's wings?"

I looked at the fossil he'd indicated; it was a colony, with four feathery branches attached to a central point. "I guess so." I bit the inside of my mouth, hard. I would not have a panic attack while prospecting for fossils.

"Do you think these fossils are wights?" I demanded. "Are they fossils at all, or just some fairy sent to spy on us?" I glanced around the gorge. We appeared to be alone, but I'd stopped trusting appearances.

Robert touched the back of my hand. "Does no' matter, lass. Even if these beasties were dragons in life, now they are well and truly dead. They canna harm us, nor report on us to her."

I ducked my head. "I guess I freaked out a bit. Sorry."

"'Tis quite all right, love." He stowed that rock and our other find in the largest of the canvas totes, then he stood and held out his hand. "Let's look for a few more o' these fossils o' yours," he said as he hauled me to my feet. "I find that I enjoy being around things that are far older than I."

About two hours went by, and Robert and I had packed all three of our totes full with fossils (that might or might not be ancient wights) and other interesting finds. Robert was a quick study, and it turned out that he had quite an eye for prospecting. When I mentioned that he laughed, and stated that he'd always loved to learn.

Eventually, we hauled our finds back to the rental. After stowing our tools and fossils in the trunk, Robert asked, "Well, Karina lass, what now?"

I blinked; what now, indeed. "Lunch?"

"Lunch sounds lovely," Robert agreed.

Per usual, Robert and I ended up eating in a pub. Our grubby state earned us a few interested glances when we entered, the bright yellow sunlight streaming in from the windows showcasing the dust motes floating around us, but no one seemed offended. And, everyone in the pub appeared to be of the human persuasion, which was yet another plus.

While Robert got us some seats I ducked into the bathroom to wash up. When I returned, I found Robert settled in at the bar with two pints standing before him.

"I ordered your meal for ye, as well," Robert said as I claimed the stool next to him.

"What did you order?"

"'T'will be a surprise for ye," Robert replied. I considered badgering him further, but figured that I'd know the answer soon enough. I flagged down the bartender instead, and asked for a glass of water. "The ale is no' to your liking?" Robert asked.

"It is, very much so, thank you for ordering it," I replied. "But since I'm driving, I can't drink it." In response to his blank stare, I added, "There are laws against drinking alcoholic beverages and driving soon afterward."

Robert looked confused, then he scowled. "What sort o' laws?"

"Um." Honestly, I had no idea of what the penalty would be for driving under the influence in Scotland, or anywhere besides the United States for that matter. I'd always figured Chris would get the first DUI, so I just kept bail money on hand. "Well, I could go to jail," I guessed.

Robert's scowl deepened. "More oppression from the English, I gather," he growled. He was still muttering away about things like Covenanters when the bartender deposited a meat pie in front of Robert, and a basket of curry and chips in front of me. Before I could mention that I was hungry for something a bit more substantial than potatoes and a condiment, the bartender returned with a plate of chicken tikka masala over rice. I glanced sideways at Robert, wondering how he even knew what Indian food was, but he merely shrugged.

"I asked the barkeep to prepare ye the best meal they offer," he said.

"Well, thank you," I said. "Why didn't you get the same for yourself?"

"What, ye will no' share wi' me?" Robert asked with a wink. "I thought we were friends by now, love."

I smiled, and took a bite of my chicken. The meat was tender, and the sauce was perfectly spiced. "This really is good. Want to try it?"

"Only if ye will try mine."

I glanced at his pie, and the thick cuts of steak and gravy that were spilling forth from the pastry. Yeah, I could do with a bite or two of that meaty goodness. I speared a chunk of chicken, coated it in sauce, and held out my fork. I had expected that Robert would take the fork from me, and eat the chicken as one normally would. Instead, he leaned closer and ate the morsel right off the tines.

"'Tis no' bad," he declared once he'd swallowed. "A wee bit peppery, but no' bad at all."

"It's not that spicy," I protested, even as I reached for my pint.

"Careful, love," Robert warned, placing his hand on mine. "I do no' wish for you to end up in this croft's tollbooth. Although, I could most likely break ye free."

"I bet you could." I took a sip of beer anyway; first of all, one sip couldn't possibly hurt. Second of all, I'd have the fairy queen's personal assassin in the car with me. As if Robert couldn't take on any ordinary police officer.

"Karina lass."

I glanced up, and saw that very same assassin holding out a forkful of steak and pastry. "For me?"

"Eat, love," he insisted, thrusting the fork closer. Since we had apparently moved on to the feeding each other portion of our day, I ate. The steak and pastry was, in a word, scrumptious.

"Oh my God, that's delicious," I said, realizing a moment too late that I was talking with my mouth full. I grabbed my napkin and hid behind it, enjoying the rich flavors. Then, I realized what I'd said. "I'm sorry."

"For what, now?"

"For taking the Lord's name in vain."

Robert chuckled. "Do no' fash, love. I do no' think He would mind a bonnie lass such as yourself enjoyin' a bite of a fine meat pie." He scooped up some more steak, and pointed it at me. My confusion must have been plain, because he added, "If ye do no' have another bite o' mine, how am I to obtain another bite o' yours?"

I grinned, and let Robert feed me. The steak was good, and the pastry crust really was to die for. "You can have more of mine if you want, but you need to get it yourself."

In response, he took possession of a rather large piece of my chicken. "I can manage that well enough."

I turned back to my lunch, only to have a chip that had been liberally doused in curry sauce thrust before my nose. "Am I supposed to eat that?"

"Ye surely are."

I accepted the chip, and washed it down with another sip of beer. What the hell, it had already been poured. "You're in an interesting mood."

"Bein' out in the countryside with ye has done wonders for me constitution," he replied, now cutting up the rest of his meat pie. "Truly, lass, there are few ills in this world that fresh air and sunshine will no' cure."

"I absolutely agree." After all, that belief was what had led me to study the earth sciences in the first place. I pulled out my crumpled map, rife with notations of all the places I'd like to visit; there had to be hundreds of marks defacing the poor thing. Since we were already a few hours outside of Crail, and it was still early afternoon, I figured we had plenty of time to visit the other site on my agenda.

"How do you feel about the sea?" I asked. "More importantly, how do you feel about castles by the sea?"

Robert cocked an eyebrow at me. "Get to the point, lass."

I shoved the map at him, and pointed to a location on the southern edge of the Firth of Forth. "Here's the other place I want to visit. It's called Tantallon Castle. The view of the sea is supposed to be amazing there, and there is this really cool volcanic plug island right offshore." I studied the map for a moment, and added, "The castle is more of a ruin, really. It's kind of on the way back to the cottage."

Robert read over the castle's description in the pamphlet, then he glanced at the map. "'Tis no' really on the way," he pointed out. "And ye mentioned earlier today that this castle may have a ghost?"

"Yep, there's a white lady," I confirmed. "No idea who she could be, though. People have all sorts of theories, but nothing concrete."

Robert snorted. "Has anyone bothered to ask her who she is?"

"Most of us don't have your unique communication abilities," I smirked.

Robert's eyes skated over the map. "And how far is this castle?"

I shrugged. "Oh, not far."

"Ye truly have no concept o' distance, do ye, lass?" he asked. I blushed and ducked my head, my dark hair curtaining my face. My fellow students had teased me mercilessly about my inability to reconcile time and space. One year, the entire geology class had pitched in to give me a state of the art GPS for Christmas, which had left me mortified. Unfortunately for Robert and me, I'd left the device back in the States.

After a moment, Robert leaned toward me and gently tucked my hair behind my ear, and murmured, "Do no' fash, Karina me love. If ye wish to visit this castle with its strange island, I shall certainly accompany you."

"You don't mind?" I ventured.

"Ye are the driver, aren't ye now? I am at your mercy."

I don't know what amazed me more, that Robert was so willing to go along with my whims, or that he could so easily turn my mood around. I smiled, and grabbed another chip. "I should teach you how to drive," I said after I'd swallowed. "I bet you'd like it."

"I do no ken about that," Robert said flatly. "I believe my skills lie in languages and swordplay, not in the taming o' metal beasts."

"Well, eat up, then," I said, taking another swig from my pint. "We have a castle to visit." I just knew that the drive, and Tantallon, would be lovely.

THE WHITE LADY

Robert and I talked and laughed during the ride toward Tantallon Castle, him regaling me with stories of his youth in Perthshire and me telling him all about life in New York. We were getting along like old friends, and I dared hope that the nonsense that had been flitting through my mind last night was gone for good. Of course Robert was grateful toward me, being that I'd liberated him from centuries of... of...

I didn't know exactly what sort of things had gone on in the fairy court, but Robert had mentioned being under Nicnevin's curse. Anything that had "curse" in the title couldn't have been all that pleasant.

Despite whatever torments or non-torments Robert had been subjected to over the last few hundred years, they hadn't damaged his good nature. What's more, all he had expressed toward me over the last few days was his appreciation over being freed from the Minister's Pine, and a cordial demeanor. His good manners, coupled with his generally chivalrous behavior, such as when he held doors for me, or walked with his hand firmly placed upon on my elbow or the small of my back, had just sent my imagination into overdrive. My flight of fancy had been nothing more than that. Maybe it was even less than that.

Once we'd arrived at Tantallon, I pulled into the empty tourist lot, parked the rental, and grabbed my Spiritual Sights tour pamphlet from the center console. Not once during this trip to the UK had I arrived at a tourist site and found it empty; even Doon Hill had had a few others wandering about the ruined kirk and graveyard, though only Chris and I had deigned to climb the fairy mound. The utter lack of visitors at a castle by the sea on a clear, sunny day made me wonder if the place had been closed down.

"It says it's still operational," I said. I flipped the pamphlet over and checked the copyright date; it had been printed only a month before Chris and I had left the States. "Where are all the tourists?"

"Perhaps they're off viewing attractions that offer more than a few crumbling stones," Robert quipped.

I scowled. "You're starting to sound like Chris."

Robert grinned at that, forcing his blue eyes to twinkle at me until I laughed. Thus disarmed, we exited the rental and made our way toward the ruins. The castle, though it had been long since abandoned, was still rather majestic, from its tall towers to its massive curtain wall to its perch on a rocky outcrop high above the sea.

"I bet no one ever invaded this place," I said as we crossed the narrow walkway to the entrance. The castle was surrounded by steep cliffs on three sides, the rocks below so jagged they resembled brown teeth jutting skyward, and the beach below wasn't any more accommodating. If you fell from the walkway and the height and rocks didn't kill you, the crashing sea would make short work of what was left of you. "Nothing could possibly be worth the risk."

"The worthiness o' the risk all depends upon what's inside," Robert said. "Some treasures are worth far more o' a trial than the crossing o' a wee bridge."

"I don't need money that badly."

"What if the treasure in question was a fair sight more valuable than gold?"

He had a point there. I was starting to hate it when he had points. We'd reached the end of the walkway, and were standing in an open area before the main entrance. I glanced about for a tour group, a docent, anything; though, since the car park had been empty, I don't know how anyone would have gotten here. Tantallon Castle wasn't walking distance from anything.

"Shall we?" Robert asked, extending his arm. I ignored him and strode off toward the tower steps. If Robert was offended he made no mention of it, though he did plant that hand in its usual spot on my back. I could hardly feel him due to my thick sweater and waterproof jacket, which was a good thing. Otherwise, who knows if I would have been able to walk on a flat surface, never mind ascend those ancient stone stairs.

The first thing we learned during our journey upward was that this tower was completely empty, devoid of everything but dust and a few crumbling leaves; there weren't even any decorative carvings or cool stonework around the windows. While complained about the lack of adornment, Robert navigated the warren of rooms until we found ourselves standing on the top of the middle tower. Once we were up there I understood why some ancient architect had had the crazy idea to build Tantallon in the first place.

The view from the tower was breathtaking, the combination of its six storey height atop the cliff below holding us far above the crashing sea in the Firth of Forth. The steeply inclined island of Bass Rock rested in the distance like a lone sentry against invasion. The salt air was cool, inviting, intoxicating, and I turned my face into the wind. I was half imagining that the wind was carrying me off, when I felt Robert's warm hand against my skin, tucking my hair behind my ear.

"That's Bass Rock," I said, stepping out of his reach and pointing toward the island. "The volcanic plug island I mentioned."

"I'm familiar with The Bass," Robert said. "Saint Baldred once kept a cell there. He was so holy that when he died his body copied itself twice over, so three kirks could be graced wi' his relics."

"Wow." Multiplying corpses was a superhero ability I'd never heard of, or particularly wanted to witness. "Do you know a lot about saints?"

"Aye, that I do."

That stubborn piece of hair blew across my face, and Robert tucked it behind my ear once again. Without thinking, I turned my face into his palm until he was cupping my cheek. "Karina," he murmured.

A bird cried overhead, breaking the spell. "Why do you always call me that?" I muttered, sliding away from him.

"'Tis it no' your name?" Robert countered.

I sighed, and looked toward the sea. "It is. It's just that everyone calls me Rina, even my professors at school."

"Oh?" Robert cocked an eyebrow. "What does your mum call ye, then?"

I pursed my lips, and walked to the opposite side of the tower. Not that the simple act of turning my back would in any way deter a gallowglass. Robert placed his hands on my shoulders, and it was all I could do not to lean back into the warmth of him. "What happened to her?" he asked.

I stared across the empty courtyard, my gazed fixed on one of the cracked blocks of the opposite tower. "Both of my parents died in a car accident while I was young. Well, I wasn't that young; I was thirteen."

"A terrible age for a girl to be wi' out her mother," Robert murmured. I nodded; in less than a heartbeat's time, I'd gone from much-loved daughter to orphan.

"Chris tried being there for me," I continued, "but he was all wrapped up with college and... And it's not like he really knew what to do with me anyway. I mean, I was just his kid sister, no one he—"

My voice cracked, and Robert spun me about and pulled me into his arms. I started to tell him that while I missed my parents they'd been gone for ten years, and that while the pain was still very much with me it had dulled with time. What's more, what Robert had obviously interpreted as a sob had really only been a cough, due to the wind having whipped up some dust or leaves or something, but his arms were so warm and strong. After what I'd seen over the past few days, I felt like I deserved a bit of comfort.

"Karina love," Robert murmured against my hair, "we truly are a pair. I am alone in this world, and ye have naught but your brother."

"It's a good thing I found you, then" I said into his chest. He tipped my head back, his blue eyes searching mine.

"A good thing, indeed." He grazed his thumb along my jaw, his face leaning closer to mine. "What would I do wi' out you, love?"

"Kill bad fairies? Rescue the wee bairns?" I clutched the front of his shirt. "W-What would you want to do?"

Robert's hand on my back pushed me closer to him. "I ken exactly what I want."

"I thought I heard visitors!"

Robert scowled, then he looked over the battlement to the courtyard below. I followed suit, and saw a middle-aged woman waving a red umbrella at us. She wore a floral button down shirt, plaid pants, and the whole ensemble was topped with a raincoat, rain hat, and galoshes in matching neon yellow. Most remarkable were her ears, long pointed affairs topped with tufts of dark fur, followed by the fangs jutting up from her bottom lip. Even if I hadn't seen those fuzzy ears and gnarly teeth I would have thought she was one of the Good People.

"I see ye ha' started the tour wi' out me," she called. "Well, since ye are the only ones in attendance, ye will ha' me undivided attention. Come along, now, let's get a wiggle on!"

"Wiggle?" Robert repeated. I slipped out of his arms, fully intending to put this latest touching incident behind us, but he grabbed my hand. "Karina."

"Let's go," I said, tugging him toward the stairs. The tone in his voice had told me that he wanted to discuss things that I'd rather not be discussing. I needed time to process what had just happened, and a few seconds on a battlement wouldn't be enough. "She's waiting for us." Robert followed me, but based on his muttering he wasn't too pleased about our—well, *his*—change in plans. And he wouldn't let go of my hand.

Once we reached the ground level, the way too chipper tour guide was nearly bursting with anticipation. "Well, good day to the two o' ye!"

"I'm sorry we went up alone," I began. "The car park was empty, so we didn't think anyone was here."

"I'm quite sure that no harm was done," she demurred. I was impressed at her elocution, what with the fangs. "I'm Morag, by the by, and I doona drive, hence the empty car park. I ha' a wee room set up for meself in yonder tower." She gestured at the other tower, which was even more crumbly than the one we'd climbed.

"You stay here all the time?" I asked. "Alone?"

"I only stay on a week or so at a time, then another takes me place," Morag clarified. "'Tis nice to be alone wi' your thoughts from time to time. And, the castle can be quite romantic. From what I saw up there, I gleaned that you and your husband have already learned as much," she added, with a sly glance toward Robert.

"He's not my husband," I protested.

"Soon enough, then." With that, Morag raised her red umbrella, as if our massive group of two might lose sight of her, and herded us out to the enclosed yard. As we followed the energetic little woman, Robert gripped my hand even harder.

"'Tis no' right," he whispered in my ear.

"What is no' right?" I mimicked.

"Morag." Robert dragged us to a halt while he stared at the back of the woman's head. "In the space of a few moments, she has told us three lies."

"What did she lie about?"

"Her name, that she only spends some o' her time here at the castle," Robert ticked off. "And that she is alone here."

I gaped at Robert; in addition to being able to see fairies and having a sword that appeared at will, he was a human lie detector as well? "How do you know?" I whispered.

"By their very nature, the Good People do no' lie," Robert replied as he grasped my hand. "When they make the attempt, they tend to do it badly."

I grabbed Robert's other hand and looked toward the car park. "Should we leave?"

Robert squeezed all ten of my fingers. "I think it's best we go along with her ruse, for the time being at least. We do no' wish to anger her."

"No, we certainly do no' wish to do that." What I really wished was to turn tail and run, but Robert's grip on my hands was firm. Just as I decided to bribe him so we could leave—not that I had any idea of what I could bribe him with—Morag planted herself in the center of the courtyard and beckoned us closer. With no other apparent options, we went.

"Now, before I begin my tale of Tantallon Castle's most illustrious history, do the two o' ye have any questions for me?" Morag asked brightly.

"Who is the white lady?" I blurted out.

"Heard o' her, have ye now?" Morag countered. "There, ye can see the window she oft appears in." Robert and I followed Morag' outstretched arm toward a second floor window, the opening secured with a black wire fence.

"Does she appear according to any sort of schedule, like on Friday afternoons?" I asked.

"No' at all," Morag replied. "Many believe her to be a lost soul, one what became trapped here in the centuries following her death." She gave us a pointed look. "But, as is the way wi' such things, that is no' quite the whole o' the matter."

"What is the whole o' it, then?" Robert demanded.

"One wi' a collar such as yours should be able to divine as much," Morag replied smoothly. Robert bristled, but remained silent. "But, since ye be so distracted by the bonnie lass here, I shall inform ye o' what happens to be goin' on right under ye very nose." Morag fell silent for a moment, her gaze flickering between Robert and me.

"Our lady is trapped here, ye ken," Morag continued at last. "Once, long, long ago, she was invited to one o' their revels, invited by the Seelie King hi' self, but the poor lass could no' manage to find her way back home. She ha' been trapped between our world and theirs e'er since."

"Trapped?" I echoed. "Can't anyone help her?"

Morag shrugged. "Perhaps a body could, but if no one has stepped forward after all this time, 'tis likely that no one e'er will."

I stared at Morag, aghast but not surprised by her indifference toward the White Lady's plight; in my brief experience with them, I'd learned that the Good People cared little to nothing for the fates of their mortal playthings. I turned to Robert, my wide eyes pleading my case before I uttered a single word.

"Lass," Robert began, shaking his head, "if she's been trapped here like as no, 'tis for a good reason. Ye should no' involve yourself."

"But you were trapped," I pointed out. "And, it wasn't with good reason, only on a crazy woman's whim. What if the same thing happened to the White Lady?"

Robert sighed, and rubbed the back of his neck. "Have ye told us all ye know of her?" he asked Morag.

"That I most surely have," she replied with a smile.

"Try again," Robert demanded. When Morag began to protest, he added, "Lie to me once more, ye meddlin' imp, and I shall demand your true name. And, I *will* get it."

Morag blanched; apparently her lies usually went undetected. "Calm yourself now, gallowglass," she hissed, "I will no' betray ye." After a short staring contest between the two of them, she continued, "As for the White Lady, when she appeared at the Good People's revel on the arm o' Fionnlagh hi'self, his wife was no verra pleased."

"Who is his wife?" I asked.

"Nicnevin," Robert replied. "Nicnevin is the Seelie King's consort, and his wife."

I opened my mouth to ask what Nicnevin had wanted with Robert when she had already been married herself, but closed it. I understood exactly why a heartless creature like Nicnevin took men other than her husband to her bed, and after hearing of her husband's affair I couldn't say I blamed her. "Did he—the Seelie King—send the White Lady away?" I asked.

"No' as far as I ken," Morag replied. "In fact, the two o' them were quite cozy, nearly as cozy as the two o' ye atop the tower, there."

My neck and cheeks heated, but I ignored it. "Then how did she become trapped?" I demanded of the tour guide/beastie.

Morag grinned, revealing rows and rows of pearly teeth. "That, I canna reveal. Been bound, ye see," she added, with a nod toward Robert. "Ye ken how inconvenient these bindings can be."

Robert grunted. "Where is the door?"

"Beneath, o' course," Morag replied. "Now, if ye have no further need of me services..."

Morag's voice trailed off as she faded from view, much like the Cheshire Cat. Her creepy teeth were even the last visible portion of her. Once she had fully disappeared, I asked, "Beneath?"

Robert sighed. "She means that the door to their world is beneath the castle, like as no carved into the earth and leading straight to hell." Robert scrubbed his face with his hands, then rested them on my shoulders. "No matter what I say, ye are goin' to want a look at this White Lady, aye?"

"Aye," I affirmed. "If she needs help, we should help her."

"And if she's a foul thing who has been rightly removed from this world, we shall let her alone." When I didn't respond Robert drew me closer. "Promise me, Karina. If I say we must leave, we leave. No discussion."

"Can we discuss afterward?" I asked.

Robert's mouth twitched, but he suppressed his smile. Mostly. "Aye, that we can."

Just as Morag—or whatever her true name was—had told us, the doorway ended up being beneath the castle. Specifically, it was in a cave far, far beneath, almost at sea level. It had taken Robert and I the better part of an hour to make our way down the rocky cliffs of the promontory, slippery as they were, though Robert would have made much better time if he'd gone on without me. He was like a mountain goat, hopping around from rock to rock and never once losing his footing. Me, I just concentrated on not falling off the cliff and landing on the beach below.

"Here," Robert called at last. "'Tis a cave."

Robert disappeared into the cliff face; a moment later, I stumbled into the cave, bumping into Robert's back in the process. The entrance had been neatly concealed, thanks to the arrangement of the spiky rocks.

"Sorry for the collision," I murmured. Robert remained silent, with his back as straight as a board. I peeked around him, and saw her.

The White Lady.

She was in the exact center of the cave, kneeling with her forehead pressed against her knees and her arms extended before her, reminiscent of the yoga position called Child's Pose. Her immaculate white gown was pooled around her, her long dark hair a stark contrast against the colorless fabric, and a golden belt hugged her hips. Beyond her was a well of sorts situated in the center of the cave floor, and I could hear the waves crashing within. Was that the way to Fairy, or hell itself? I didn't think those angry sounds boded well for any of us.

"Is she asleep?" I whispered. "Does she know we're here?"

"I do no' ken, and most likely," Robert replied. "Karina, stay behind me, love."

I nodded, even though he wasn't looking at me. I was fully content to let Robert take the lead on this expedition. "Should we approach her?"

"No."

Well, that was firm. Robert and I stared at the White Lady for what seemed like an hour; the only sounds I heard was the sea crashing against the cliff, and my heart thudding away in my ears. The regular beats had lulled me into a sort of half-sleep; after a time, I caught myself drowsing, leaning against Robert's back. He hadn't moved a muscle.

"Maybe we should go," I said as I straightened. "I don't think she wants to be disturbed."

"You have already disturbed me." The White Lady stood in one fluid motion, rising bonelessly like a marionette. Now that she was upright I saw that she was beautiful, a near-perfect example of womanhood, from her piercing green eyes to her lush curves. No wonder Fionnlagh had been interested. "Take care that I do not disturb *you*."

"We mean ye no harm," Robert said. "The one called Morag told us o' ye, and o' your plight."

"And?" she asked archly.

"And we wanted to know if you needed any help," I said.

"Help?" The White Lady threw back her head and laughed. "I fail to see how a few mortals could help me. Have you ever loved? Has your passion ever been used to make another jealous? Once you had filled your purpose, were you cast aside like so much garbage? Has your very existence ever caused the one you love embarrassment?"

Her voice caught on the last word, and my heart went out to her. I was all too familiar with unrequited love. I stepped around Robert, but he caught me and dragged me against his side.

"It's terrible, isn't it?" I said, for all that Robert was trying to muffle me. "Loving someone that doesn't love you back. But you don't have to be a prisoner any longer. We can help you."

She cocked her head to the side. "Help... me?" Her gaze moved between Robert and me, just like Morag's had, then it settled on Robert's silver collar and her eyes widened.

"You're him, aren't you?" the White Lady asked as she took a step forward. "You are the assassin, the foolish man that refused Nicnevin, then forsook her for a mortal girl." She placed her hands on her hips. "Tsk, tsk. All of Elphame has been tasked with searching for the queen's rogue gallowglass. Your head will fetch me a mighty price."

"What?" I looked up at Robert, but his face was like stone. He'd known all along that Nicnevin would come after him, he just hadn't been sure of how long it would take her to pinpoint his location. What the White Lady said next answered that question beyond a shadow of a doubt.

"With your traitorous hide in my grasp, I will at last be able to bargain for my freedom!"

The White Lady lunged toward us, her green eyes transformed to a burning red and her fingers elongating into curved claws. Robert's sword materialized in his hands and he lunged at her, slicing off her arms below her elbows. Black, stinking blood sprayed around the cave, soaking her white gown and making the ground iridescent and slick.

"I thought she was human," I shrieked.

"As I said to ye above, that Morag is no but a liar." Robert planted his feet and squared his shoulders, gripping his claymore with both hands.

The White Lady laughed. "A lack of hands? Think you that will stop me, gallowglass? Think you that will even slow me?" she taunted as she moved before the mouth of the cave, blocking our retreat. Pulpy pink hands were already growing from the stumps of her arms, and her body was morphing into some sort of winged abomination. "Did you learn nothing whilst you were amongst my kind?"

Robert moved so fast I couldn't track him, then the White Lady's head was rolling away for her body.

"Karina!" Robert grabbed my arm, rousing me from my fascinated staring; never had I thought I'd see two bodiless heads in one week. "Can ye swim, lass?"

I looked up, and nodded. The next thing I knew Robert had an arm around my waist, and we were running toward the caverns' well.

"Love, now we jump!"

IT'S A TWO-WAY STREET

"Jump? We can't jump," I shrieked.

"We have to," Robert shouted.

"We don't know how deep the water is," I said. "We don't even know if there's a way out!"

"There's a monster behind us," Robert said.

"But her head," I began, then I looked beyond Robert to the White Lady. The bloody stump of her neck was already regenerating some kind of gross mushy lump.

"Her head's re-growing." I covered my mouth with my hand, re-sisting the urge to vomit. "It's growing back."

Robert stashed his sword, then he pulled me against him and we leapt into the well. The water was deep, so deep that my feet didn't touch the bottom. When I surfaced I felt along the sides for a crack or crevice, something to steady myself, but the walls were smooth as glass.

I was wet, I was terrified, and damn it all but if I lost the rental's keys I had no idea how I'd open the trunk and get to my fossils from Dob's Lin. Since I couldn't do much about any of those things down there in the well, I screamed all of them at Robert.

"The water comes from somewhere," he said, grabbing my shoulders. "There must be a connection between this well and the Firth."

I stared at him, momentarily forgetting to tread water and slipping under. After I'd come back up, I asked, "And you expect us to swim out to sea?"

"Aye, I do expect us to survive," he replied. "Wait here, love."

"As if I can go anywhere," I muttered, but Robert didn't hear me, having already sunk beneath the waterline. He reappeared less than a minute later.

"A tunnel," he gasped. "Wide enough that we may pass through."

"How long is it?" I asked, trying to remember how far the cliff was from the water's edge. "What if we can't make it?"

"Lass, we do no' have a choice," Robert said. "Deep breaths now."

I nodded, and took in several gulps of air. I remembered reading about endurance swimmers taking deep breaths to saturate their bodies with oxygen. I'd always wondered if you really could saturate your body in such a way, or if it was just a widely-held superstition that made people strive for Olympic greatness. Right then, I would take any advantage I could get.

Deep breathing accomplished, Robert grabbed my hand. "Stay close. Grab a hold o' me if ye need to."

"How can you swim with me holding on to you?"

"I will manage." Robert released my hand and placed his on the back of my neck, pushing his fingers into my hair. "Karina love, I will see ye to safety."

I nodded, then cringed; the White Lady had roared, the sound echoing off the rock walls. So, now we knew how long it took to regenerate a head, or at least a set of vocal chords and a mouth. Robert pressed his lips against my forehead, then he took a final deep breath and slipped below the water; a moment and a deep breath of my own later, I followed.

The tunnel wasn't very long, and there was an air pocket against the ceiling about thirty seconds in, which meant that it was probably low tide. Low tide meant that we had a chance. Low tide meant that we might not die.

Robert and I didn't speak as we stole a few moments breathing against the tunnel's ceiling, our faces pressed against the rock as we gulped the precious air. He nodded, then as one we ducked beneath the water and pushed off the tunnel wall.

The rest of the tunnel was dark, so dark I'd assumed we'd signed our death warrants. Suddenly I saw light overhead, and the tunnel opened out into the Firth of Forth. I grinned as I swam upward and broke the water's surface, twisting my body around to get a look at the shore. Then a wave smashed into the back of my head, and I saw stars.

I hadn't been properly prepared for the impact, and ended up with a mouthful of seawater. Then the second wave hit, and it pushed me under. My clothes and boots were soaked, heavy as concrete, and I couldn't get break the surface. I did the worst possible thing one can do in open water: I panicked.

Despite my flailing arms and legs, I managed to break the water's surface and steal a lungful of air. Then another wave crashed into my face, forcing me back under. That third wave was stronger than the last, and pushed me farther down than the last two had. Like a corpse, I drifted toward the sea floor.

I'm going to drown. I'm really going to drown.

No! Kick off your boots! Swim!

I kicked weakly as I struggled out of my coat, and got tangled in my own arms. My mouth opened of its own accord and letting more seawater into my lungs. I coughed and my chest burned, desperate for air I'd never get.

At least I'd get to see my mom again.

Strong hands grabbed my shoulders, and something firm pressed against my cheek. I opened my eyes, and saw Robert's face against mine. His fingers forced my mouth open, seawater rushing in before he sealed his lips over my mouth. I struggled against him at first, my half-drowned brain not understanding that he was sharing his breath with me, easing the burning pressure in my lungs the only way he could. Then our feet had made contact with the sea floor, and we rested for a moment, our limbs and mouths tangled together. I wondered if this was how mermaids kissed.

We couldn't remain under water for long. Robert poked my cheek; I opened my eyes, and saw him pointing toward the surface. I nodded as I drew back from him, then we pushed off the sea floor. A few moments later (had I really been that close to air the entire time?) we broke the surface and swam toward the beach. I crawled onto the shore and flopped onto my back. That was a bad idea, and I started hacking up seawater.

"On your side," Robert said as he rolled me over. I spit up blood-warm water and phlegm, not caring how disgusting I must have looked. "Can ye breathe, love?"

"Yeah," I croaked. "Couldn't we have just walked out while she was headless?"

"And given the beastie a chance to attack from behind our backs?" Robert stroked my forehead, moving my soaked hair out of my eyes. "No, thank ye verra much."

I scowled at him, but he was right. "I am never leaving dry land again."

Robert snorted. "Tough claim to make, bein' that we're on an island."

I glared at him. "I'll manage."

Robert got to his feet and extended a hand to me. "I've no doubt ye will, love."

We trudged up the hill side, wet footwear squelching away, in the general direction of the car park. Morag and the White Lady were nowhere in sight, probably because they were off terrorizing a whole new set of tourists. I hoped that the rumor of the White Lady being bound to the castle meant that she had to stay inside the castle and the cave below, and wasn't free to wander about the grounds.

Robert whistled away as we walked, quite pleased with himself at having evaded not just the White Lady but the sea as well, but I was nothing short of miserable. I'd almost died—twice—in the last thirty minutes, and climbing up a rocky slope while wearing completely soaked clothes was not helping my mood. It was like I'd been transported to my own Sisyphean level of Hades, my wet clothing having replaced the boulders.

"Surely, 'tis no' that bad," Robert quipped.

I bit my lip; I hadn't realized I was muttering out loud. He had rescued me, not only from the White Lady but from drowning as well, and I was whining away like a spoiled brat. "Thank you."

"For what, now?"

"For saving me."

"I was only returnin' the favor. Ye saved me first, love, back on Doon Hill."

I peeked over my shoulder and smiled. "I did, didn't I?"

Robert's smile stretched into a grin. "That ye surely did."

At length we reached the car park; after fishing around—literally—in my pocket, I was grateful to learn that the rental's keys were still with me. I popped the boot, gave my fossils a hello pat, and grabbed my duffle bag. As anyone with a history of field work will tell you, never go anywhere without a change of clothes, or three.

I dropped the duffel on the ground, yanked off my boots and threw them in the boot. My coat (so much for waterproof) followed my boots. Next, I grabbed the hem of my sweater.

"Lass, what the devil are ye doin'?"

I glanced up, and saw Robert staring at me in mingled shock and curiosity. "I'm getting out of these wet things," I explained. I unzipped my duffel, and pulled out a pair of Chris's old basketball shorts and a tee shirt. "Here, these should fit you."

Robert accepted the items, but didn't drop his gaze. "And you're going to remove those wet things here, in the open, in front o' God and everyone?"

My lips twitched into a smile, which surprised me as much as it scandalized Robert. I wondered if he would appreciate any of my Haz-mat training stories, during which students of both genders showered together in mock decontamination drills. Believe me when I say that those coed showers were way not sexy. "I'm not driving like this," I said, gesturing at my soaked jeans and sweater. "Besides, there's no one here but us."

Robert spluttered something about how someone could enter the car park at any moment, but I ignored him as I turned my back and stripped off my sweater, followed by my t-shirt; after a moment's hesitation, the bra followed. No one likes clammy boobs.

I pulled a long sleeved thermal shirt over my head; since it fell well past my thighs, my jeans, socks and underwear were the next to go. As I was about to toss the tangled mess into the boot, I heard a strangled noise from behind me. I turned around and found Robert, still in his wet clothes, staring at me with eyes so wide they were about to fall out of his head.

"Were you watching me?" I asked.

"I was *keeping* watch," he growled. "What if someone came up from behind and saw ye in such a state?"

"I'm just changing," I said, giving him my back again. "It's not like this is a strip tease or anything." The grumbling started up again, so I added, "You won't be so grumpy once you're wearing dry clothes. Go ahead. Change."

Dead silence followed that, then a bit of grunting and the cold, wet smack of Robert's clothes as he flung them into the boot. I continued ignoring him, and his muttering, as I pulled on a pair of bright turquoise gym shorts. Curiosity got the better of me, and I peeked over my shoulder.

Robert had evidently thought it best to strip completely before donning the dry clothing, and was standing not more than two feet away from me, completely, totally naked. Muscles rippled in his back and arms as he grabbed the tee shirt from where he'd laid it on the rental's bumper, his shoulders bunching as he pulled the garment over his head. My gaze traveled lower, taking in his smooth back, trim waist, and truly magnificent butt. As Robert raised his foot to step into the shorts, I spied of something between his legs that brought the fires of hell to my cheeks. Then the most embarrassing moment of my life happened: I moaned.

Flustered, I coughed and turned back to the duffle.

"Are ye all right, lass?" Robert asked.

"Yeah. Sea water." I dug around in the duffle, and emerged with a couple pairs of flip flops. "These might fit you," I said, holding the brown pair over my shoulder. I'd decided on wearing the neon orange pair.

"Exactly what am I supposed to fit them on?" he countered. I stood and turned, and saw a now-clothed Robert staring at the footwear.

"Your feet."

From the look on his face, you would have thought I'd suggested he hook them onto his ears. Although that would have been cute, too. He tossed the flip flops into the boot with a, "No, thank you." Then he got into the passenger side and slammed the door.

I tossed my duffle in the boot and shut the lid, then I slid into the driver's seat. We were silent until we were on the main road.

"Lass," Robert murmured. "You're shivering."

I glanced at my arms; I was covered in gooseflesh. "The water was pretty cold," I muttered as I turned on the heat, cranking it as high as it would go. Of course, the car hadn't warmed up yet, and the blast of cold air wasn't all that soothing.

"'Tis no' just the cold."

I glared at him out of the corner of my eye, but—as always—he was right. "Is it wrong for me to be a little freaked out?" I demanded. "I mean, our tour guide was some kind of disappearing imp, and then a ghost woman turned into a monster and tried to kill us. And we almost drowned. Drowned, in the fricken' ocean! How am I supposed to—"

I slammed on the brakes, stopping the rental right in the middle of the road. Since the sheep did it all the time, I figured I could get away with it too. "Wait. The ghost monster woman recognized you."

"Lass—"

"She said there's a price on your head!"

"Lass—"

I laid my forehead against the steering wheel. "What the hell are we going to do now?"

"Karina!"

Startled, I looked at Robert.

"First, ye will quit your haverin'. Then ye will get this metal contraption moving, and have it return us to the cottage. When we get there I shall get ye warmed and calm. Once all that has taken place, I, and I alone, will decide what is to be done regardin' this mess."

I stared at him, stunned. He'd just spoken to me like I was a child, not a fully grown woman, and one that had saved his arse on a few occasions as well. I threw the car into gear and stepped on the gas, speeding down the winding country road.

"Karina," Robert said. When I ignored him, he reached for me.

"Don't touch me," I said as I slapped away his hand. He clenched his fist, but respected my wishes. We rode to the cottage in silence, two long, uncomfortable hours' worth of silence, my fury simmering the whole way. And no, I didn't stop once. Once we were inside the cottage and the door had clicked shut behind us, I loosed all of my pent-up anger on him.

"How could you talk to me like that?" I demanded. "I nearly died—I have never been so fricken' scared in my entire life—and you spoke to me as if I was some stupid kid! Well, I'm sorry I if I was worried about you! I'm sorry I didn't want the monster woman to turn you over to Nicnevin! If me worrying about you is such a burden, there's the fricken' door!"

I stood shaking, while Robert stared at me. "Lass—"

"Don't you 'lass' me," I snapped. "This is a two-way street, buddy. If you get to care about what happens to me, I get to care about what happens to you."

His jaw dropped, and I turned around so he wouldn't see my tears. I'd always hated that I cried when I was pissed, almost as much as I hated crying when I was just plain upset.

Ignoring the fact that I was ignoring him, and my hands that swatted wildly at him, Robert put his arms around me. "Forgive me, Karina me love," he murmured against my hair. "O' course, ye are correct. I was foolish to dismiss ye. I should ha' realized that you only wished for me safety. I... When it comes to ye, I just wish to keep ye safe from her and her games. I did no' mean to belittle ye in any way." He tightened his arms around me. "I hope ye can find it in your heart to forgive me."

"I'll check, but I'm not positive," I snuffled.

Robert turned me around, and tucked my head under his chin. "There, love, do no' weep," he murmured, wiping my cheek with his thumb. "We shall rest tonight, and in the morning we shall discuss this new matter. Together, we shall determine our next course of action."

I snuffled again, and peeked upward. "You promise?"

"I promise."

SMALL MESSES

The next morning found Robert and I not discussing the matter of Nicnevin's assorted minions so much as straightening up the smaller messes we'd made the day before.

Last night, after Robert had apologized, and apologized again, for not considering my feelings, I'd taken a scalding hot shower and retreated to my room. It had been a bit early for sleep but after the day I'd had, what with a total of six hours of driving, prospecting for fossils, and almost shuffling off this mortal coil in a variety of manners, I couldn't face anything more than my pillow and a few blankets. When I woke my stomach was furious, not at all pleased that I'd denied it dinner the night before.

When I emerged into the common room my gaze instantly landed on Robert, whose dark head was bent over the kitchen table. He had one of my textbooks open and was scribbling away on a notepad. Holy hell, there is nothing sexier than an attractive man doing research in the morning. Or evening. More important than said man and research, I smelled coffee.

"Did you make this?" I asked, following the aroma like a bloodhound. In addition to coffee, there was a plate of toast waiting for me, which meant that the two basic food groups, caffeine and carbs, were present and accounted for.

"And a good mornin' to ye," Robert said. "Yes, I managed your black brew all on me own."

I smiled at him over my shoulder, then I poured myself a mug. It smelled perfect, tasted perfect...until my second mouthful, which was a bit chewy. I pulled out the basket, and noted the lack of a filter.

"Next time, put one of the paper cones in first," I said as I dumped the grounds. After rinsing the basket I plopped in a filter, then I located a mixing bowl in one of the cabinets. I placed the bowl on the burner, and poured pot's contents through the filter, and *voila*! Real, groundless coffee. Sure, I could have made a new batch, but wasting perfectly good coffee went against my entire belief system.

After transferring the new coffee from the mixing bowl back to the carafe with a minimum of splashes, I joined Robert at the table. "Try that," I said, switching a mug of my new and improved coffee for the chunky stuff he had been drinking.

"Much improved. Truly, love, I would be lost without ye," he declared after sampling the filtered coffee. My cheeks heated a bit at that, so I brought my mug up to my face. Surely, I could blame any excessive pinkness on the rising steam.

"What are you reading?" I asked, after I'd grabbed a piece of toast. I lifted the book's cover, and discovered that it wasn't one of my textbooks; it was an encyclopedia about the healing properties of crystals that I'd picked up at a New Age shop in Glastonbury.

"I was considering our pending discussion," Robert began, responding to the new, as yet unarticulated question in my eyes, "and, being that you are a scientist as well as a scholar, I was curious if any headway has been made in the last few hundred years with regard to hiding oneself from the Good People."

"Science isn't much interested in fairies," I pointed out. "Most people, like Chris, believe that magic died out centuries ago, and that fairy tales are just children's stories."

"Would that they were," Robert said, pushing his notes toward me. "See here, I've made a list of stones that protect the wearer from harm, from spiritual attack, and such."

I put down my mug and looked over the list. I opened my mouth to ask if we were supposed to trudge around with rocks in our pockets all day, only to shut it. As a geologist I did that anyway. "Why are these here?" I asked, pointing to the column titled "Summoning".

Robert's eyes darkened. "Just in case."

I nodded; based on the things I'd seen of late, I was perfectly all right with him not telling me the whole truth. If he thought I didn't want to hear it, he was probably right.

"This is good," I murmured. "Very good." I mentally organized the stones he'd listed, sorting the ones we could easily obtain from the rarer—and heavier—items. Then I spied the plastic laundry basket tucked away in the corner of the kitchen and remembered our seawater-soaked clothes, moldering away in the rental's trunk.

"Before we can get working on this list, we have an important job to do," I said as I finished off my toast.

"Oh?" Robert cocked an eyebrow. "What sort o' job might that be?"

"I am taking you to a Laundromat."

After Robert and I had loaded the laundry basket full of our dirty clothing, including the stinking waterlogged mess from the rental's trunk, we drove to the closest Laundromat. It was a large establishment, with three rows of sparkling white machines, and there was only one other patron—a human patron, thank all the gods—was present. We claimed the aisle farthest from the other person, and set to work.

"Yet another modern miracle," Robert said as I tossed items into the washer. "No' having to waste one's time with such mundane tasks as the washin' and such will free one for research."

"Agreed." I stuffed one machine full, added a packet of detergent, and started the wash cycle. Once that task was complete, I dumped the rest of our clothes into its neighbor. "Hand washing is definitely not one of my preferred ways to pass the time."

Once the second machine was full and washing away, we investigated the magazine rack. Robert and I flipped through all three of the outdated tabloids, and caught up on all the latest celebrity antics. When I finished reading the third one, I checked the first washing machine's timer; it still had a few minutes left in the cycle.

Bored, I hopped up onto the machine's lid. Robert rose from his seat and stood directly in front of me. My perch brought me to just above eye level with him. I liked being taller.

"What do we do now?" he asked.

"We wait for the wash cycle to be over with, then we put the clothes in the dryer, and then we wait some more," I replied. "Doing laundry is not the most exciting activity."

Robert nodded, his blue eyes glinting as he moved closer and positioned himself between my knees. "Karina me lass, I've a confession to make."

"Oh?" I was feeling a bit coquettish; something about Robert's and my clothes tangling together in the machine beneath me was turning me on. "What sort of confession?"

Robert set his hands on my knees. "When ye were getting out o' those wet things yesterday at the car park, I caught a glimpse o' your bum."

"Did you now," I murmured. "Why, reverend, I'm shocked."

He smiled lazily, blue eyes at half-mast. "'T'would have taken a stronger man than I to look away."

I returned his smile, and hooked my finger in the collar of his shirt. "Since we're confessing, I have two to make."

Robert's eyes widened. "Please. Share them with me."

I looked down, studying Robert's hands where they lay on my knees. "At the castle, after we made it through the tunnel and into the sea, the waves just overwhelmed me. I really thought I was going to drown. Then you helped me breathe, and... And I felt like a mermaid kissing you. I know you weren't really kissing me, but it felt that way."

"Karina love," Robert murmured, sliding his hand up my outer thigh. I caught it, and laced my fingers with his. "What... What is your second confession?"

I looked up, and speared him with my gaze. "When we were changing in the car park, I saw a bit more of you than just your bum."

Robert stared at me for a moment, then he burst out laughing. "And how did ye find me?"

"Everything appeared to be in order."

"In order? Is that all ye have to say about the sight o' me in the altogether?"

"You didn't say anything about my bum."

Robert gently tugged his fingers from mine, then he slid his hands up my legs, coming to rest on my hips. "'Twas such a sight, me heart nearly stopped."

"I'm glad it didn't."

"Me, as well. 'T'would be a shame if I expired before getting me hands on such a bum."

My breath caught in my throat; up until then, we'd been engaged in a bit of harmless flirting centered on how we'd accidentally seen each other naked, but Robert's last comment had ratcheted our flirting up from 'harmless' to 'dangerous'. And those hands gently squeezing my hips weren't helping.

Robert pulled me forward, pressing me against him as he tilted my hips upward, his hands splayed across my butt. I laid my hands against his chest, and stared down into his eyes.

"Tell me, love," Robert murmured, "do mermaids kiss on dry land?"

"They'd probably suffocate," I said, my nerves sending my mouth into full on babble mode. "I mean, they probably breathe with gills or something, so they'd flop around like a fish out of water."

As the words left my mouth, I realized that I'd ruined the moment. Gills? Really? Here I was, dying for Robert to kiss me, and all I could manage to talk about were gills. Before I could figure out how to salvage things, the washer buzzed underneath me. I didn't know if I was irritated or relieved.

"Um, the clothes are done," I said. "We need to take them out."

Robert nodded, then he pulled me the rest of the way off the washer, keeping his hands firm against my butt. He held me against him for a moment, then he said, "I am glad ye are no' a mermaid. I like ye just the way ye are."

"Oh, um." Amazingly, I didn't blush. "Thank you."

Robert relaxed his hold on me, and I slid down his body while his hands slid up my back, eventually cupping the back of my head. "Ye are quite welcome, love."

I wet my lips with my tongue and heard bells; someone had opened the Laundromat's front door. Remembering we were in a public place I pulled away from Robert, and busied myself with emptying the washer and flinging the clothes into the adjoining dryer. A few moments after that task was done, the other washer buzzed, and I repeated the process. All in all, the laundry gave me about ten minutes of focused activity before I had to face Robert again. Should have filled a third machine.

I turned toward Robert, my hands jammed in my back pockets, and said, "So." The dryers were drying away, I had nothing to do for at least an hour, and I had no idea of what I should say to the man. Having limited options, I decided to babble in the truest sense of the word.

"It will probably be another hour before everything's done. Drying takes a lot longer than washing, though I've no idea why. Then we can fold everything, and bring it back to the cottage. Or, if you want, we can separate our clothes here, or we can just throw everything into a basket and separate things at the cottage. Or—"

"Karina. Quit your haverin'. Just sit here wi' me until these machines finish their tasks."

Robert smiled, and extended his hand. I accepted it, and let him pull me onto the bench beside him. Robert dropped his arm around my shoulders; after a moment, I leaned my head against him.

"Robert?"

"What is it, love?"

"I'm glad you're not a mermaid, too."

He snorted. "O' course you are, being that mermaids are female."

I laughed softly; I hadn't thought of that. "Well, I'm glad you're not a merman, either."

Robert pressed his lips against my forehead. I shut my eyes, and hoped that the moment would never end. "As am I, Karina love."

HER

"Christopher."

It took me a moment to realize I was being addressed. I hadn't heard my own name in so long I hardly remembered it. Not that I needed it. I had her, and she was all that mattered.

Her.

Sorcha.

When she'd first led me into her home, I'd expected a house with regular walls and floors and furniture made of wood and upholstery. Instead we'd stepped into a grand room as large as a concert hall, where the ceiling was speckled with stars and the chandelier shone like the sun. It was so bright I couldn't see who else was there, but I felt their hands as they took my coat, removed my shoes, stroked my hair. Gentle, cool fingers put a goblet to my lips, and I drank deeply of a nectar that was almost as sweet as Sorcha's mouth.

The hands guided me to the center of the room, and I laid down on a bed made of vines, covered in tiny white blossoms. Somehow the bed became a garden, and then a ballroom, and Sorcha and I were dancing as we spun across the polished floor. Or maybe we'd been standing still, and the stars spun around us. That would make sense, since Sorcha was the center of my world, my beginning and my end. She was everything.

Afterward, we lay on velvet cushions, her people fanned out around us. They brought us sweet drinks, wove flowers into Sorcha's hair, mopped my brow when I sweat. Loving Sorcha was heady work.

"Stay with me forever," Sorcha murmured.

"Where else would I be, but with you?" I replied. I moved and the silk sheets fell away, revealing my nakedness, but I didn't care. Let everyone in the world know that I loved Sorcha, and that I would never leave her side.

"What of Olivia?" Sorcha pressed. "What if she desired you to return to her?"

"Who is Olivia?"

Sorcha smiled, and drew me down beside her. "No one," she murmured, as I bent to kiss her. "No one at all."

TENDER SWEET HEARTS

After whiling away the morning at the Laundromat, and all of the associated flirting that had occurred, Robert and I returned to the cottage. He spent the afternoon reading the crystal text, while I explored the newly reorganized bookshelves. It was stocked with titles Chris would like, Shakespeare and Burns and various other deceased poets; as for me, I'd take a good science fiction tale over poetry any day. Once I'd thumbed through the volumes and found all of them lacking, I sighed. And no matter how much I wanted it, that pile of unfolded laundry was not going to fold itself.

As soon as I started separating the clothes, Robert joined me. Despite the confessions we'd shared at the Laundromat, and all the butt squeezing that had happened, Robert and I kept our hands to ourselves once we returned to the cottage. The repetitive work of separating and folding our clothes certainly didn't lend itself to any romance, real or imaginary.

And imaginary was just what it was. There was no way Robert would have any sort of interest in me; first of all, he'd made it crystal clear that he only sought to have "relations" with a woman he was married to, or intended to marry. Since we'd known each other for all of one week, marriage was not exactly on the table.

As for me, I'm not exactly the marrying type. No, I was the type to scramble over hill and dale searching for shiny rocks and other treasures, the sort of uncouth girl who thought nothing of belching the alphabet or stripping naked in a car park.

Robert had looked pretty good in the car park. Good enough to make my belly flutter, good enough to make me wish we'd stayed at the bottom of the sea a bit longer. Good enough for me to take a fricken' bite out of his—

"Lass."

I looked up from my laundry and saw Robert standing over the pile of clothes, eyeing me intently. "What is it?"

"What has that garment ever done to wrong ye?"

Confused, I looked down, and saw that I had twisted one of my shirts so much it resembled a cigar more than something one would wear. "Nothing," I muttered, smoothing the shirt across my knees.

Robert touched my chin, and tilted my face upward. "Tell me."

"Tell you what?"

"What e'er fashes ye so."

I took a deep breath; there was no way I was going to tell Robert that I had been fantasizing about him kissing me, and me kissing him back. "I suppose I have a lot on my mind," I hedged.

Robert's eyes narrowed; too late, I remembered that he had some sort of built in lie detector. But, I hadn't lied, not really anyway. There were more thoughts flying around inside my head than I knew what to do with. He didn't call me on the half-truth; instead, he skirted the edge of the coffee table our laundry was heaped upon. Then, he crouched before me and took my hands, his thumbs gliding across my knuckles.

"Karina lass, believe me when I say that I never intended to drag ye into this mess," he said. "Truly, if I were a better man, I'd wish ye had never freed me from Nicnevin's curse."

"But you're still cursed," I pointed out, rather unnecessarily. As I gazed at my reflection in his silver collar, my mind grasped something else he'd said. "What do you mean, if you were a better man?"

"I canna wish to have never met ye, my lovely Karina."

My mouth dropped open, and if I hadn't been sitting I would have fallen. Me? Lovely? I could think of quite a few adjectives to describe my appearance—pale, freckly, awkward—but lovely was not one of them. Maybe he needed glasses.

"I'm not lovely," I whispered. "I'm not even that pretty."

Robert caressed my cheek with the back of his knuckles. "'Tis a shame ye do no' see yourself as I do."

With that, he stood and returned to his side of the laundry pile. I didn't know if I should feel flattered by the compliments, offended that he just kept touching me whenever he felt like it, or if I should just stick with my present confused state. In the end, I decided to go with flattered.

"Thank you," I said. "It was nice of you to say that."

Robert looked up, and smiled. "Ye are quite welcome, love."

"Let's get out of here," I said, rising to my feet. "All this domestic work is driving me bonkers."

"Bonkers?" Robert repeated.

"You know. Stir crazy." I rooted through the as-yet unfolded laundry, and found my sweater from the day before. "And I'm pretty hungry," I added as I pulled the sweater over my head. "Aren't you?"

"I suppose I could do with a wee bite," Robert said, his amused gaze following me as I searched for boot socks. When I pulled on my hiking boots I realized that they were still damp, which was just gross.

And I did not want to go out to eat wearing orange flip flops, or any color flip flops, for that matter; it was bad enough I'd worn them to the Laundromat.

An idea bloomed in my mind, so I entered my bedroom and dragged out my suitcase from where I'd stashed it below the bed. I unzipped it, and took out my black high heeled boots. I'd packed them to wear at dinners in nicer restaurants, and other activities that weren't appropriate for hiking boots. Sadly, this was the first time I'd worn them; they hadn't even made an appearance at the Italian restaurant.

After I put on the boots, I considered my sweater. It was one of the traditional cable knits, bulky and warm and more than appropriate for the early fall air. However, since Robert had said I was lovely, I decided to show him just how good I could look when I made the effort.

I pulled off my chunky sweater and opened the top dresser drawer to assess my shirt situation. I chose a form-fitting midnight blue v-neck knit top, which made my blue eyes pop while revealing just enough cleavage. I layered a black tank top underneath, mostly so I wouldn't freeze in nothing but a thin shirt, and slipped on the v-neck. I then loosened my ponytail and combed out my hair, added a touch of mascara and eye shadow, and rejoined Robert in the common room. He was standing at the counter with his back toward me.

"I'm ready if you are," I said. He turned around, and I saw that he'd been taking more notes from the crystal book. Remember what I said about hot guys and research? It was like he was trying to give me a heart attack.

Robert looked me up and down, his gaze coming to rest on my feet. "How can ye walk, balanced as ye are on those wee stilts?" he asked.

"They're not that high," I pouted. I had just put on makeup for the man, and he was complaining about my footwear?

"As ye say." Robert grabbed our coats, then he extended his arm to me. "Come, love," he said. "Let's find out if this old man can show a pretty young lass like yourself a pleasant evening."

"I'm sure you'll manage." Robert opened the door, but we found our way blocked by a herd of butterflies.

"The wights," I murmured, realizing that the butterflies were actually the garden's tiny, colorful inhabitants. "They seem upset."

"That they do," Robert agreed, then he addressed the swarm of color. "Well? Let's have it, then. What news have ye?"

"She knows, gallowglass," they said in unison, more of a song that a reply. "She knows about the gallowglass and his lass."

"She? Oh." They meant Nicnevin, of course. "What does she know?" I asked.

"That the gallowglass lives, that he walks her land," they replied. "That he looks on a mortal lass, and how he will surely hold her hand."

I ignored that last part, and turned to Robert. "The White Lady?"

"Most likely her or Morag," he replied. "Does she know where we are now?" he asked the wights.

A blue-winged wight, probably the one that had landed on Robert's head the other day, perched on my shoulder and looked Robert in the eye. "'Tis only a matter of time," said the wight, while the rest flitted around us. I wondered if the blue one was in charge, Head Wight or something. "As long as you walk her island, her minions will continue searching for you. They will not rest."

Robert nodded, eyes solemn. "Thank ye for the warning. I will do everything in my power to keep her from this location, and your homes."

The wight bowed. "We, in turn, shall misdirect them whenever possible. The two of you are good for the garden, bringing it life and light. We will do our best to keep you with us."

With that, the blue wight leapt into the air toward the garden, the rest of the swarm following like so many glittering, floating jewels. Once they'd disappeared around the corner, I turned to Robert. "Should we stay in tonight?"

"Absolutely not," Robert stated. "Never once have I hidden from her, not even when she was displeased with me, and sought to flay the skin from my back." I gasped, my hand covering my mouth. "Do no' fash, love, 'twas a long time ago, afore I was her gallowglass."

Despite his assurances, I was certain that being flayed was a fash-worthy event. "But if she sees you—"

"She will not," Robert insisted. "'T'would be only o' her minions, as the wight said." He took my hands in his. "Love, do ye trust me to keep ye safe?"

My stomach rumbled loud enough for Robert to hear it. "I guess that's your answer," I said. "If we see any monsters, can we come back home?"

"O' course, love."

I really shouldn't have been reassured by that; if anything, I should have turned around, bolted the door, and booked a flight out of Scotland. But I'd gotten dressed up—dressed up for me, anyway—and I was starved, and... And I really wanted a night out with Robert. I mean, we'd gone out to eat together nearly every day since we'd met, but I wanted tonight to be different. I wanted tonight to be something like a date.

Not that I was in any way going to admit that to Mr. Kirk. "I believe you have convinced me, reverend," I admitted, tucking my hand into his elbow.

Robert grunted. "Ye do enjoy referrin' to me as a reverend, don't ye?"

"As much as you like calling me Karina."

He threw back his head and laughed. "Ye have me there."

We left the rental in its spot behind the cottage and walked down the gentle hill to the town proper. Eager to explore the depths of Crail, we avoided the pub where the Ice Princess tended bar and wandered through the streets, passing by the Mercat Cross with its super cool unicorn finial, and getting ourselves turned around more than once. Eventually, we made our way past the piers and the sea wall, and stood on the beach gazing out over the Firth of Forth.

"Did you ever come to Fife?" I asked. "You know... Before?"

"Aye. I studied at St. Andrews, before going on to Edinburgh," he replied. "'Tis where I became a minister, ye ken," he added.

"Oh, maybe you should have gone to St. Andrews with Chris," I said. I wondered what he and Ethan were up to. Knowing the two of them they were getting drunk and challenging each other with facts about obscure Elizabethan literature like the party animals they were.

Robert cocked an eyebrow. "Tired o' me, are ye? Wantin' to pass me off to your brother?"

"Never," I declared. "I just thought you might like to visit. Old times, and all."

Robert nodded, then turned his gaze back to the water. "I believe I prefer these new times with ye, Karina me lass. No, I think I'll stay here, and see where these days take us."

It was a good thing he was looking at the sea instead of me, because I was staring at his profile, opening and closing my mouth like a fish. Unable to formulate any sort of response to Robert's declaration, I followed his gaze out to the water. Three seal pups floating on the waves captured my attention; while I watched, one flopped onto the shore and looked right at me.

"Look," I said, dropping into a crouch. "Isn't he adorable?" As if on cue, the pup rolled onto his back, and waved his flippers at me.

"Have a care, love," Robert warned. "'Tis a wild animal, and one ye should not agitate."

"It's a baby," I protested. "What could he hurt?"

"I'm sure that the local fish can tell a tale or two." Robert placed his hand on the back of my neck. "Come along, love. I can hear your belly rumbling from here."

"You can*not*," I grumbled, but I stood and let him lead me away from the water. Robert offered me his arm, as he was wont to do, and I leaned against him as we walked. It amazed me how comfortable I'd become with him in such short a time, how I no longer found it odd when he reached for my hand, or found random excuses to caress me. I planned on finding a few random excuses for me to caress him.

But how long was this fairy tale really going to last?

We found a restaurant with outdoor seating, thankfully with a few tables set in the dwindling sun. After the server had taken our orders, I found myself staring at the store fronts that lined the road. Robert seemed content to leave me to my thoughts, but the notions swirling through my head wanted out. And out they were getting.

"Have you learned anything more?" I asked. "About the crystals?"

"Aye, that I have." Robert withdrew a carefully folded sheet of paper from the inner pocket of his coat, and spread it on the table between us. "This column represents those with especially protective qualities," he indicated the column on the far left, "this next, has ones for summoning the Good People, and this last column attracts luck."

"Luck?"

"I feel we could be needin' a wee bit o' luck," he quipped. I nodded, studying the list.

"What we need are stones that we can get quickly," I mumbled. "I have the amethyst brooch you gave me, that might cover us for the protection aspect, but—"

Robert laid his hand over mine. "Quickly? Do ye ken somethin' I do not?"

I sighed, and sat back in my chair. "Robert, I don't live in Scotland. I live in America, which is... Well, it's nowhere near here."

He nodded. "I am aware of this."

The server appeared with our wine, and our soup; I'd gone with potato leek, Robert with Scotch broth. He let me eat a spoonful of my soup before he continued.

"You were saying," he prompted.

I set down my spoon, and looked him in the eye. "My research grant ends soon. I can't stay in Scotland after it's over."

He raised an eyebrow. "Cannot, or will not?"

"Can't," I repeated. "The grant is what's funding the cottage, paying for our food, the rental car." The first rental, at any rate. "I'm still a student. I'm not rich like Chris. I don't have the money to stay here after it runs out."

"When will that happen?"

"A few weeks," I replied. "By the end of September, I'll be out of money."

Robert's brow furrowed. "I gave ye the *sgian dubh* and brooch," he said. "Each is worth a goodly sum."

"I know, and I appreciate both of them. But I have no idea of how to turn those items into money."

"Ye just take them to a banker and request their worth in coin."

I held up my hand. "It's not like that any longer. If you try to sell something like that, and you don't have the correct documentation proving ownership, you could go to jail."

Robert nodded, slowly. "I would no' wish for ye to be imprisoned."

"Neither would I." I resumed eating, mostly since soup tasted much better hot than cold. Also, if I was eating I didn't have to talk.

The moment I swallowed the last bite of soup Robert's questions started up again.

"Why did ye just inform me of all o' that?" Robert asked.

I shrugged. "I just thought you should know."

"That's no' the whole of it, love," he pressed.

"I... I just need to know where we stand." Robert looked confused, so I elaborated, "I mean, I only have a few weeks left here, and I might not ever be able to come back."

"And ye are concerned as to what will happen to me." Robert reached across the table and grasped my hands. "Worry not o'er me, lass. I can take care o' meself quite well."

Hot blood spilled up my neck, and my voice shook when I spoke. "There's not just you to think about. There's an us, you know."

Robert blinked. "Us?"

That blank look in his eyes pushed me right over the edge. "You go around, touching me whenever you feel like it, kissing my hand, grabbing my butt, making me feel all these things for you and all you can say is that when my grant dries up you'll take care of yourself," I said in a rush. "What about me?"

Robert's eyes widened. "Hear me, Karina love. I thought ye were but humoring an old man, I did no' suspect—"

The server—who had either the best or worst sense of timing in the world, depending on how you looked at it—arrived with our meals, thus saving Robert from what would have surely been a heart wrenching explanation. Heart wrenching for me, at least. Once the server departed Robert reclaimed my hand.

"Love," he began.

"Please." I withdrew my hand and grabbed my fork. "Not now."

"Karina, please," he said.

"I'm sorry. I shouldn't have laid all that on you. But I really would like to just enjoy my dinner, if that's okay with you." I didn't add that we had a very small number of shared meals left.

Robert scowled, but he didn't argue. "As ye like, love."

We began our meal in silence. I'd ordered lobster, since I'd probably never get fresher seafood than here in this fishing village, while Robert had decided upon capon stuffed with cranberries and nuts. After my temper had cooled off, I said that the capon looked a diminutive Thanksgiving turkey.

"Thanks giving?" he repeated. "Is that a breed o' fowl?"

"It's a holiday in America," I explained. "You celebrate it by eating a ton of food, and everyone goes around the table and says what they're thankful for."

"It sounds verra nice."

"It is."

After a moment, he asked, "Well then, what are ye thankful for?"

"My brother, my education," I said. "And my dinner, of course." I glanced up. "What are you thankful for?"

"Many things; good food to eat, good air to breathe, me faith," Robert replied. "Mostly, though, I am thankful for ye, Karina me love."

"I'm sure someone would have sprung you from the tree eventually," I said as I struggled with a lobster claw.

Robert laughed and held out his hand. "Give it here, lass."

I handed over the claw, and watched as Robert cracked the shell, then as he grabbed my fork and picked out the meat. "Strange creatures, lobsters are," he murmured. "'Tis so difficult to get at the meat, one wonders if they ken how tasty they are."

I giggled. "So the tough shell is the lobster's last stand?"

"Perhaps." Robert dipped a forkful of meat in butter and held it out to me. "Or perhaps a tough shell merely masks a tender, sweet heart."

I smirked and took my fork; being that I was still mad at him there was no way I was letting him feed me. "Funny."

"Lobsters are many things, but funny is no' one of them." Robert laid his hand on my wrist. "And, love, I am no' just thankful for ye for freeing me from the tree."

I stared at him, the lump of lobster meat like concrete in my throat. "Oh."

Robert smiled and turned his attention to his own plate, and didn't bring up the taboo topic of us again. At least, not while we were eating.

The food didn't last long with our appetites. Once the plates had been cleared, and we had finished our after dinner coffees, Robert cajoled me into walking around the village with him. The sun had almost completely set during our meal, and we strolled up and down the dark streets until we found ourselves once again past the sea wall, staring out over the dark, swirling water. I imagined that the thoughts crashing about my head were similar to the waves; endlessly cycling back and forth, but never making any headway.

"Karina," he began. Robert took my hand, and immediately forgot what he'd been about to say. "You're positively frigid, love!"

"I am not frigid," I snapped, realizing a moment later that he meant cold, temperature-wise. "Well, maybe I'm a little chilly."

He chuckled softly. "What else could I be meanin'?"

"Oh, hush."

Robert moved behind me and wrapped his arms around my shoulders. "Better?"

I turned sideways, and rested my cheek against his chest. Robert widened his stance, and tucked my head underneath his chin. "Better." We remained that way for a time, silently sharing our warmth as if I hadn't bitten his head off a scant hour ago. "I don't think you're old."

He snorted. "I am a verra, verra old man."

I shrugged, as much as one could shrug while wrapped in a gallowglass's arms. "I'm a geologist. I deal with things that are millions or even billions of years old. You've got nothing on that."

"I suppose not." He pressed his face against my hair, and murmured, "About these things I make ye feel."

I so did not want to have that conversation. Lucky for me, a distraction had arrived just in the nick of time. "Look, it's one of the baby seals from before." I wiggled out of Robert's arms, and crouched before the barking pup. "I think he recognizes me."

"Karina," Robert warned, but I ignored him.

"Here, boy," I coaxed, reaching toward him. The little guy barked, and started flopping his way toward me. Just as I was about to ask Robert if he could run to the store and grab a can of tuna for my new friend, the pup roared.

Roared.

"Wha—" I fell backward, scrabbling away from the pup. Robert grabbed my arm and yanked me to my feet, his other hand brandishing his claymore.

"'Tis one o' the *fuath*," he yelled as he thrust his sword into the not-seal's neck. More abominations erupted from the sea; some were finned humanoid creatures, almost like the Creature from the Black Lagoon, some resembled mammals, some snakes. I. Hate. Snakes. All of them were terrifying, and all of them were striding and slithering toward us. Robert and I broke into a run as the skies opened above us.

Not How Mermaids Kiss

We ran from the *fuath* as they dragged themselves from the sea and fell from the clouds, my stupid high heeled boots first getting lodged in the wet sand, then skidding across the slick cobble stones. I couldn't see anything except Robert's back as he ran in front of me, and all I could hear was the rain hitting the road mingled with the otherworldly shrieks from the *fuath* that chased us. Every bone-chilling sound called up images of their crazed red eyes; long, needlelike teeth; their filthy claws; what they would do to me with those teeth and claws. I pushed myself to run faster.

My heel caught in a joint between the cobbles and I went down hard. Robert crouched beside me and yelled something, but his words were lost in the downpour. Then he grabbed me by the shoulders, hauled me upright and flung me against a hard wall. The impact made me see stars.

Once my senses dribbled back to me, the first thing I realized was that I wasn't being rained upon. The second thing was the massive pain blooming at the base of my skull, probably from hitting my head.

I groaned as I rubbed the sore spot, then Robert clamped his hand over my mouth.

I tugged his hand away, and whispered, "My head. I think I hit it."

Brows furrowed, Robert threaded his fingers through my hair, and gently explored the back of my head. While he did that, I peeked over his shoulder at our surroundings. We were standing underneath an archway that I assumed was the support for a bridge, or maybe the terminus of an alleyway; the stone wall behind me was what I'd hit my head against. Robert had wedged us into the far corner, beyond the pool of dim light that filtered in. I shivered in the cold, musty air; if the *fuath* figured out this little ruse and found us, we would be trapped.

I gasped, wincing, when Robert found the lump on the base of my skull, but otherwise remained silent. He massaged my head for a moment, then he pressed his lips against my ear.

"Och, love," he breathed, "Forgive me. I did no' mean to hurt ye."

I pulled back, about to tell him that I understood that he hadn't done it on purpose. It wasn't like he'd had a lot of options, what with the monsters chasing us. Before I could say as much I heard hoof beats rattling across the rooftops, followed by an all too close howl. To my horror, the howl was answered from somewhere on ground level, followed by scratching near the arch's opening. I bit the inside of my mouth, the pain doing little to center me.

As the scratching moved closer I started shaking, and I pressed my hands to my mouth to keep my teeth from chattering. Could the *fuath* hear teeth chattering? Then a chorus of those bone chilling howls sounded from directly above us. I squeezed my eyes shut, and moved my hands from my mouth to my ears.

"They're going to find us," I whimpered, remembering too late that we were supposed to remain silent. Robert's fingers slid from my hair to my jaw, and he titled my face up. I wouldn't open my eyes, so he was forced to whisper.

"Be still," he murmured, his lips a hair's breadth from mine. "I will protect ye."

My lips parted, which was a bad idea since the creatures howled again. Since my hands were covering my ears I couldn't stifle this latest round of sobs. Robert pressed his mouth to mine, swallowing my cries. Figuring we were going to die anyway, I fisted my hand in Robert's shirt and kissed him.

Robert drew back and we looked at each other for long moments. Even in the dim light I could see his blue eyes, the emotions skating across his face: wariness, determination, hope. I liked hope the best.

I slid my arms around Robert's neck and kissed him again, softly at first, but he wasn't in the mood for a quick peck. He kissed me hard, his hands gliding down my sides to encircle my waist, then his hands were under my thighs as he lifted me against the wall. I locked my ankles behind his waist, opened my mouth beneath his, and let him devour me.

This wasn't how mermaids kissed. This was how two people who had no idea if they would survive the night kissed.

I don't know how long we stayed that way, wrapped in each another's arms beneath that bridge. It could have been a year, an hour, perhaps even the barest second. I forgot about the creatures pursuing us, the pouring rain, Nicnevin's curse; I forgot everything but Robert. He, however, managed to keep his wits about him.

"Lass," he murmured. "I believe they ha' moved on."

I blinked, unsure what "they" he was referring to, when I remembered the *fuath*. I unwound my limbs from Robert's body, listening for their howls and scratching, thankfully hearing neither. Robert held me against him as I slid down the wall, his hands lingering on my waist as I steadied myself. His release was sudden, my body cold where he'd held me. He went to the mouth of the arch and peered down the alley. "The rain continues," he said. "Like as no', they have lost our scent. We'd best return to the cottage before they retrace their steps, to keep them unaware of where we lay our heads. We have a promise to keep to the wights."

I was trembling again, but not because of the *fuath*. As Robert assessed our situation with military precision, far more concerned with a herd of tiny fairies than me, I realized that our kisses had meant nothing to him. He had just wanted me to shut up, and distract me from imminent death.

I just threw myself at a preacher. I am such an idiot. A hot tear slid down my cheek; I dashed it away and rubbed my nose. Robert picked that moment to turn around; based on his expression, he saw a sniveling girl who had gotten the wrong idea. *Or he thinks I'm a whore*, I thought, remembering how I'd wrapped my legs around his waist.

If he thought that, he didn't say as much. "Karina," he murmured, "take my hand." I did, mostly because I didn't have a lot of options either, and followed him out into the night.

The rain had lightened from a downpour to a light drizzle, not that it mattered since I was already soaked to the bone. We walked in blissfully uneventful silence for a while before we reached the part of the village with street lamps. I turned my face toward the light, and wondered if I could avoid darkness for the rest of my life. The dark was where you found things like evil fairies and seal pups that wanted to eat you, not in the bright light of day. Well, except for that *fuath* that had taken over the old lady at Inchmahome, and the White Lady at Tantallon... Still, the light was safer. It had to be. While I contemplated how many lamps it would take to keep the cottage blazing like the sun twenty-four hours a day, Robert grabbed my shoulders, pulled me to him, and kissed me hard.

At first I was startled, then I was mad. What, did he think he could just maul me whenever he wanted? I opened my mouth to yell at him but he slid his tongue against mine, silencing me and defusing my anger in one fell swoop.

"Why did you do that?" I asked when we parted.

"Because," he replied, his hand cupping the nape of my neck, "I do no' want ye to think I only wish to kiss ye when we're being chased by foul beasts."

"Oh," I mumbled. "I thought—"

"'Tis plain what ye thought, love," Robert said, brushing his lips across my knuckles. "I did no' mean to upset ye. Forgive me if I have."

I nodded, having lost the ability to speak. Robert smiled, and we resumed walking.

Once we were inside the cottage, and had locked all the doors and windows, I retreated to the bathroom. I contemplated a hot shower, then decided that I'd been wet enough that day. I towel dried my hair as best I could, the rain having darkened the brown strands to nearly black, and after dragging a brush through it I returned to the common room.

Robert had stripped out of his wet clothes, and was wearing black sweats and that old Iron Maiden shirt that had become his favorite. After he shut the bathroom door I entered my bedroom and got out of my second set of waterlogged clothes in as many days, then I pulled on a long-sleeved charcoal gray sweater and black yoga pants. The sweater was tissue paper-thin, but it was soft. After the day I'd had, soft was winning.

I was sitting on the edge of my bed, trying to decide if I wanted to wear socks, when Robert returned to the common room. A few cushions hit the floor and bounced into view through my bedroom doorway, which meant that he was getting ready to pull out the couch.

"Robert."

"What is it, Karina love?" His large frame filled the doorway, all but blocking out the light from the kitchen. "Do ye be needin' anythin'?"

I swallowed. "Stay with me tonight." His eyes widened, and for a terrible, heart-stopping moment, I thought he would say no. "Please."

"As ye wish." He disappeared into the common room; from the rattling, I understood that he was checking the locks one last time. Then he was in the bedroom with me, softly closing the door behind him.

He approached the bed and stood over me for a moment, then he bent to kiss my forehead. I closed my eyes, memorizing the feel of his lips against my skin. With that, I got under the covers and turned toward the wall. I felt the mattress dip under Robert's weight, the warmth of his body, and was grateful that he was lying between me and anything that could hurt us.

KARINA ME LOVE

It was still dark when I woke, but the moonlight streaming through the window told me that the rain hadn't started up again. No rain was good, since it meant that the *fuath*, water demons that they were, were denied a rather convenient means of transport.

As my eyes adjusted to the soft light, I realized I was staring at the bedroom door, which meant I was lying on the outside edge of the bed. That was more than a bit strange, since I was positive that I'd taken the side next to the wall, and that Robert had laid down between me and the door. In the midst of wondering when Robert had left, I realized that his arm was wrapped around my waist.

I almost laughed aloud, practically giddy with the knowledge that he hadn't left me. I pressed back against him, soaking up his warmth, pretending that we were a perfectly normal couple, in bed together for perfectly normal reasons, not because we were marshaling our defenses against a jilted fairy queen.

A cloud floated across the moon, plunging the room into darkness. Figuring that was as good a time as any, I rolled onto my back and looked at Robert sleeping on his side, the preacher I'd made out with under a bridge, and then invited to my bed. Even though he had never been celibate like a priest, I couldn't help the guilt that fluttered in my belly. As I traced his strong jaw, I was overtaken with a different sort of flutter.

I tried to keep my touch light, but his eyes opened anyway. After he'd blinked a few times, I asked, "How did we switch sides?"

Robert propped himself up on his elbow, and gazed down at me. "Ye did a fair bit o' thrashin' about." He smoothed the hair back from my forehead. "Bad dreams, was it?"

"If it was, I don't remember them," I replied.

"Just as well," he murmured. The moon picked that moment to come out from behind the clouds, filling the room with light and making it nearly as bright as day. Robert's eyes widened and his jaw tensed; I followed his gaze, and saw that the intense moonlight had made my thin sweater all but transparent. And I wasn't wearing anything underneath my sweater.

"I'm sorry," I mumbled, yanking the blanket up to my chin. "I didn't mean—"

"Do no' fash," Robert murmured, tracing the contour of my jaw, and then my neck. "Ye are lovely to look at, Karina."

My cheeks heated, and I hoped that Robert couldn't see my blush in the moonlight; when he grazed his thumb across my cheek, I knew I'd failed. Since I was already red-faced, I decided to add in some daring. "You should take off your shirt."

"Why is that, pray tell?"

"We'll, um, be even that way."

Robert's eyes glinted, and his mouth twitched. "Fairness is a virtue," he said, then he sat up on his knees and pulled his shirt over his head. I almost gasped at what he revealed, all smooth golden skin and rippling muscles. Who would have thought that a man of God would have such a sinfully beautiful body?

Robert tossed his shirt onto the floor, then he pulled the blanket off of me and swung his leg over my waist, straddling my hips. He gave me a good, long look, and asked, "Pleased?"

"Yeah." I raised myself up on my elbows, and looked him in the eye. "I like... fairness."

He smiled, then he leaned forward and captured my lips with his. When we'd kissed beneath the bridge, we'd been ravenous for each other, but this time was different. Now, Robert was kissing me like a man who came from a time before television, before the internet and a thousand meaningless distractions. He came from a time when the best way to spend your evening was making love.

Robert kissed a path from my lips to my jaw, then he worked his way lower, pausing to nuzzle my neck. He kissed my breast through the sheer weave of my sweater, his calloused hand kneading the other. I moaned, but when I tried to return his favors, he grabbed both my hands in one of his and pinned them above my head. I swore, desperate to touch him, wrap a leg around him, anything, but he only laughed.

"Let me touch you," I said, struggling beneath him.

"Love, I ha' been waiting to touch you for so long," he murmured, pressing a kiss between my breasts. "To sleep so close to you, yet so far apart, was worse than any torture visited upon me in Elphame. Please, just this one time, let me."

"And next time?"

Robert's laugh rippled across my skin, the sound arousing me as much as his hands. "If ye are so concerned about when next I love ye, I must no' be doing such a good job now."

He kissed me before I could protest, and laughed into my mouth when I bucked my hips against his. Once he was sure I'd stay silent, he resumed his journey down my body. Robert's lips meandered from my breasts to my belly, then he pushed up the hem of my sweater and took his sweet, delicious time acquainting himself with my navel. He paused when he reached the edge of my yoga pants.

"Strings?" he murmured. "Why have ye black strings about your waist?"

I looked down, and saw him tracing the side strap of my lacy string bikini. Not only had I packed such an impractical garment for a research trip to Scotland, I'd purposefully donned it earlier that evening. "That's the side of my underwear."

"Under wear?" Robert's rich brogue made it sound like *oondahrr weahrr.*

"You know, what you put on before your pants. I got you a package at Hamilton's." God, were we really having this conversation?

"Ye mean those wee trews that came folded up like a trio o' handkerchiefs?"

"Yeah."

Robert chuckled. "I have no' worn them but once. They were chafing me where I do no' care to be chafed."

"Oh." My gaze moved lower, and stopped on the bulge below his waistband. I shivered, achingly aware there was only a thin layer of cotton keeping him from me.

His fingers slipped under the waistband of my yoga pants, tracing the top edge of my panties. "Perhaps I am just needin' to observe how this under wear is meant to be worn," he murmured, tugging the stretchy black fabric down and over my hips, inching backward until he was standing at the foot of the bed. Once the pants were off, and he saw the scrap of black lace I was wearing, he stripped out of his sweats and returned to my side of the bed, looming over me like some sort of erotic god, all golden skin and blue, blue eyes.

"Karina, love," he murmured, "tell me you will ha' me."

I rose up on my knees, and pulled my sweater up and over my head. "Robert, love, I will have you."

He kissed me hard, placing a knee on either side of mine and backing me down the bed until his body covered mine. Robert kissed my cheeks, my eyes, my mouth, then his lips traveled from my mouth down to my navel and then back to my jaw. My panties disappeared, and I was finally able to hook a leg around Robert's hips, eager to have as much skin to skin contact with him as possible. I gasped when he slipped a finger inside me, and whimpered at the second.

"Are ye maiden, love?" Robert asked, his voice thick.

"No. Is that bad?"

"No' at all," he murmured, trailing his lips across my neck. "I do no' wish to hurt you, 'tis all."

I shifted my hips; based on the weight pressed against my thigh, I seriously doubted that this would be pain free. "I don't think you'd ever hurt me."

"Aye, I'd die e're I let ye come to harm."

He withdrew his fingers and replaced them with his heavy, hot erection, slowly, gently stretching me. When he was fully inside me, he paused, his forehead pressed against mine, and kissed me softly. "Love," he murmured against my lips. "Karina, me love."

Instead of replying, I kissed him back, long and demanding. He answered by withdrawing ever so slowly, then thrusting into me, faster and faster until I forgot my name. I gripped his shoulders, my nails digging into his skin, and saw stars exploding behind my eyes. The last thing I remembered was Robert, whispering in my ear and holding me as if I was cherished.

CATHARSIS

T he next morning dawned bright and glorious and perfect, my
opinion of the day owing no small part to the man in my bed.
Making love with Robert had been amazing, trashy bodice ripper
paperback romance amazing, and I was almost able to forget about
Nicnevin and the killer seal pups and the rest of the monsters. Almost.

Still, we had escaped from all of them so far, and I'd been with
Robert, and... and the morning was just good, you know? After
Robert had woken me in the most delightful way possible, I suggested
that we bathe. I soon learned that sharing a bathroom with a man
from the seventeenth century was somewhere between hilarious and
annoying.

"I have been meanin' to ask ye, love, why do ye require so many
kinds o' soaps?" Robert asked, staring bewildered at all the tiny bottles
arrayed next to the sink.

"They're not all soap," I said, peeking around him; it was a rather
small bathroom, and it definitely hadn't been built for two. "That
one's conditioner, which is for after shampoo."

"Shampoo?"

"Shampoo is soap for hair," I explained.

"Your hair requires its own soap?"

"And that one's hair gel," I continued, ignoring his last question, "and that one—"

"Is something else to make me bonnie lass even more beautiful," he finished. "Really, love, with all these potions ye apply on and about your person, I am beginnin' to wonder what ye really look like."

"Careful, or I'll stop using them." I mimed claws and crossed my eyes. "Then you'll be stuck with another wee beastie."

Robert laughed, a deep rumble that was fast becoming my favorite sound in the world. "Wee ye are, but beastly ye shall ne'er be."

It was an unusual compliment, but we were an unusual couple. I turned on the shower, and waited for it to get steamy. Robert eyed the spray warily, and I couldn't say I blamed him. Probably because the cottage was a rental, the bathroom hadn't been updated for decades, and the combination of Pepto pink tile and metallic floral wallpaper was enough to give anyone the creeps. Despite the lackluster décor, the water pressure was at least ten times stronger than what was delivered by the elderly pipes in my apartment back in Queens.

"Love, ye have no plugged the drain," Robert said as he reached toward the stopper, but I caught his hand.

"We don't need a plug," I said as I stepped into the tub. "This is what we modern folks call a shower."

"Ye intend to bathe standing up?" Robert stared at the showerhead, intrigued.

"Yes. And you're going to stand up with me." I tugged Robert's hand, and once he was in the tub I pulled the pink plastic curtain closed and positioned him directly below the showerhead. At first he looked a bit scandalized, then he rolled his shoulders and shook his head like a dog.

"'Tis warm." He looked down at me, and grinned. "'Tis nice."

"Told you." I nudged him out of the way, and got my own hair wet. "Can you hand me the shampoo?"

"Which bottle was that one, now?"

"The one that says shampoo."

That remark earned me a gentle slap on the rear, but he grabbed the correct bottle. That led me to re-explaining that yes, shampoo really was a soap designed only for use on one's hair, and a subsequent demonstration with Robert as the test subject. Robert insisted that he wash my hair next; he was something of a hands-on sort of guy.

"You are in incredible shape," I murmured as we rinsed our hair, me tracing the puffy white suds as they slid across his shoulders and down his chest. I wondered if the term "chiseled abs" had originated with gallowglasses. I never thought men really looked like that without airbrushing. "These muscles are all... muscle-y."

"Swingin' a claymore for three centuries will do odd things to one's form," Robert said, as he massaged conditioner into my hair. I never knew that the scalp was an erogenous zone, but holy crap was it ever. "All me life, I only wished for the soft, white hands of a scholar, not anything close to this warrior's form."

I looked at my own hands, and how my years of gathering rocks and fossils had left me with ragged nails and rough, calloused palms. "I suppose I'm a scholar, but I don't think I'll ever have hands like that."

Robert plunked a kiss on my forehead. "'Tis one o' the many reasons why we're a match."

I leaned my forehead against his chest, enjoying his hands in my hair, the warm water cascading down my back. All too soon, he backed me underneath the spray and rinsed my hair.

"About your collar," I began, as I reached for the body wash. "It really doesn't hurt?"

"It does not," he murmured. I soaped up the sponge and went to work on his chest, giving the collar a few pokes in the process. "Ye can no' remove it."

"Why not?"

"Because," he replied, grasping my hands and kissing my soapy fingertips, "ye do no' have the key." He plucked the sponge from my hand, turned me around, and began washing my back. He almost distracted me away from my line of inquiry.

"So, where is this fabulous key?" I asked, then I moaned as he did something positively decadent to my lower body. After he explained this key situation to me, I was asking him if he'd really been alone for the past three hundred years.

"Nicnevin herself possesses it. And," he continued when I opened my mouth, "I will no' have ye tryin' to obtain it."

"But why?" I turned around and traced the edge of the collar; despite Robert's insistence that it didn't cause him any pain, I knew it weighed upon him, just maybe not physically. "If she has the key, then she still controls an aspect of you."

"Aye. That she does."

"So—"

"So nothing." Robert dropped the sponge, and drew my face close to his. "Karina, heed me. I do no' wish ye to be goin' after this key. Dealings with Nicnevin ne'er end well, and ye are far too dear to me to allow that."

I touched his face, and traced a line from his cheekbone to his strong jaw. "What if you're too dear to me to allow her to continue controlling you?"

He smiled, but his eyes were sad. "I am already damned. You, love, still have all the chances in the world."

A smart girl would have let it end there. "I'll undamn you!"

"Karina, leave it be."

I scowled. "I don't want to leave it be! I want to—"

"Tell me about the boy what gave ye the stone," he said over me. "Jared, was his name?"

Frowning so hard my forehead ached, I turned off the water, whipped back the shower curtain and grabbed a towel. Robert put his hands on my shoulders, but I shrugged him off. "Karina, love, I meant no harm."

"Jared and I both attend Carson University in New York City. It's where Chris teaches, too." I rubbed my hair with the towel so intensely the friction could have started a fire. "When we met, Jared was a junior, and I was a freshman. I had a rough time when I first got to Carson; too many classes, bad study habits, things like that. He saw me struggling and gave me the stone. He told me it was lucky."

Robert grabbed a second towel, and set about drying my back. "And ye loved him from then on."

I nodded, but I didn't look at him. "Yeah. I did." I combed my hair in silence for a few moments before I continued. "Whenever that stone was in my pocket, I aced whatever test I was up for, whether it was English or geology or calculus. I began to think it really was lucky. When I told Jared about my newly stellar grades, he laughed and said that rose quartz was for love, not luck."

Having finished drying both himself and me, Robert dropped the towel and put his hands on my hips, his forehead resting against the back of my head. "We started hanging out after that, studying together. When he became a TA—that's a teacher's assistant, they help the university professors—he always asked me to help him with lesson plans, grading, stuff like that. We were together all the time."

I dropped the comb, and gripped the counter. "When I decided to go for my masters and then doctorate, Jared pulled some strings and got me admitted into his program. He'd already earned his undergrad and was working toward his masters, and had worked for the department since then as an adjunct. Things between us were just like they had always been, us working and studying together, then one night we were in the office late, grading tests, and since it was the last week of the summer session, he'd brought a bottle of wine..." I squeezed my eyes shut, remembering the warm, alcoholic haze that had surrounded us that night.

"Did he hurt ye, love?" Robert demanded, his fingers tightening on my hips.

"No. Not then. Then was nice." Robert slid his arms around my waist, but I didn't move. Now that the floodgates were open, everything was coming out.

"The next morning, I got up early and picked up his favorite coffee and some bagels." I glanced up at Robert's reflection, and saw that perplexed look on his face. "A bagel is like bread. You can spread cheese or jam on it."

He nodded. "Bread. Go on."

"I wanted to surprise him with breakfast. When I got to the floor with the offices, his door was open a bit, and I heard him talking to another TA. Jared was saying how he never felt stressed by all the work the professors piled on him, because he had a bunch of dumb students do all his work for him. He said he only picked girls, so when he got bored he could... he could..."

Robert turned me around, and held me so tightly I could hardly breathe. "Tell me ye flung the coffee in his face."

I laughed shortly. "I wish I had. I left the coffee and bagels on the floor next to his office door, and I ran. I was a coward."

Robert tilted up my face. "Karina, love, there is nothing cowardly about ye. Ye ha' the heart o' a lioness, o' that I am certain," he said as he bent to kiss me. When we parted, he smoothed back my hair. "Did ye e'er confront the scoundrel?"

"No. Right after that, everything happened with Chris and Olivia, then this research grant came out of nowhere. Since summer classes were over, and Chris and I both really needed to get away, I accepted the grant. And, you pretty much know the rest." Chris and I had arrived in Scotland less than three weeks after I'd signed the grant paperwork.

"He bedded ye, but he ne'er e'en tried to speak wi' ye again?" Robert demanded.

"He did," I replied. "He called and sent messages. I never returned them."

"And yet ye kept the stone."

"Good thing I did, being that it freed you." I took a deep breath, and realized that a dull weight had been lifted from my heart. Even though telling Robert about my stupid fling with Jared had been number one on my Things Not To Do list, I'd apparently needed some sort of catharsis. I'd needed to say out loud that Jared was a jerk, and tell someone how horribly he'd treated me. I should have talked about it sooner, but I'd been so embarrassed about the whole situation. Now that I had, I hoped could leave him in the past and move on with my life.

I'd rather see a million more fairy monsters than Jared's smug face when I returned to Carson.

I opened the bathroom door, leaving my robe hanging on its hook next to the shower. Why bother covering myself in front of a man that now knew my every detail? Unencumbered, I entered the kitchen and was greeted by the heavenly scent of coffee. Automatic coffee makers were possibly the world's greatest invention, right up there with the wheel and microwave popcorn. I poured myself a cup, and turned toward Robert. He'd decided to hang out naked, too. Nice. "Why did you ask me all of that?"

He shrugged. "Curiosity, mainly. And I was needin' to know if there was a lad across the sea that would challenge me for your heart."

"No chance in hell of that happening."

Robert took the mug from my hand, and set it on the counter. "Good. I do no' like to share," he said as he drew me into his arms. After he held me for a few moments, he asked, "Tell me, love, have ye any regrets?"

I snorted. "About Jared? Tons."

"Not about the boy."

I was about to ask Robert what sort of regrets he was referring to, when I remembered who he'd been before he was a gallowglass. "Is this the first time you've had sex when you weren't married?"

Robert laughed through his nose. "No' hardly."

I leaned back and looked at him. "But you were a minister. I thought you found sex with anyone other than your wife wrong."

"Aye, I was just that, a minister, not a saint. And what I told ye was that I need a pretty heart far more than a pretty face." Robert widened his stance so we were almost at eye level, and pressed his forehead to mine. "Karina me love, ye have a beautiful heart and mind, the most perfect compliments to your lovely form. The only regret I have is no' lovin' ye sooner."

"Oh." I wound my arms around his neck, twisting my fingers into his damp hair. "I guess I have that regret, too. But that's the only one," I added.

Robert grinned. "I'm glad to hear that. But I must correct you on one other matter."

"And what matter would that be?"

"Ye said we 'had sex', such a cold, clinical term." Robert grazed his thumb across my cheek, while his other hand glided down my back, coming to rest on my bottom. "We, Karina me heart, did nothin' short o' makin' love."

"Did we?" I traced the muscles of his arm, stroking the hills and valleys. "Maybe you should show me what you mean, so I'm certain I understand."

He laughed, the throaty sound awakening all sorts of sensory receptors across my skin. "That I shall do, love."

FEY KISSES

Agood while later, our rumbling bellies drove Robert and me out of bed and back to the kitchen. We'd even gotten dressed—couldn't be naked all the time—though we'd only put on what we'd originally gone to bed in. I had, however, remembered to layer a tank top beneath my gray sweater.

Robert stretched out on the couch while I reheated the coffee and took an inventory of the kitchen: we had bread, cheese, butter and jam, two jars of olives, and a bunch of grapes. There would definitely be grocery shopping in my future. After I had most of the food arranged on one of the larger plates, and poured the coffee, I delivered everything to the living room and settled on the couch next to Robert.

"Is it the key to your heart? Is that what will unlock your collar?" I asked without preamble. Robert's gaze slid toward me, but he wasn't annoyed. Based on his lazy, sated grin, he was in a mood to reveal everything.

"No, because a heart must be freely given," Robert replied. "One canna just lock it away." He bit into some bread, and I crossed my legs under me and watched him chew. One did not remain in the same academic program for as long as I had without learning patience. Finally, Robert said, "My soul."

"Your—oh!" I put down my coffee mug as Robert set down his bread, and slid my leg across his hip so I sat facing him on his lap. "Your soul," I murmured, fingering the end of the silver chain that dangled from the collar. The broken link that I'd first noticed after Robert had applied the fairy ointment to my eyes was still there, tenaciously clinging to its mate.

"Aye. 'Tis how she bound me in the first place." Robert settled his hands against the nape of my neck, and rested his forehead on mine. "Which is why ye will no' seek a way to free me. My heart, I canna risk ye losin' your soul as well."

I stared into his icy blue eyes, forcing a smile while my stomach roiled. I wanted to argue with him, but he was right. I didn't want to risk my soul. I just wanted Robert's back.

"Did it change you?" I asked. "Losing it?"

"It made me capable of killing," he replied. "And no' just killing for farm and family, but for the sake of it alone."

"What do you mean, killing for family?" I adored my brother, drunken sot that he was, but I couldn't imagine committing murder for him.

"My youth was different than yours. We raised livestock, chickens and sheep, and me brothers and I shared in the butchering. I've been killing things for as long as I can remember."

"But then she made you kill for her," I prompted when he fell silent.

"Aye. That she did, and while I canna say for certain, I believe that had I ne'er encountered her, I would have stopped at chickens and the like." Robert raised his gaze to mine. "Please, Karina, I do no' want ye to end up like me. Leave it be."

My stomach still churned, so I slid off of Robert's hips and wedged myself between his leg and the armrest, and grabbed a piece of bread.

Coffee on an empty stomach hadn't been my best idea, and reheated coffee at that. "I don't like sharing, either," I grumbled.

"She only has a part o' me soul," Robert quipped. "The remainder is all yours, love. No' to mention the whole o' me physical form," he added, with a wink.

Just because I held the majority didn't mean that I was the winner. Before I could impress upon Robert that I wanted all of him, even the invisible bits, my brother came crashing through the front door.

"Don't you two look cozy," Chris sneered, dropping his bags next to the door.

"Hello to you too," I retorted. "There's coffee."

"Thank fricken' God," Chris grumbled, then he caught Robert's eye. "No offense, padre."

"None taken," Robert said evenly. "I trust St. Andrews was to your liking."

"Sure was," Chris said between gulps of coffee. "I might have worked out a job there."

If I'd been standing, I would have fallen. "Like, a permanent job?"

"Yeah. I would be teaching Elizabethan literature alongside Ethan."

Chris turned his back to Robert and me, and started rummaging through the cabinets. Chris's words had shocked me, so much so that I couldn't even tell him that pretty much all of the food was already out on the coffee table. Instead, I slumped against Robert's chest, my head spinning. If Chris could stay in Scotland, did that mean I could, too?

I could definitely finish up my degree in the UK; there were lots of schools here, not to mention some of the best universities in the world. I could complete my thesis on supernatural phenomenon as it related to bedrock composition in the place where my theory had been born. Instead of cramming my research into a few short weeks, I could spend months or even years perfecting my arguments. And I could stay with Robert.

I looked up, examining Robert's profile, wondering if he wanted me to stay in Scotland with him. We'd never finished the discussion we'd begun at dinner last night, when I'd freaked out and told Robert that my grant funds would be tapped out in a few weeks, and that despite the fact that he could look after himself quite well there was now an "us" to consider. Then again, maybe our marathon lovemaking session had been my answer.

Despite how strongly I felt for Robert, in the back of my mind I'd just assumed that once my grant ended, I would tell him goodbye, return home, continue my studies, and avoid Jared at all costs. Of course, avoiding Jared would mean either switching schools, or taking a leave of absence and hoping he graduated in the meantime, and got a permanent teaching position somewhere other than Carson University. Assuming that he even could graduate without his dumb girl doing all of his work for him.

Yeah, I'd rather stay in Scotland.

"When will you know if you have the job?" I asked Chris, my eyes never leaving Robert.

"It's pretty much a done deal," Chris replied. "I just need to work out a few loose ends."

I nodded, wondering what loose ends I had. "Robert," I murmured, but he didn't look at me. "Robert, what do you think of Chris's news?" Since Robert kept on ignoring me, I followed his gaze. He was staring at weird mark Chris's neck.

"What's that on your neck?" I asked. The mark in question was a shiny whitish spot, about the size of a thumbprint, peeking out of his collar.

Chris rubbed at his neck, then he buttered a slice of bread. "No idea," he said. He wolfed down the bread, finished off his coffee, and stretched. "I'm going to take a shower."

Once he was in the bathroom, and we heard the water running, I turned back to Robert. "That was weird."

Robert nodded. "Ye saw the mark on his neck?"

"I did. It looked like an old scar, but I don't remember him having one there."

"'Twas no scar." Robert turned to me then, his eyes hard. "'Twas the mark of a fey kiss. Your brother was no with academics the past few days, likely he was not at St. Andrews at all. He was cavorting with the Good People."

ETHAN SPILLS THE BEANS

After Chris finished his shower, he emerged from the bathroom, announced that he was exhausted, and disappeared into his room. That was just as well, since I didn't have the slightest idea of how I was going to approach my brother about his extracurricular activities with the Good People.

After I'd stared at Chris's closed door for a solid minute, I asked Robert, "Do you think he knows he was with a bunch of fairies? They could have glamoured themselves around him."

"The question is no does he ken, but does he care," Robert replied. I shook my head; I was not about to let the Good People have my brother. Chris and I didn't always see eye to eye, but he was all the family I had left. He was my family, dammit, and I wasn't going to let the fairies have him.

Spying Chris's briefcase where he'd dropped it near the front door, I grabbed it and placed it on the kitchen counter, and then I swore loudly enough for Robert to rush to my side. The briefcase had one of those combination locks, and I had no idea what it could be.

"This... This is a problem," I muttered, running my thumb over the little dials. "What would he have used as the code?"

Robert snorted. "It canna be too complicated. The man is not exactly an enigma, ye ken."

On a hunch, I dialed in Olivia's birthdate. When that didn't release the clasps, I cleared the numbers and set the dials to June twenty-fifth, Chris and Olivia's planned wedding date. The lock popped open, and I smiled.

"He may not be an enigma, but he is a hopeless romantic," I said as I rifled through Chris's paperwork.

"What are ye searching for?" Robert asked. "Evidence of a sort?"

"Of a sort." I found Chris's appointment book, and flipped it open to the contact sheet; for a man with a cell phone that cost more than a car, he was such a Luddite. Having found the information I needed, I grabbed my own cell phone. Hands shaking, I punched in the top number on the sheet, then I activated the speakerphone feature and set it on the counter.

"What the bloody hell is that?" Robert demanded upon hearing it ring.

"You've seen my phone before," I reminded him. Before Robert could freak out any further, the line was answered.

"'Ello?" said a rough voice.

"Ethan? Ethan Jacobsen?" I asked.

"In the flesh," he confirmed. "Voice, rather. Who might this be?"

"It's Rina Stewart, Chris's sister."

"Sweet little Rina!" Ethan bellowed, earning a laugh from me, and a scowl from Robert. "Still playing with your rocks and bones?"

"You know it." Robert's scowl deepened, so I gave him my back. "So about your little get together with Chris," I began.

"About that," Ethan interrupted. "When is the lunk planning on getting here? I know you're dragging him all across the countryside, looking for fossils and fairies and such, but this land is not so big. Get out here, already! I have quite the time planned for us."

A chill took me, shaking me so hard I wrapped my arms around myself. "That's what I was calling about," I said, willing myself to remain calm. "Chris isn't feeling all that well; he must have caught a cold or something. He's going to take it easy for a few days, then he'll make it out to St. Andrews, maybe by next Friday."

"Sounds like you caught a bit of something yourself," Ethan observed. "Get yourself some rest, have a wee dram as the locals call it, and I'll see you both next weekend."

Ethan and I said our goodbyes, then I pushed the end call button. I took a deep breath and gripped the edge of the counter, centering myself before I spoke.

"Chris did not go to St. Andrews," I said, rather unnecessarily since Robert had heard Ethan's and my entire conversation. "He hasn't even talked to Ethan. He was... I have no idea where he was." I shook my head. "No, I know exactly where he was. He was with them."

Robert placed his hands on my shoulders, his thumbs rubbing the back of my neck, but I needed more. I turned around and buried my face in his chest, willing myself to concentrate on the slow, steady thump of his heartbeat rather than remembering what Ethan had said.

"There, love," Robert soothed. He was always soothing me, always helping me. In that moment I decided that I would stay in Scotland, maybe for the rest of my life. There was no way I could give Robert up, not now that he meant so much to me. I just had no idea of how I was going to do it. But before I figured all of that out, I had to help my brother.

"What do we do now?" I asked. I assumed that Robert would know where Chris had been, and what manner of creatures he'd been with.

I imagined that he'd brew up one of his worts, and that by sundown my brother would be safe again. Once again, I was wrong.

"I have no' the slightest idea," he murmured. God. I hate this no lying crap.

POOR DENTED PINEAPPLE

S ince there was nothing Robert nor I could do about Chris's situation, at least not until he woke up, we set our sights on something we could handle: grocery shopping, Scottish style. Like the orderly scholars we were, we proceeded to make a list, and then we emptied our tote bags of the fossils and other treasures from Dob's Linn. After we'd shaken out the dust and debris, we headed out to the Marketgait in the center of Crail. We hadn't made it too far into town before I realized that our plan might have been overly ambitious.

Mind you, the groceries themselves weren't the problem. Since it was Sunday, the open air market had taken over the downtown streets, the very same streets Robert and I had fled through just last night, pursued by the *fuath*. Then, the streets had been cold and dark and wet, slippery and stinking of death.

Now, the streets were clean and bright, packed with stalls offering produce, meat, and baked goods; there was even a tent offering ale and whisky, along with the free samples that were something of a national custom. Robert and I had sampled and purchased aplenty, but that wasn't what was irritating me about this particular outing. The issue arose when Robert, who had repeatedly claimed to have traveled into the world on many, many occasions at Nicnevin's behest, had to stop and study the ingredient list of every cellophane package and canned good we came across.

"I'm really starting to doubt that you were ever in the modern world before we met," I commented, as Robert scrutinized the ingredient list on a canned haggis. "And we are *not* getting that."

"Agreed," Robert said, replacing the can on the table. "Haggis should be served hot and steamin' right from the oven, no' closed up in a wee bit o' tin." I shuddered; in my opinion, meals stuffed into sheep stomachs shouldn't be served at all unless starvation was imminent, and even then I'd prefer a few stale bread crusts. "Now, as to this cock a' leekie," he continued, picking up a different can from the display.

"It's chicken soup," I said, snatching the can from his hands and tossing it and another of the same into our basket. "If you like chickens, and soup, it will be fine." Robert eyed me, but said nothing. Based on the general nosiness of Scottish shoppers, he didn't have to.

"Now lass," said a woman, who herself was lugging a basket laden with canned haggis, both beef and lamb versions, "do no' be so hard on your man. Even in these days o' workin' women and such, 'tis rare for a husband to go out and do the shopping."

My cheeks flamed in mingled embarrassment and outrage. Why did everyone just keep assuming that Robert and I were married? "He's not my husband," I pouted. "He's old enough to be my father. Grandfather, even."

"Och, no," the woman said, "he does no' look a day over thirty." She leaned closer, and added, "But then, I hear that a young lass can have all sorts of pleasant effects on a man."

She patted my arm before she trundled off, while my cheeks ratcheted up the heat to nuclear. I glared at the chuckling Robert, and noticed that he was standing in direct sunlight, without a hint of shade softening his features. With the exception of a few laugh lines around his eyes and mouth, he didn't have a single mark of age.

"How old were you when you were, um, you know?" I asked, my gaze darting about. We hadn't seen any of the Good People at the market, but they were slippery little buggers. "Were taken."

"I was forty-seven years of age," he replied.

"Wow." Somehow, the twenty-two years that separated our mortal ages seemed like a far greater span than the three centuries he'd spent in Fairyland. "Why don't you look forty-seven?" I pressed.

"And how should I be lookin'?" he countered.

"I don't know. Older." I stood on my toes, and examined his skin while I raked my fingers through the dark hair at his nape. "Wrinkly, at least. And why don't you have any gray hair?"

"The elixir, most likely." He had mentioned Nicnevin's elixir before, describing it as a sweet drink that burned away one's mortality. While I was contemplating that, Robert grasped me about the waist and pressed a quick kiss to my lips. "At last, you admit that me bein' an old man bothers ye."

"That's not what's bothering me." He loosened his hold, and I slid away from him. "Are you immortal?"

"Truly, I do no' ken." Robert pursed his lips. "I was while I regularly imbibed the elixir. Now, who's to say?"

I watched him for a moment, then I turned away and paid for the cans of soup. Once that was done, and I'd transferred the cans from my basket to one of our tote bags, I wandered off to a produce stall. Robert followed, not that I'd expected him to do anything else. After I'd added carrots, potatoes, and celery to our basket, he asked, "One thing I would like to ken, are ye wishin' for me to age and die, or remain as I am?"

"I don't want you to die," I snapped. "I just... I just don't want to be all gray and wrinkly while you stay looking like that."

"Like what, exactly?"

"That." I gestured, encompassing his entire form. "Like you just walked out of a photo shoot. People are going to think I'm your grandmother."

Robert's brows shot halfway up his head, and I bit my lip. I'd just made the most shallow statement of my life, and was more than a bit mortified. I turned away and examined the fruit displays, wondering if it was worth it to purchase a fresh pineapple. While I debated between that and a few mangoes, Robert slipped his arms around my waist. "Are ye keeping me that long, then?" he murmured, his lips against my temple. "Until we're grandparents?"

"I'll keep you only so long as you behave," I said, swatting away his hands. "This is a public place, you know."

"You did no' mind the last kiss."

"I don't mind any of them," I admitted. "It's just... It's not polite. For the other shoppers."

"Oh, we do no' mind," chirped the woman with the canned haggis, who was now busily fondling a tomato. "'Tis a wonderful thing to see a young couple in love."

That comment generated a round of approving nods from the fruit seller, and several other market patrons. "Is that woman one of the *fuath*?" I asked, jerking my head toward Ms. Haggis.

Robert glanced at her. "Most certainly not."

"So, you can't kill her?" I pressed.

"Karina!"

"Too bad," I grumbled. "Let's pay for the stupid fruit."

We paid the fruit seller, and after we picked up a few loaves of bread and boxes of pastries at the next stall, we decided to head back to the cottage. It was our only option, being that we had three tote bags full of food, and only myself and my gallowglass to carry it.

"Perhaps I'll try me hand at brewin' up a batch of the elixir," Robert said out of the blue.

"Do you even know what's in it?" I asked. I didn't imagine the Seelie Queen was big on sharing recipe cards.

"Wine, assuredly. And 'twas quite sweet, so I imagine honey is involved." He rubbed his chin. "Perhaps a bit 'o mint, as well, or rose petal..."

"Well, I do hope you figure it out. We wouldn't want you losing your good looks." I stomped on ahead, foolishly hoping to outpace a man with a stride twice as long as my own. Even the tote of canned goods didn't slow him down.

Robert stepped in front of me, halting me with his hands on my shoulders. "Love, the elixir would no' be for me, but for you."

I opened my mouth, shut it, and looked up at him. "Why for me?"

"To even us out, ye ken." Robert's eyes twinkled, his lopsided smile working its way into my heart. "Now that I've found ye, Karina, me love, I canna imagine going forward in this life without ye by me side."

I stared at him, my arms going limp as the tote bag slid from my shoulder and landed on the street; poor, dented pineapple. As much as I had tried not to acknowledge it, there had been a nagging little voice in the back of my mind that had always agreed with Chris: Robert was a freeloader and a gigolo, just using the dumb tourist girl until he got what he wanted. And after last night, I was afraid that he'd gotten it, and soon would be on his way. That was pretty much what had happened with Jared.

But Robert was no Jared.

"Do you really mean that?" I whispered.

Robert set down his totes, and looked me in the eye. "Love, I really do."

Just like that, the little voice in my head was silenced, never to pipe up again. I squealed, right there in the street, and leapt into Robert's arms. He laughed as he caught me, his strong hands under my hips as I wrapped my legs around his waist, raining kisses onto his face.

"I'm keeping you," I said between kisses. "Forever and ever and ever, I'm keeping you."

"Hear that?" Robert yelled over his shoulder. "She's keepin' me!"

I peeked over the top of his head, and saw Ms. Haggis and the rest nodding their approval. Somehow, they weren't bothering me as much anymore.

DINNER WITH THE FAIRY LOVER

A noise somewhere between a gasp and a moan escaped my lips, and I collapsed against Robert's chest, clutching his shoulders as his hips bucked beneath me. I was drenched in sweat, sore as all get out, and a fair bit happier than I could ever remember being.

I was keeping Robert. Even better, he was keeping me.

I had been on cloud nine after our little PDA session at the market, and my feet had hardly touched the ground as we walked back to the cottage. All of my doubts about Robert, which had already been dwindling away at a steady pace, had been replaced by a single certainty: this man from the seventeenth century had been made for me.

"'Tis unfortunate I needed to wait so long for ye to come along," he had said, when I shared why I was smiling. We'd been leisurely walking along the village streets, lugging our groceries while Robert's arm was draped around my shoulders.

"I'm sure you found a few ways to pass the time," I'd said. "She must have kept you pretty busy." We both avoided saying Nicnevin's name aloud, especially in public.

"Not as much as ye would think," Robert murmured. "When she had no need of me, she would ignore me for weeks or months at a time."

"That must have been nice," I said, imagining that having all that free time to explore Elphame was a folklorist's dream come true. Robert snorted, and explained how wrong I was.

"'Twas more of a torture than the collectin' o' the teind. Without her leave, I was confined to the tree where ye found me, me sword raised and at the ready. I was no' to eat or drink or even sleep without her say so." Robert squeezed me against him. "I was kept alone in the blackness, as yet another one o' me punishments for refusing her."

"You must have been so lonely," I said. "How did you manage?"

"Faith," he replied. "Faith in God, faith that He had a purpose for me, faith that Nicnevin would find a reason to send me out into the world... Faith that a bonnie lass would happen by that infernal tree, and loose me from my torment," he added, kissing my hair.

"You just made that last part up," I accused.

"Perhaps," he admitted. "Still, 'twas an act o' faith on me part, and I ha' been richly rewarded."

Once we had reached the cottage, and had set the tote bags packed full of groceries on the counter, I checked on Chris. He was still sleeping, so I'd helped Robert unpack the food and restock the cabinets and fridge. Foodstuffs thus secured, I then asked Robert how we should spend our time until Chris woke. I'd assumed that he would suggest we work on some research, or maybe take a walk by the harbor to check for signs of the *fuath*, but the glint in his blue eyes told me that he had an entirely different activity in mind. One that I was more than willing to participate in.

Now, I was lying atop Robert's chest, waiting for this latest round of aftershocks to subside. "You're insatiable," I mumbled into his shoulder.

"I do no' hear ye complainin' one bit." Robert shifted so he was on his side, and propped himself up on his elbow. "Fancy another o' your standing baths?" he asked, tracing a bead of sweat along my collarbone.

"You mean a shower?" I teased, then I sobered and added, "We can't be showering together with Chris in the next room. That would be... Well, it would be weird."

"Mmm. Surely, you and I sharin' a bath will no' be the strangest thing he has encountered o' late." Robert rolled onto his back, and stretched his arms over his head. I laid my head on his chest, and toyed with the dark curls scattered across it.

"How much longer is he going to sleep?" I grumbled. Robert and I had gotten back from the market around two, and the sky I could see through the bedroom window was painted in twilight's purples and oranges.

Robert grunted. "I've seen mortals sleep for days or e'en weeks after revels. Like as no', he was no' doin' much restin' while he was there."

I wrinkled my nose; if there was anything I didn't want to think about, it was whatever Chris had been doing with the fairies.

"I guess we'll leave him to it, then." I got out of bed and stretched. "I call dibs on the shower!"

Robert let me get to the bathroom first; he even let me start the shower and step under the spray, but he didn't let me get much farther than that. There I was, helpless with a head full of shampoo suds, when a gallowglass invaded my bathroom.

"What are you doing?" I shrieked when he stepped into the tub.

"I'm here to wash your back, o' course," he replied, his blue eyes feigning innocence.

"Only washing," I said. "I mean it. Chris is sleeping right on the other side of this wall," I pointed at the offensively cheery pink tile, "and no brother in the world wants to be woken up by hearing his sister doing *that.*"

"I suppose ye have a point." Robert backed me under the spray, working his hands into my hair as he rinsed away the shampoo. Then we were kissing, and his hands were following the bubbles as they slipped down my body and toward the drain.

"Behave." I bumped him away with my hip, and reached for the conditioner. Once I'd slicked on the creamy liquid, I turned around to grab a washcloth. That was when Robert bumped me with something of his own. "I said behave!"

"'Tis no' my fault," he replied. "Blame my condition on that bum o' yours."

I turned around, and rubbed the washcloth across his chest. "You're just showing off," I said, gliding the washcloth lower. "You can't possibly have anything left in you."

"Oh?" Robert grabbed my waist, then slid his hands lower to squeeze my butt. "Care to make a wager on that?"

Robert kissed me as I closed my hand around his shaft, stroking one, twice, thrice... Then we were interrupted by a slamming door. Specifically, the slamming of Chris's bedroom door. I sighed, and backed under the spray; it just figured that as soon as Robert had swayed me to his cause, my brother woke up.

"Let me talk to him first," I said, once I'd rinsed off the soap and conditioner. "Join me in a minute?"

Robert pressed a kiss to my forehead, and squeezed my butt once more for good measure. "Aye, love, that I will." With that, I toweled off and slipped into my terry robe, and went out to the common room to confront my brother, the fairy lover.

I found Chris staring at the coffeemaker, as if he thought it would get up and perform a grand trick or two. "Welcome back to the land of the living," I greeted.

"Why isn't there coffee?" he grumbled. "You always wake up first and make coffee."

"Chris, it's past eight o'clock at night," I said. He grabbed his phone from his back pocket, eyes widening as he read the display.

"When did I get home?" he asked.

"Early this morning," I replied. "You've been sleeping all day."

"I guess that's why there's no coffee," he muttered, as he set his phone on the counter.

"Are you hungry?" I asked. "We went shopping. There's enough food here to feed an army."

"We?" Chris echoed. As if on cue, Robert emerged from the bathroom, dripping wet and wearing only a towel around his waist. So much for letting me talk to my brother alone first. Chris scowled at Robert, and asked, "Showering together now?"

"It saves water." I was so not letting him bait me, not while he had that shiny mark on his neck. "How was St. Andrews?"

"Good, very good," Chris replied. He turned away and opened one of the cupboards. "Ethan's the same old party animal. You would have thought that being a professor would have mellowed him out some, but not that guy."

"I called him."

"Called who?"

"Ethan."

Chris's back went rigid, but he didn't turn around. "Why did you call him?"

"When you came home after being gone for two days, and with a fairy kiss planted on your neck, I was worried."

Slowly, Chris shut the cupboard door, then he took a deep breath. When he turned around he was smiling. "It was good of you to worry, Rina, but I can take care of myself. Ethan and I—"

"You weren't with Ethan," I interrupted. "You were off—somewhere—with the Good People."

"Good People?" Chris repeated.

"You know. Fairies."

"Don't start with all your magic woo-woo," Chris warned. "You know I don't buy into that." He reached up and rubbed the back of his neck; as his sleeve rode up, I saw another silvery mark on the inside of his wrist.

"Then how do you explain this?" I demanded, rushing forward and grabbing his arm. I shoved up his sleeve, and saw many more of the shiny ovals dancing up his flesh. Sickened, I said, "You're covered in them."

"So what?" he said, yanking his arm free. "What's wrong with me having a little fun? Don't you think that after all I've been through these past few months, I deserve a little fun? Isn't that what you're doing with this guy?" I glanced at Robert; he was standing with his feet planted wide and arms folded across his chest, looking more like a general surveying a battlefield than a man who'd just gotten out of the shower. Even the damp towel about his waist did little to detract from his dignity.

"The difference is that Robert won't hurt me," I said. "The Good People are only out to play with you. They care nothing for mortals."

"They seemed to care about this guy," Chris said, jerking his chin toward Robert. "Wasn't he shacked up with their queen? Or so he claims?"

"I was a prisoner to her whims," Robert said, his voice dead calm. "And my name is Robert. Robert James Kirk. No' 'this guy', and not any o' the other insults ye lob my way." Robert came to stand beside me. "Everything Karina said to you is correct. There is nothing good about the Good People, for all that we call them that. Ye would do best to leave them be."

Anyone in their right mind would have been terrified after receiving such a speech, especially from someone who exuded such menace as Robert did, but Chris laughed. Not a chuckle, or a simple giggle, he laughed so hard he needed to lean on the counter for support. "You expect me to listen to a wet, naked guy lecture me about fairies? Really, Rina, this is nuts, even for you."

That comment stung, but I tried to hide it. When Robert touched my elbow and murmured in my ear, I knew I hadn't done such a good job.

"Leave it for now, love, he is no' himself," he said. "I am going to dress. Try to talk some sense into him."

I nodded, and Robert retreated to our bedroom. As soon as he shut the door, I attacked the coffee maker.

"What are you doing?" Chris asked.

"I thought you wanted coffee," I said. "I might as well make the whole pot, since I have field notes to go over."

"What about—"

"Do we have to fight all night?" I faced my brother, and caught a glimpse of more fairy kisses trailing under his collar. Gross. "Listen, I'm sorry I called Ethan. Really. Can't a girl worry about her older brother?"

Chris's brow furrowed. "What about the guy?"

"Robert," I corrected. "I'm keeping him," I said, as I filled the carafe.

"Keeping?" he repeated. "Keeping as in *keeping*?"

"Yes." I poured the water into the reservoir and grabbed the packet of filters. "So, you and he had best learn to get along with each other."

Once the coffee maker was set up, I left my stunned brother staring after me, and escaped to the bedroom to throw on some clothes. It looked like I was going to have a long night ahead of me.

Once Robert and I had dressed and formulated a bare-bones plan for helping Chris, whether he liked it or not, we returned to the common room and started on dinner. Since I'm not much of a cook—and Robert didn't know how to use the stove—we opted for the canned cock a' leekie soup. While it simmered away, Robert sliced up a loaf of bread, and I ate a few olives straight from the jar. Chris, most unhelpfully, loafed on the couch, flipping through the channels on the tired old television and complaining about the lack of suitable Scottish programming.

"Then why don't you read a book?" I suggested, cutting off his diatribe about how sitcoms were the lowest form of humor. Chris made a face, but he got up and perused the bookshelf. After a few minutes, he returned to the couch with a battered copy of *Hound of the Baskervilles*.

"Dinner is served," I proclaimed a few minutes later, ladling the soup into a few mismatched earthenware bowls. The three of us sat around the table, Chris as far from Robert as he could manage, and we proceeded to eat. Somehow we managed to make generic small talk instead of arguing, with most of our conversation centering on the food. The cock a' leekie wasn't bad for canned soup, and the bread was excellent.

"Want help with the dishes?" Chris offered, once we had finished.

"Nah," I said. "Just leave them to soak, for now. I want to get started on my notes."

Chris gathered up the dirty dishes and deposited them in the sink before returning to the couch and Mr. Holmes's phosphorescent dog. I hacked up the pineapple for dessert, and once I'd delivered a plate of the yellow fruit to Chris, I took possession of the kitchen table. While my laptop powered up, I spread out my research notes, and refilled my coffee. Not surprisingly, Robert opted to join me with a mug of his own. I wouldn't want to sit next to my cranky brother, either.

"What's all this, love?" Robert asked, eyeing my laptop warily. "A wee version of the talking box that so irritated Christopher earlier?"

"Um, in a way." I popped a wedge of pineapple in my mouth as I clicked open a few files, and angled the screen so Robert could see it. "It's like a research library I can take with me. I enter all my notes and fieldwork into it, so I don't have to carry random stacks of paper everywhere I go."

Robert nodded, his face thoughtful. "I remember when I first learned o' microscopes. The description was so fantastic I thought they were the stuff o' fiction. Then, I saw one wi' me own eyes, and I realized that there are many worlds just waitin' to be discovered."

I nodded. "I know exactly what you mean."

"How do ye write on it? With a certain type o' stylus?"

"Like this." I called up a blank document, and typed *Karina Siob-han Stewart.*

Robert's eyes widened, then he tugged the keyboard toward him. "Why aren't the letters in order?" he demanded.

"I think they're organized based on how often they're used," I replied, though I really had no idea how the Qwerty keyboard had been, um, Qwerty-ized. There must be some practical reason, right?

"It was created by telegraph operators transcribing Morse code," Chris called over.

Scowling, I muttered, "Know it all."

"Those who teach tend to know things," Chris retorted.

"How do ye create a capital letter?" Robert asked, so I introduced him to the shift key. He grunted, and then very, very slowly, he typed *Robert James Kirk.*

"Very good," I murmured. Feeling mischievous, I took back the keyboard and typed:

Robert and Karina

Sitting in a tree

K-I-S-S-I-N-G

First comes love

Then comes marriage

Then comes Karina

With a baby carriage!

"Baby carriage," Robert's deep voice rumbled.

I flushed, and hit delete. "I didn't mean it like that. I didn't really think past the kissing part."

Robert stayed my hand, leaving most of my juvenile rhyme intact, and pressed a kiss behind my ear. "Let me see if I have the hang o' this contraption," he murmured, reclaiming the keyboard. After an agonizingly long time, he turned the laptop back to me.

rObert James Kirk would gladly wait another three hundred years just to be kissing his Karina Siobhan Stuart once more

I laughed, though it was cut short when Robert kissed me. "I do no' think much past the kissing, either," he murmured when we parted.

"You spelled my surname wrong," I said.

Robert glanced at the screen. "Forgive me, love. I was thinkin' of our King James."

A cough reminded Robert and me that, unlike the past few days, we weren't the only ones in the cottage. I looked up, and saw my silver-spotted brother standing in front of us. "Since you two obviously want to be alone, I'm going out for a drink."

"Okay," I said. "Maybe we'll meet up with you in an hour or so."

"Sounds good," Chris said. He nodded toward Robert, then he grabbed his coat and was out the door.

"That worked surprisingly well," I said as I shut down my laptop. "I figured it would take hours for him to work up the nerve to leave on his own."

"Ye forget, love, like as no' he is under the Good People's thrall," Robert pointed out.

"Why weren't you ever under Nicnevin's thrall?" I asked, as Robert held out my coat for me. Once my arms were in the sleeves, he kissed my temple.

"She could no' offer me anything I wanted," he replied. "If Christopher does prove to be enthralled, likely he has been given a glimpse o' something he desires greatly. Do ye ken what that desire may be?"

I considered Chris's floundering careers, both as an English professor and as an author, his relentless pining for Olivia, the friends and colleagues that had abandoned him, the lawsuits that were threatening to break him. "I can think of a thing or two."

Robert opened the door, and we stepped out into the chill night air, intent on following my enthralled brother. Just like the oft-quoted movie line, I had a bad feeling about this.

OUT FOR A PINT

I leaned back against the cottage door, relieved and amazed and wondering what my sister was really up to. After Rina had told me she called Ethan, I worried that she and Robert were going to attempt some kind of woo-woo intervention on me. I probably could have convinced them that, even though I'd lied about being with Ethan, I was just having some fun with a local girl. Then again, my sister had inherited the Stewart stubbornness, seemingly undiluted, from our father.

There was also the fact that I still hadn't told Rina about Sorcha, and I honestly had no idea why I hadn't. Before Rina had started interrogating me, and leaping to her ridiculous conclusions that I had been spending time with imaginary creatures for the past few days, I'd fully intended to. Even after she'd calmed down and dropped the subject, I'd wanted to tell her all about Sorcha, but my mouth couldn't form the words.

Then, after we'd eaten, Rina and Robert had started making eyes at each other. There was no way I wanted to stay around and watch that. And what the hell did she mean by keeping him, anyway? Instead of asking her, or him, what had happened between them while I was gone, I left.

Before, I never would have left. If I'd thought anything was coming at Rina, be it a mosquito or a full grown Scot or anything in between, I'd have stayed right there and demanded answers. Hell, I still didn't really know what had happened at Inchmahome, and who that Robert guy really was. But instead of asking any of those questions, as soon as Rina was distracted, I left to find Sorcha. Brother of the year, that's me.

I shook my head, and started toward the center of the village. As I walked, hands stuffed into my pockets and collar turned up against the night breeze, I considered what I really knew about Sorcha. It had only been a few days since we'd met, so I didn't know much, but I had been inside her home. It was a grand house, with marble floors and hand painted scenes on the walls, but I didn't think it had any heat; despite the many blankets and cushions on her bed, I'd woken up shivering. In fact, the entire house was stuck in winter, from the cold stone floors to Sorcha's icy fingertips. Only her kisses were hot, especially when her pink lips had wrapped around my—

"Christopher."

As if thinking her name had made her appear, I turned and found Sorcha leaning against a brick wall beside me. I'd been so deep in thought, I hadn't noticed my heart's desire was mere inches away. She was wearing a deep green sweater and a tan suede skirt, along with chocolate brown riding boots. Her dark hair was piled atop her head, with a few stray tendrils curling about her ears. I couldn't wait to wind those tendrils around my fingers, kiss the soft skin of her neck.

"Were you looking for me?"

"I was," I replied, gathering her in my arms. "I told my sister I was stepping out for a pint, but I really only wanted to find you."

Sorcha smiled. "Then let us get you that pint."

She led me to a door, and we entered the pub, weaving among the other patrons as we headed toward the seats in the rear of the room. The blonde woman behind the bar gasped when she saw us, though a glare from Sorcha quieted her. Before I had time to wonder what that was all about, we were sliding into a corner booth. The bartender then appeared before us, bearing two pints on a tray.

"My lady," the bartender murmured, then she bowed her head and disappeared.

"Did she just call you 'my lady'?" I asked.

"Did she?" Sorcha asked. "I hadn't noticed. I was busy looking at you."

I smiled, then I sipped my beer. As long as I was with Sorcha, I couldn't be anything but happy.

REVELATIONS

E ven though Chris had a good ten-minute head start on Robert and me, it didn't take long for us to track him down. Really, all we had to do was check the pubs. He was in the second pub we entered, the one where the Ice Princess worked behind the bar. Chris was seated in the farthest booth from the door, cozied up with a rather normal looking young woman.

"She looks mortal enough to me," I said. The woman in question had dark hair, so dark that it seemed to absorb the light, artfully coiled atop her head, creamy olive skin, and big, dark eyes. Chris was so wrapped up in her that he didn't notice Robert and me until we were standing right at the edge of their table, and I'd said his name three times.

"Chris," I repeated. Finally, he tore his gaze away from the woman and acknowledged me. "Robert and I decided to have a drink, too."

Chris nodded, then he grabbed the dark haired woman's hands. "Rina, this is Sorcha," he said.

"Ah, the famous sister," Sorcha murmured. Good to know that Chris hadn't completely forgotten my existence while he'd been off doing whatever he'd been doing with her. "A pleasure to meet you."

"You as well," I mumbled, taken aback by the fact that maybe Chris had been spending time with a not-fairy person after all.

"And who might this be?" Sorcha asked, with a nod toward Robert.

"Oh, he's my…" I blinked; what was Robert to me? The term boyfriend had always sounded a bit trite to me, and calling him my lover would be revealing too much to a stranger. "Robert."

"Your Robert?" Sorcha asked, raising an eyebrow. "It's a pleasure to meet you as well, Rina's Robert."

Robert grunted a greeting to Sorcha, then he took my elbow. "We do no' wish to disturb the two o' ye. Karina and I shall take our pints at the bar." He led me to the bar, where we claimed some stools and waved at the Ice Princess. She acknowledged us with a nod, and started filling two pint glasses.

"I guess he wasn't with the Good People," I whispered. "She's obviously human."

"Do no' be so deceived," Robert warned. "The wort I prepared for ye only allows one to see around the most basic o' glamours. Some creatures hardly use any glamour at all."

"You mean, like how the *fuath* inhabited that old woman at the priory?" I shuddered, remembering the monster's needlelike teeth, its head as it rolled away from its body, and all the black, sludgy blood that had soaked the ground.

Robert put his hand on my knee and squeezed. "Yes, love, exactly like that."

"Then how will we know if she's one of them?"

"We watch. And we wait."

I scowled; I wasn't much for watching or waiting. I like to be doing, or at least researching my options in preparation for doing. Before I could express my displeasure about this lack of activity to Robert, the Ice Princess arrived with our pints.

"Do no' allow your brother to leave wi' the likes o' her," she hissed, without preamble. "He has spent far too much time wi' them already."

"What do you mean?" I hedged. And how did the Ice Princess even know that Chris and I were related? "Chris and Sorcha seem to be getting along well enough."

"Do no' play games wi' me, lassie," she said. "Ye ken as well as I that she be no mortal."

My eyes widened, and I bit my lip. "What makes you say that?"

The Ice Princess leaned forward and tapped Robert's silver collar. "Oh, I do no' ken, mayhap a good guess on me part?"

I was stunned; she had known all along that we could see her, and hadn't once betrayed us. "Why did you keep our secret?" I asked.

She shrugged. "Ye are no threat to me and mine. And ye tip well."

"Where has she been taking him?" Robert asked.

The Ice Princess shrank back. "No, ye canna go there," she whispered, then she said to Robert, "Especially not ye."

Robert's mouth became a slash across his face. "We canna leave the boy to them."

Ice Princess nodded. "Ye always were a noble one, I'll give ye that, e'en while ye were carryin' out her whims. 'Tis no wonder ye endured far longer than the rest."

"The rest?" I asked.

"That I did," Robert said. Neither answered me.

The Ice Princess nodded, then she rummaged under the bar, and produced a pencil and notepad. "Are ye familiar with the bens beyond the paved roads?"

Robert and I affirmed that we were, and the Ice Princess quickly sketched out a map to the hollow hill where Chris had been spending his days and nights. Once that was done, she gripped both of our hands, then without another word, she retreated through the swinging doors to the kitchen. I hoped she was really our friend, and not a double agent running off to tell her fairy friends to spring the trap.

"What did she mean?" I asked Robert, my eyes still on the swinging doors. I didn't want to ask him about this, but I had to. The Ice Princess had piqued my insatiable, and somewhat foolish, curiosity. "About that enduring comment?"

"What about it?" Robert countered.

"She said that you lasted longer than the rest," I said. "The rest of whom?"

"Before I was taken, she had had her fair share o' gallowglasses," Robert replied, not bothering to explain which she he was referring to. I was most certainly aware of *her* identity. "Most lasted less than a year; a few had survived for a decade or so, but no' much longer than that."

I blinked at him. "But you were one for over *three hundred years*."

"Aye, and I am still. As long as I wear this collar, I am *the* gallowglass, naught more than a murderer." Robert raked a hand through his dark hair. "To retain my lofty position as her assassin, I killed all those she pitted against me. I... I canna imagine the amount of life that has been sent to hell by me own two hands."

I watched his profile as he took a long pull on his pint. I'd known that Robert had had to kill the gallowglass that had come before him, but I'd just assumed that was the end of it. I mean, he'd told me that he was Nicnevin's assassin, but he'd gone on to describe himself as more of a guard than a killer, and I'd ended up deciding that he was a gallowglass more in title than deed. I had no idea that he'd killed anyone and everyone that had gotten in his way over the next few centuries.

I pressed my hand to my mouth, hot bile burning my throat. How could I reconcile the two halves of Robert: the man that held me as if I was precious, and the one who described himself as a murderer?

Robert glanced at me, my clenched hands and blood-drained face, and set down his pint. "Now, love, do no' be frightened," he murmured, cupping my cheek with his hand. "I only wish to speak honestly to ye. Ye ken well I would ne'er harm so much as a hair on your head."

I opened my mouth, but I was distracted by a flash of dark hair: my brother and whatever she was were exiting their booth. "Chris and Sorcha are leaving." I left some money on the bar, and slid off my stool. "We should follow."

"Karina." Robert captured me in his arms, and tilted my chin upward. "Tell me you are no' frightened o' me."

"I..." I pursed my lips. "I don't want to lie to you."

Robert nodded, his face grim. "Fair enough," he murmured, his lips against my forehead. "I love ye, Karina me heart, ne'er forget that. No matter what may come to pass, promise me ye will no' forget that I love ye."

"I won't forget. I promise." With that, we left the pub, and followed my brother and Sorcha out into the night.

DOORWAY TO ELPHAME

Robert and I trudged through the dark, chilly streets, following Chris and a woman who probably wasn't a woman, presumably to save my brother's life, and I wasn't thinking about Chris at all. Instead, I was fixated on what Robert had said in the pub: *As long as I wear this collar, I am naught more than a murderer.*

I'd always known that Robert was a warrior, but it turned out that he had been more of a killer. And a rather effective killer, at that. A man whose sole purpose these past three centuries had been to remove whatever—whomever—Nicnevin had desired removed. Based on all accounts, including my own eye witness experiences, he was exceedingly good at his job.

How was this killer the same man who had held me as if I was dear to him, who had washed my hair, made pots of bad coffee with the best intentions, and defended me from the *fuath* on more than one occasion? Of course, when he had been defending me, he had been killing. The thing he was best at.

After about ten minutes of walking, Chris and Sorcha stopped under a streetlight for an impromptu kissing session. Robert placed his hand on the small of my back, and drew me deep into the shadows, and we waited. And waited. You'd think they were going for the Guinness Book of World Records title in snogging.

"Why did you refer to yourself as a murderer?" I asked suddenly. "When you described what you did a few days ago, it sounded like you were more of a guard." Robert sighed and pulled me against his chest.

"If she ordered me to kill, I killed," he said. "I had no quarrel with any o' them; they were merely me prey."

"Prey." I squeezed my eyes shut, pressing my forehead against his chest. "What if she told you to kill me?"

Robert grabbed my chin and jerked my head upward. When I opened my eyes, I saw his blue eyes blazing into mine. "I would kill her instead. If I could no' manage to kill her, I would fall on me sword and end it. Nothing—*nothing*—could make me harm ye, not even Nicnevin herself." Robert swept his thumbs across my cheeks. I hadn't realized I was crying. "Karina, love," he murmured, "can ye no' believe in me?"

"I... I want to." I stepped back, and rubbed my nose. "I really, really want to. More than anything. It's just, when you called yourself a murderer, it rattled me."

"I only spoke the truth," Robert said, then he was distracted by something behind me. I looked over my shoulder; Chris and Sorcha had finally ended their snog beneath the street lamp, and were on the move again. "Come, love. They are once again afoot."

Robert laced his fingers with mine, and we resumed our pursuit. "You told me you love me," I said, realization dawning, albeit a bit late. "In the pub, you told me you love me."

"Aye, that I do," Robert replied. "Surely the words did no surprise ye."

"I guess they didn't," I said. "I just wish you'd said them before we started talking about all this killing stuff."

"Me as well, Karina love," Robert said, "me as well."

We pursued Chris and Sorcha until they entered a rather innocent if grandiose looking apartment building. It was set far back from the street, and looked like it had once been a stately mansion, but had long ago been carved up into smaller apartment units. It was comprised of gray stone, which reminded me of the greywackes that made up Dob's Linn. Surrounding the elegant mansion were similarly elegant grounds, so well cared for that not a leaf or blade of grass was out of place. An apple tree grew next to the main door of the building, its fruit-laden branches arching over the entrance. It would have been a postcard perfect scene, if not for the windows. Every one of them was filled with a cold blackness, so dark it seemed to swallow the sunlight.

The building practically pulsed with darkness, like the haunted mansion in a horror film. And my brother was in there.

Robert stalked across the front yard, and looked in one of the side lights alongside the door. "There are no rooms, no corridors inside," he announced. "This home is a doorway to Elphame."

"A doorway?"

"Some would call such a thing a portal," Robert said. Huh. I guess we wouldn't need the Ice Princess's map after all.

Robert turned to me, the streetlamp's glare transforming his face into harsh planes. "Love, do ye trust me well enough to accompany me to that most terrible place? I will no' lie to ye, Nicnevin's portion o' Elphame is filled wi' naught but evil and monsters, but I swear on me very life I will no' allow them to harm ye. If ye do no' wish to make the journey, I will leave ye in safety with the wights and retrieve Christopher meself."

I looked at him for long moments, this man that I hardly knew, yet felt closer to than anyone I'd ever met. Was I still terrified of him? Absolutely. But he loved me, and I loved him back, and I sure as hell wasn't going to let him go to that place of horrors and nightmares without me.

"I have to go," I said. "What if Nicnevin tries to capture you again? You need someone to watch your back."

Robert raised an eyebrow. "Will ye challenge her for me?"

"You're mine. She can't have you." I stepped up to his side, and pushed open the heavy oak door. Just as Robert had said, the interior was devoid of floors and walls, and was nothing more than a gaping black hole, winds and debris swirling within. I swallowed, and said, "So let's go already."

Robert wrapped an arm around my waist, pulling me close as he pressed his lips to mine. "Aye, I am yours. Until the end o' forever, I am yours." He draped my arms around his neck, then he gripped my waist. "Hold on to me with all your might, Karina me love. These passages are no' for the faint o' heart."

NOT FOR THE FAINT OF HEART

He hadn't been kidding with that faint of heart comment.

Robert and I had stood together under the apple tree for a few heartbeats longer, our arms wrapped around each other, a moment's reprieve before we plunged headlong into who knows what. After we'd shared a few good luck kisses, we tightened our hold on one another, and stepped over the threshold and into the darkness.

Remember that movie about tornadoes that had been popular a few years back, the one that had the cow caught up in the funnel cloud and flying helter-skelter across the countryside? And back again? As soon as we'd stepped inside the apartment building that wasn't an apartment building, I knew exactly how that cow had felt. We were spinning, and twisting, and flying across—Well, I have no idea what. My feet weren't on the ground, or anything else for that matter; leathery wings beat perilously close to my ears, and, thanks to all the debris whipping around us, I couldn't open my eyes. Although, I probably didn't want a good look at the scenery in this place.

Throughout it all, the howling winds and strange noises and the unseen creatures, Robert held on to me. I had my fingers hooked into his shirt, one of my hands on his shoulder and the other on his waist, clenched so tightly I worried I'd claw right through the fabric and score his skin. He didn't complain, or even try to shift my hold on him. Instead, he kept his hands firm on my waist, all the while whispering in my ear. I had no idea what he was saying, his voice having been lost to the maelstrom, but his warm breath and the vibration of his voice comforted me. Robert was my constant, my talisman in that dark, windy hell.

All at once, the wind and noises stopped, and I was aware of standing upon something solid. Even better, my feet were fairly convinced that this something solid was real, actual ground. Slowly, I raised my head and opened my eyes, but I did not relax my hold on Robert. After that hellish ride, I doubted I'd ever let go of him.

"Are we there?" I asked as I took in my surroundings. If this was Elphame, the legendary Fairy Realm, it looked pretty ordinary. We were standing in a meadow, a rather lovely one at that, filled with wildflowers. The sun shone brightly overhead, and there were rolling hills off in the distance. "It looks just like Scotland."

"We are here, all right," Robert declared. "And Scotland is a fair sight lovelier than this wretched place."

"I'm sorry you had to come back," I said. "Chris'll be sorry too, once he understands." I ran my finger along Robert's silver collar. "Will she know you're here?"

"Aye," Robert replied. "Like as no' she already does."

That chilled me. I rested my forehead on Robert's chest, wondering how we could possibly retrieve Chris while staying out of Nicnevin's way. I burrowed into his arms, grateful for his warm solidity.

"I love it when you hold me," I murmured. "I feel so safe in your arms."

"No' like you're bein' held by a murderer?" he asked.

I peeked upward, and was glad to see him smiling. "From now on, let's call you a warrior instead of a murderer."

"Agreed." Robert kissed my forehead, then we untangled ourselves from one another. "Walk with me, Karina love. Let us find your fool brother, and take him forever away from this place."

As Robert and I traversed the green fields of Elphame, the glamour that had been placed on our beautiful surroundings peeled off like cheap wallpaper. First, the hills in the distance shimmered like heat waves rising from asphalt, their edges smudging as if touched by a pencil eraser before they faded away. After the hills had faded from view, the wildflowers scattered throughout the grass withered and died, one by one.

Far worse, however, than the departure of the hills or flowers was what happened to the trees. Before our eyes, the stately columns transformed from green-leafed and healthy into gray, hulking beasts, with hollowed out trunks scarred by blackened scorch marks. By the time Robert and I had reached the edge of the forest, our surroundings resembled nothing so much as a burnt out battlefield. The birdsong in the distance went from chirrups to wails, a dirge for the loss of their homes.

"Why is everything changing? Isn't the point of putting a glamour that we don't know about it?" I murmured. "Why even use a glamour in the first place? It must take up so much energy."

"Nicnevin has no concerns for wastin' the efforts of others," Robert replied. "She only wishes to amuse herself. At the moment, it would seem that she is quite pleased at the sight o' you and I crossin' the plains o' hell."

I shuddered. "I don't know how you endured all of this."

"Faith," Robert said.

"You must be the most God fearing man that has ever lived," I mumbled, making a mental note to name our firstborn Faith, provided that said firstborn was female, and that we survived long enough to even have a firstborn. Or a second or third born, for that matter.

A bird—at least, I think it was a bird; for all I knew it was a fricken' pteranodon—alighted on the tree next to me. Its deep brown feathers reminded me of an eagle, but it had a vulture's bald, wrinkly head. It stared at us for a few heartbeats, then it let out a horrible, rattling scream, and it was all I could do not to turn and run. Then, the bird-pteranodon-monster spoke.

It fricken' spoke.

"She will not let you leave again," the creature rumbled.

"Who said anything about leavin'?" Robert countered. "We only just got here."

The creature let out another series of caws, then it flung itself into the air. As I watched it circle overhead, I asked Robert, "Friend of yours?"

"Merely one o' Nicnevin's watchers," he replied. The creature was soon joined by two other, equally monstrous friends, and they circled high above us. "It seems that we shall be dealin' with her gloriousness, after all."

"Oh," I mumbled. "Awesome."

"Faith will see us through," Robert reminded me. That's it. Our firstborn is getting named Rebecca.

We walked on in silence, save for the screams emanating from the bird-pteranodon-monsters above, picking our way among the boulders and diseased trees scattered across the field. After a time, the debris thinned out, and a large rusty gray castle loomed in the distance.

This castle was eerily similar to the ruins of Tantallon Castle, mostly because the castle before us was in ruins itself. The battlements were crumbling away, and the open portcullis was littered with stone blocks that at one time had been part of the surrounding walls. Dry leaves and grasses had gathered in the corners, and what was left of the towers bore ugly black stains. But this castle wasn't situated on a cliff overlooking the sea, so if we encountered the White Lady, or any other monsters, at least we wouldn't almost drown like we had at Tantallon. I supposed that was something.

"Should we go inside?" I asked. As much as I wanted to turn tail and run, something was pulling me toward the castle. It was as if an invisible lasso had been looped around my waist.

"No. We should run as far away as we can, and ne'er speak o' it again," was Robert's frank reply.

"This is her home, isn't it?" I asked. "Nicnevin's."

"Aye, that it is."

"Why is it falling apart?" I wondered. I would have thought that a fairy queen would have a nice castle, or at least one that wasn't collapsing into dust.

"The abode mirrors its mistress," Robert replied. "A home needs a heart, and Nicnevin is altogether devoid of one. Wi' out a heart, the body crumbles away, ye ken."

I swallowed. "Is Chris is in there?"

"Yes, me love, I am certain of it."

Without further conversation, Robert placed his hand on the small of my back and guided me amongst the rubble and into the Fairy Queen's home. The interior was just as run down and squalid as the exterior, with once-colorful tapestries rotting off the walls, rats scuttling in the corners, and layer upon layer of cobwebs and dust blanketing every surface. I wanted to ask Robert why any queen, even a heartless one like Nicnevin, would live in such filth, but I was so terrified I couldn't speak.

The corridor was endlessly long, and silent save for our footsteps and the occasional ratlike creature scurrying by. Eventually, we spied light at the end of the corridor, and followed it to a room large enough to be an auditorium. It was just as dilapidated as the rest of the place, but at least the floor had been swept somewhat recently. The room was crowded, packed with every sort of creature imaginable, and a few I had never, ever wanted to consider, not now or ever again.

The mass of them parted as Robert and I entered, creating a living corridor that led to a dais carpeted in frayed and faded red. Sprawled across the steps lay my brother.

"Chris!" Heedless of the nightmares that crowded around me, I ran forward and crouched before my brother. He was breathing, but was in some sort of stupor. I wondered if he had been drugged. "Chris, can you hear me?"

"The correct question is, does he want to hear you?"

I looked up, and saw Sorcha sitting on a throne upholstered in dusty purple velvet, the bright gilding flaking off the edges to reveal the wood beneath. Beyond the dais, I spied Morag, the disappearing tour guide from Tantallon, as well as the White Lady and a few of the child-stealing fey. Behind them grinned Ms. Haggis, the nosy shopper from the market. I'd been positive she was evil, I just hadn't known what sort of evil.

"Of course he wants to hear me. I'm his sister," I shouted, but Sorcha shook her head.

"You see," Sorcha explained, "I have offered our dear Christopher his heart's desire, and he readily accepted. Rest assured, that desire was not for his sister." Sorcha swept her arm to the side, and Olivia melted out of the crowd.

"You bitch!" I shrieked, leaping to my feet and charging at my almost sister-in-law. "You just love ruining Chris's life, don't you? Are you some kind of succubus, or something?"

Olivia shrugged. "Or something. Our queen desires creative minds. It was my task to locate the best and brightest for her, and bring her their essence."

"Queen?" I repeated, my gaze returning to Sorcha. Before my eyes, Sorcha's dark hair transformed into a fiery red, and her blue eyes grew larger, slanting upward at the tips. Her body's feminine curves went from attractive into something altogether decadent. While Sorcha had certainly been striking, the woman that now stood before me was nearly perfect, her unearthly beauty shining so bright she cast the White Lady of Tantallon in shadow.

"Nicnevin," Robert growled, coming to stand beside me. "I had hoped to ne'er again set eyes upon ye terrible form."

"Oh, but surely you missed our games, Robert my dear?" Nicnevin purred. "Truly, while I very much crave the young scholar at my feet, it was your loss that stung me to my core."

"Wait, what?" I said. "I thought you sent Olivia for Chris."

"Yes, I did," Nicnevin allowed. "But when she shared with me how brilliant our Christopher truly is, I just had to see him in the flesh. First, we ruined his career. A simple thing, that. Once that was done, we used your foolish ideas about counting rocks and such to bring him here, to my island."

I blinked, wondering what geology had to do with this nutcase, when the last piece fell into place: my research grant. Every one of my fellow grad students had found it odd that a heretofore unknown grant for furthering the study of supernatural occurrences and their correlation with the surrounding bedrock in the UK had just appeared practically out of thin air. What's more, the grant had also arranged the Spiritual Sights of the UK tour, and rented us the cottage in Fife that had come with a garden chock full of wights. While it seemed that Chris and I had been manipulated by monsters from the get go, it didn't mean that I was going to back down from Nicnevin.

"Why did you let me free Robert?" I demanded.

"I had nothing to do with that," Nicnevin snapped. "You stole my gallowglass all on your own, foul girl. Luckily, your brother's presence in my home more than makes up for his loss." Nicnevin descended the dais, then she knelt beside Chris and ran her fingers through his blond hair. "This one is so free with his affections. Others at my court were beginning to wonder if Robert had been made eunuch, or if he'd perhaps been born *without*."

The nightmare creatures around us laughed and jeered at Robert's expense. He stiffened, but said nothing. Based on my hot cheeks, my face had done an ample job of defending his manhood.

"Is it so?" Nicnevin asked. She rose and peered first at Robert, then at me. "It is! You *have* bedded the frail human wench! My people, my gallowglass has at last found his sword!"

The jeers became a roar, the comments and jibes bandied about at Robert's expense were enough to make me want to crawl underneath the throne. After enduring a few minutes of that torture, Robert said, "Take me, in place o' the boy."

"What?" I demanded, but Robert ignored me while Nicnevin smiled a slow, evil smile.

"Ah, so all is not well between the lovers," she purred. "Robert, if I agree to your bargain, our relationship will need to be somewhat more *complete* than it was before."

"No!" I stood between them, my back to Nicnevin as I faced Robert. "What are you doing? You're finally free of her!"

"Yes, but at what cost?" Robert's pale blue eyes had darkened; he had long ago resigned himself to his fate. "I am long since damned. Young Christopher still has his life spread out afore him. I canna leave him to such a fate wi' the likes o' her." Yeah, that made sense, but my life had stopped making sense a while ago.

"Don't leave me," I said, hot tears slipping down my cheeks. Robert caught my tears with his thumb.

"Would ye trade me for your brother?" he asked.

"There is another way," I insisted. "There is always another way." I wanted them both, my lover and my brother, well and hale, as Robert would say. "There has to be." Robert murmured something, but I didn't pay it any mind, my gaze having landed my reflection on his silver collar. A plan formed in my mind, and I spun to face Nicnevin. "I want Robert's soul back."

Nicnevin arched a perfect red eyebrow, then she jerked her arm. The short silver chain that had been innocently dangling from Robert's collar lengthened by inches and then feet until the end was coiled around Nicnevin's arm, and she dragged Robert toward her by his neck. He landed on his knees before the dais. "You dare challenge me for my gallowglass, child?"

I steeled myself, trying not to betray how much the sight of Robert splayed at her feet disturbed me. "Yes. And, when I win, I will get both Robert *and* Chris."

She laughed, a beautiful sound that penetrated my heart and made it sing. I dropped to my knees and stared up at Nicnevin, the desire to serve her so strong I could taste it. Then she sneered, revealing the layer of tarnish upon her beauty.

"Robert and Chris," I said as I struggled to my feet. "Both of them. Say it."

"You will not be victorious, so I accept your terms," Nicnevin declared, then she pranced up the steps to her throne, and sat upon it with all the pomp of a little girl hosting a tea party. She shifted on her seat, and a puff of fetid dust escaped from the tired velvet cushion. "But let me ask you this, child, how well do you know our Robert?"

"My Robert," I corrected. "And well enough."

"So you know of the many fell deeds, the terrible acts, the horrible things he has done?" Nicnevin pressed. "For if you are to reclaim his soul, you will need to experience all of those acts. Here. Now."

I glanced at Robert, huddled at Nicnevin's feet, my stalwart man that had gone white as a sheet. "What do you mean, here and now?" I demanded.

"He will transform from one creature to the next, each more terrible than the last," Nicnevin explained. "Each creature will represent an aspect of his past deeds."

That didn't sound so unbearable. "And? What am I supposed to do?"

"You must hold on to him throughout each and every transformation," Nicnevin continued. "If you relinquish your hold, if only for a moment, you will lose both your gallowglass and your brother."

"Love, do no' do this," Robert implored. "You are young, with all the goodness o' life yet to be experienced. Leave me here, live your life, and move on from this madness."

"I... I can't." I approached him where he crouched on the dais's steps and put my arms around his neck, staring into his icy blue eyes as I ruffled my fingers through his hair. "I love you."

Robert's eyes widened, then he pressed his forehead against mine. "Karina, me love, ye are more dear to me than I can e'er put into words. I love ye, so much so that me heart may burst." He kissed my forehead. "Forgive me, me dearest love, for the things I have done."

"Forgiven. All of it." I glanced up at Nicnevin, full of unearned courage. With Robert by my side, I felt like I could accomplish anything. "Well? How do we do this?"

"As a token of my endless generosity, I will let you pick the first creature," she declared. "What will it be, foul girl: snake, newt, lion, or stag?"

"Um, newt," I said, mostly because newts were small, and, I imagined, easy to hold, and therefore a good animal to begin with. And there was the fact that I had no idea how I'd hold on to the other three.

Nicnevin's face broke into a grin; maybe a newt hadn't been the wisest choice. The Seelie Queen produced an hourglass the length of her arm, and said, "When I turn this glass over, the transformations will begin. They will continue until the last grain of sand has fallen."

"How long will it take for the hourglass to revert to a zero state?" I asked. I was trying to rattle her with my science speak. It didn't work.

"As long as it takes," she purred.

I nodded, and turned back to Robert. I wrapped my arms around him and kissed him, deeply, hungrily. God only knew if I'd ever get to kiss him again. Then there was fire in my mouth, and I screamed.

SNAKE, NEWT, LION, STAG

When Nicnevin had listed the animals Robert would transform into—snake, newt, lion and stag—I'd assumed that by newt she had meant a small lizard, like the little orange critters I used to find under large-ish stones and rotting logs when I was away at summer camp. My fellow campers and I would carefully scoop them up, giggling as their tiny, cool bodies skittered across our hands.

Robert had not transformed into one of these tiny, harmless creatures. The man that had so tenderly made love to me a few hours ago had become a fire breathing newt, more akin to a mythical dragon than a salamander, and he was breathing fire down my throat.

I screamed again, but no sound emerged. My throat was already charred, my vocal chords having long since turned to ash and flaked away. Robert's hands became claws and his talons ripped into my flesh as he struggled against me. Frantic, I tried breaking our kiss, my fingers slipping across the smooth scales of his back. My hand caught on the bony ridge that followed his spine an instant before I lost my grip on him.

I would not lose him.

I refused to lose him.

He was mine, goddammit.

Newt-Robert took his mouth from mine and craned his neck, and an icy blue eye looked down into mine. Robert's eye. Suddenly, I realized that this was all an illusion, just another one of Nicnevin's games. My throat wasn't a column of ash, it was flesh and blood and bone, and Robert didn't have claws that were slowly shredding my back. He had normal hands with normal fingers, the same fingers that had caressed me so many times before, that would caress me so many times again. We were okay, the two of us were truly okay. Having figured out her trick, I smiled.

Then Robert became a snake.

Have I mentioned that I hate snakes?

Robert lengthened until he was ten or twelve feet from his snout to the tip of his tail, and as big around as my thigh. His smooth, muscular, slippery body kept twisting away from me, and I could hardly hold him. Just as I gripped him securely behind his head, one of Nicnevin's creatures threw some sort of liquid onto us and Robert almost slid out of my arms.

"Not fair!" I shrieked, glaring at Nicnevin. The Seelie Queen was sitting sideways on her throne, her feet dangling over the armrest.

"All is fair in my court," Nicnevin drawled. "Or unfair, depending upon your view of things."

I wrapped my arms and legs around snake, which really only served to make snake-Robert mad. His head reared up, jaws wide and fangs extended. Robert was going to bite me.

If he bit me, his teeth would be sunken into my flesh, and I'd have an easier time holding on to him.

I rolled, wrapping the snake's length around my torso, clutching him behind his head. Furious, Robert reared up and buried his fangs into the curve where my shoulder met my neck. The venom burned with the heat of a thousand fires as it entered my bloodstream, setting my nervous system on fire. The edges of my vision went black and spotty, and I wondered if that venom would be the end of me. I heard Nicnevin laugh, and the snake became a stag.

My hands, which had been clasped around the snake's body, now clutched the stag's foreleg. Stag-Robert kicked, so I grabbed handfuls of his short, wiry fur, pulling my way almost to his belly. Then he bucked, trying to fling me forward; I wondered if he meant to impale me with his antlers. I grabbed his foreleg above the knee, pulling him off balance and down to the dusty floor. Once he was down, I scrambled onto his back, and grabbed him by the antlers.

"You're not getting rid of me that easily," I panted. "I'm not leaving this place without you."

The stag screamed as I pulled his head back, then it became a roar. Just as I was wishing that stags had easy to hold manes like horses, the antlers dissolved in my hands, and the bony tissue transformed into a mane. Robert had become a lion.

The big cat tossed his head, and I fell forward over his shoulders, but I retained my hold on his mane. I grabbed his paw, trying to still him, only to have lion-Robert swipe at me with the other.

"Robert, why are you fighting me?" I pleaded. "Can't you just hold still?"

"He is reliving the fell deeds of his past," Nicnevin offered, as if I hadn't already known that. "I imagine that those memories are quite upsetting."

Lion-Robert swiped again, scoring my cheek with his claws. I cried out, but I didn't loosen my grip. He struck me again, this time dragging his claws across my back. Frustrated, I smacked his nose. That was not the smartest thing to do to a lion. Robert bit my shoulder, snarling and tearing the flesh from my bones.

"Bite me all you want, you bastard," I growled. "I'm gonna remember this."

Then, he was gone.

I blinked, wondering if I'd somehow failed, when I opened my hand. In it was an ordinary lump of coal.

Was Robert the coal?

Nicnevin hadn't mentioned coal. But then, she's a liar.

Does this mean I've won?

No, it didn't. Before my eyes, the coal began to glow red hot.

I screamed, the coal's heat being even hotter than that of the newt's, the burning pain worse than the snake's venom or the lion's claws, but I didn't let go. I fell to my knees and doubled over, clutching the coal to my breast.

"Not letting go, not letting go," I murmured. "Robert, I'm not letting go of you." I fell to my side, the intense heat sapping my strength. I closed my eyes, not remotely resigned to my fate but unable to alter it. Even though I could hardly think for the agony, one coherent thought formed in my mind: Nicnevin had won.

I'd lost both Robert and my brother. I was alone.

"Enough!"

My eyes tracked the voice, and I saw a man striding toward me and my lump of superheated coal. He was tall and lean, with a fall of dark hair that swept across his shoulders, and deep green eyes. He wore a long leather cape with no shirt beneath, a gold torque, brown leather leggings, and an antlered headdress. Even though I'd never seen him before, I knew that he was the Seelie King, Fionnlagh himself.

"Nicnevin, the girl has proven herself many times over," Fionnlagh boomed. "Cease your petty games and grant the mortals their freedom."

"But I saw him first," Nicnevin pouted.

"You forget who holds the true power here." Fionnlagh turned to me, and held out a silver chalice filled some sort of shimmery liquid that reminded me of mercury. "Here, child, pour this onto the coal."

"I can't let go," I said around gritted teeth; the coal was so hot I was about to pass out from the pain. "If I let go, I'll lose him and my brother."

Fionnlagh smiled. "Perhaps I shall assist you in your trial." The Seelie King tipped the chalice forward, the cool liquid hissing as it made contact with the red coal and my blackened flesh. Then, the coal vanished from my hands.

"You tricked me!" I shouted at Fionnlagh. My pain was gone, just as Robert was, and I rose onto my knees. "He's gone! After all we went through, he's gone!"

"Turn around, girl," the Seelie King ordered.

I did as Fionnlagh said, and looked over my shoulder. There was a naked man lying on the floor behind me, his skin covered in ashes and wounds; some of the wounds were burns, some were punctures, and yet others were terrible slices in his flesh. Most notably, there was a length of snakeskin wound around his ankle.

"Robert," I whispered. I crawled to him, and cupped his face in my palms. "Robert, wake up. Please, wake up. Wake up for me."

Robert didn't move for such a long time, so long that I feared he was gone. Then he blinked, his icy blue eyes the most welcome sight I'd ever seen. After a moment he coughed, and blinked some more. I waited as he rolled onto his side and spat. "Did we win?" he croaked, rolling back to face me.

I moved to lay my body alongside his and stroked my fingertips along his neck, which was now free of the silver collar that had bound him to this terrible place. "We did."

He smiled. "If anyone could best Nicnevin at her worst, o' course 'twould be ye, Karina me love."

I grinned. "You know it."

I stood, helping Robert to his feet. I looked toward the dais, and saw that Chris was awake and sitting up, blinking as he took in the scene before him. His eyes settled on me and Robert, his gaze darting between my wounds and Robert's nakedness.

"What," Chris began, then his gaze moved around the room, ultimately settling on the creature that had called herself Olivia. "And now, I shall believe in unicorns," he muttered. Turning his gaze back to Robert and me, he asked, "Is this hell?"

"Near enough," Robert replied. He turned, and gave his full attention to the Seelie King. "My lord, on behalf of meself and my beloved, and my beloved's brother, I thank ye for your most generous boon."

"Naught but a trifle," Fionnlagh demurred. "You have served Elphame well these last three centuries, Robert of Aberfoyle. The least I could do was end your beloved's torment."

Robert nodded, then asked, "What is the price of your assistance, my lord?"

"You will remain a gallowglass," Fionnlagh replied. "My gallowglass. Should I have need of your services, I will summon you."

"Aye, and I shall serve ye as ye see fit, my lord," Robert replied. As he spoke, the padded leather armor and chain mail that Robert had been wearing when I'd freed him from the Minister's Pine atop Doon Hill materialized around him, along with his claymore and shield. "Aught else I must do?"

"Yes. Stay away from Nicnevin. Far, far away." Fionnlagh turned, and speared Nicnevin with his cold gaze. "I have grown weary of your dalliances with mortal men. Stray from my bed no longer, wife."

Nicnevin smiled sweetly, deadly. "I will remain as true to you as you are to me, husband."

While the fairy royalty glared at each other, Chris got to his feet and joined Robert and I. "I think now is a good time for us to be going," he said. He spared a last, longing look at Olivia, then he turned away.

"I could no' agree more," Robert said. He took my hand, and turned his back on the unhappily married pair and the rest of the fairy court. "Karina me love, I shall take ye away from this place."

I laced my fingers with Robert's, then I hooked my other arm around Chris's elbow as we left the Seelie Court. God willing, we'd never see it again.

REPARATIONS

As it turned out, the Seelie King's assistance hadn't ended with the breaking of Nicnevin's curse.

When the three of us finally returned to the cottage, we were greeted by a pile of paperwork heaped upon the kitchen table. First and foremost, there was a Scottish birth certificate for Robert, which listed him as only thirty years old, two years younger than Chris. Next to the birth certificate was a US passport, citizenship papers for both the US and the UK, and various other credentials, including diplomas from St. Andrews and the University of Edinburgh. Just as he had been in his first mortal life Robert was once again a scholar, though this time around he had doctorates in literature and philology, but not divinity. I suppose it would have been difficult to explain to my colleagues that my boyfriend was also a preacher.

Fionnlagh's assistance extended beyond Robert's modern identity. Lying next to Robert's diplomas was a letter from Chris's lawyer, advising him that Olivia hadn't appeared at any of the scheduled hearings regarding her plagiarism charges. As a result of her many absences, and her being utterly unreachable by all other means, the judge had thrown the suit out of court. There was also a letter from Chris's publisher, expressing their sincere happiness that the suit was over, and encouraging him to cash the advance payment for his next book as soon as was convenient for him. Would an early summer publication be agreeable?

"This is amazing," I mumbled, staring at the documents before us. "We can actually go on with our lives now. It's like he fixed everything."

"He made reparations," Chris murmured, his eyes scanning the letter from his publisher. He put it down and retrieved another document from the heap on the table. "Reparations for his wife's misdeeds."

"Aye, that he did," Robert murmured, draping an arm around my shoulders. He was still wearing his gallowglass getup, and the chain mail was pretty uncomfortable against my tender, semi-burnt and lacerated flesh. But those pains also meant that Robert was alive and safe and holding me, so I didn't complain. As long as he was with me, I might never complain again.

"My sister, you have real estate," Chris announced.

"What?" I asked. I'd never owned property in my life, even though Chris had often encouraged me to buy my apartment in Queens. "Where?"

Chris handed over a piece of paper. "Right here. You and Robert are now the deeded owners of the cottage we are currently standing in."

I stared at the deed, which listed Robert James Kirk and Karina Siobhan Stewart as the owners of said cottage. I guessed I was keeping the herd of wights, along with my gallowglass. "Does this mean that I live in Scotland now?" I asked, wondering how hard it would be to get a dual citizenship, which also seemed to be the only document Fionnlagh had forgotten.

"Ye live wi' me, love," Robert murmured. "Whether our home is here or across the sea in your America means little to me, so long as ye remain by me side." He tightened his arms around me, and I sighed. Robert was right; from now on, home for me would be in his arms.

"Oh, crap." I wiggled out from under Robert's arm, and powered up my laptop. "If Olivia vanished without a trace, what about my grant money?" I said to Chris and Robert's confused stares. "What if we don't have enough left to get home?"

"Rina, I can pay our way back to the US," Chris said. "I'm a real author again, remember?"

"Yeah, well," I grumbled. "All of my research had better not be gone too."

My fingers flew over the keys, and I pulled up my bank account. The balance in my checking account had remained unchanged, but when I clicked over to savings I gasped so loudly both Robert and Chris rushed to my side.

"What has happened, love?" Robert demanded, while Chris asked, "Is it all gone?"

"Not gone." I angled the screen toward them, and watched Chris's eyes widen, while Robert still looked confused. "I'd say it's all there. There, and then some."

"Three million dollars, US," Chris said, then he looked at Robert. "Looks like you are going to be on the Seelie King's payroll for quite a while."

Robert nodded, his eyes grim. "Aye, that it does."

GALLOWGLASSING AROUND

Later, after we'd all eaten and showered and tried to restore some semblance of normalcy to our unnormal lives, Robert and I cuddled on the couch and watched a romantic comedy. Chris, who was worn out from his many apologies to me and Robert, had gone to bed early, and we were enjoying our alone time.

"Love, I have yet another confession to make," Robert murmured during the end credits.

"Confess away," I said. "Whatever you have to say can't be nearly as bad as when you bit me. Or poisoned me. Or breathed fire down my throat."

Robert scowled. "Do no make light of such a harrowing experience. And," he added, grazing his teeth along my neck, "I rather thought ye liked a wee nibble."

I giggled, completely in love with the sweet, caring man nestled beside me on the couch. "You better get on with this confessing before we get too distracted to talk."

He gave me another nip for good measure, then rose and retrieved his gallowglass armor. From an inner pocket in the leather tunic, he withdrew two corked vials.

"Remember when I told ye about the elixir?" Robert asked, once he'd returned to the couch. I was about to say that of course I remembered, because who could forget about a magic potion that made you live forever, when my eyes widened.

"That's it?" I asked.

"One and the same," he replied. "I imagine that your brother was correct, and that our lord Fionnlagh will be needin' me services for some time yet."

"Oh. I guess that's good." I dropped my gaze, altogether unpleased that Robert was going to remain cover model hot while I got all wrinkly and my hair fell out. How long would it be before Robert grew tired of being with an old woman?

Apparently, my concerns were pretty obvious, because Robert said, "Love, the second bottle is no' for me. 'Tis for you."

"Me?" I squeaked.

"O' course," Robert replied. "Do ye really think I could go on wi' out ye, me sweet, sweet Karina, who broke me free from Nicnevin's curse no' once but twice?" He uncorked the larger of the vials, then his brow furrowed. "Despite that I want ye by me side for all eternity, I will no' force ye to take it. If ye prefer a mortal's life, I will understand. And no, I will ne'er forsake ye o'er a few silver hairs. I am yours until the end o' time, Karina love."

I grabbed the vial from him. "That's right you won't forsake me." I downed the contents in one gulp; it was as sweet and thick as Robert had described. "There is no way I'm going to let you out there, gallowglassing around without me. We don't know what Fionnlagh has planned for you. You'll need someone to watch your back."

Robert smiled, and took the now-empty vial from my hands. He recorked it and set it on the coffee table, and then he gathered me against his chest. "Aye, me love, o' that I surely do."

I hope you enjoyed Karina and Robert's first adventure. You, the reader, make all of this worthwhile.

Reviews matter! Please tell the world what you thought about Karina and Robert's adventures Thank you so much!

The next book, Walker, is available now. Keep scrolling for a sneak peek!

WALKER-CHAPTER ONE

"What is that?" I asked.

"I've no notion, love," Robert replied. When the warrior who'd spent three hundred years in fairyland didn't know what the supernatural creature in front of him was, that was bad. Very bad indeed.

"Is it dangerous?" I peeked around Robert's arm for a better look. The creature in question was short, squat, and crouching at the mouth of an alley. Thanks to the deep shadows I couldn't tell what color it was, but it did have lumpy, cracked flesh, reminiscent of a burn victim. Gross.

"These sort o' beasties usually are."

"Maybe it's just hanging around, and we can leave it be." We hadn't come across very many supernatural creatures since we had left Scotland and relocated to New York—specifically, my apartment in Astoria. I didn't know if the steel and concrete infrastructure was holding them at bay or what, but this critter was only the fourth such being Robert and I had encountered in the city. Which meant that it was the only supernatural creature in the city, since Robert had killed the other three.

Before Robert could comment on my rather naïve statement, the creature thrust its hand into the alley's deep shadows. We heard a frightened squeal, then it unhinged its jaw and shoved a live, wiggling rat into its maw. I clamped my hands over my ears, wishing he would just hurry up and swallow the thing so I didn't have to listen to it crunching away.

"It has teeth like one of the *fuath*," I said, remembering the water demons that had hunted us in Scotland. "Could it be an American version?"

"Possibly." Robert held his right arm away from his body, and a moment later his sword—a massive claymore like the ones that had been popular in the Highlands a few centuries ago—appeared in his hand.

"Do you have to kill it?" I asked. "Maybe it just eats rats. We could do with less rats."

Robert gave me a look. "And what o' when its tastes turn to children? How would ye feel if the beastie we let get by us snacked on a wee bairn?"

I made a face, and whined, "We're going to be late."

Robert chuckled, then he leaned down and pecked me on the lips. "Do no' fash, love. 'Twill take but a moment."

"Okay," I grumbled. "Go on. Kill it."

Robert chuckled again, then he stalked toward the creature; the first time Robert had wielded a sword in broad daylight I'd been convinced we would get arrested. I'd had nothing to worry about, since the average New Yorker was far too jaded to find a sword interesting or unusual. Since this altercation was happening after dark, I only worried about Robert ending up on social media.

The monster was engrossed in its rodent snack, and didn't notice the man with the sword until said blade was crashing down on its head.

"Don't let the blood get on you," I yelled as the creature's head bounced onto the sidewalk.

Robert looked over his shoulder, the corner of his mouth curled up. "The Karina of a few months ago would ha' been in a terror over such an act," he said. "Now your only concern is that I keep tidy."

"Oh, hush." I helped Robert hide the body under some trash bags that had already been in the alley, then I gave him a once-over as he wiped his sword clean. "Are there any more?"

"There does no' seem to be," he replied, as his sword vanished to wherever it went when it wasn't slicing and dicing evil creatures.

"Good," I said, looping my arm with his. "I can't wait to get to the party."

Need to know what happens next? Find Walker at your favorite retailer here: https://books2read.com/walker-gallowglass2

GLOSSARY

Alchemy [**al**-*kuh*-mee] – a form of chemistry and speculative philosophy concerned with discovering methods for transmuting baser metals into gold, finding a universal solvent, and an elixir of life.

Christopher Stewart – an Elizabethan scholar and bestselling author who resides in Manhattan, and older brother of Karina.

Dob's Linn – a site near Moffat, Scotland. It is the location of the Global Boundary Stratotype Section and Point which marks the boundary between the Ordovician and Silurian periods.

Doon Hill – a hill near Aberfoyle, Scotland that some believe to be a gateway to Elphame. Some believe that Robert Kirk is still imprisoned in the Minister's Pine at the crest of the hill.

Elphame [**el**-faym] – Fairlyand; abode of the fairies.

Fairy ointment – an ointment applied to a mortal's eyes that allows them to see fairies in their true form.

Fash [fæʃ] – to worry, trouble, or bother.

Fath-fidh [fath fee] – a spell to keep things close, yet hidden.

Fionnlagh [**fin**-lay] – the Seelie King.

Fuath [fuə] – malevolent water spirits. Their name literally means "hate" in Gaelic.

Gallowglass [**gal**-oh-glas, -glahs] – a heavily armed mercenary soldier. In Elphame, the gallowglass is the Seelie Queen's assassin.

Glamour [**glam**-er] – an illusion that conceals flaws or distractions.

Good People – a euphemism for fairies.

Habetrot [**hay**-*beh*-trot] – an imp concerned with household chores.

Haver [**hey**-ver] – to equivocate; vacillate.

Karina Stewart – an American geology student traveling in the UK to further her doctoral work. Younger sister of Chris.

Ken [ken] – knowledge, understanding, or cognizance.

Kirk [kurk] – a church.

Leannan sìth [leh-**nan** shee] – a fairy woman who acts as a muse and offers inspiration to an artist in exchange for love and devotion. In time, she siphons off all of the artist's creativity.

Leprechaun [**lep**-*ruh*-kawn, -kon] – an Irish dwarf or sprite employed in making or mending shoes.

Loch [lok] – a lake.

Nemeton [**neh**-*meh*-ton] – places sacred to the old Celtic religion, primarily trees but also including temples and shrines.

Nicnevin [**nik**-*neh*-van] – the Seelie Queen.

Robert Kirk – a minister, Gaelic scholar, and folklorist, best known for writing *The Secret Commonwealth of Elves, Fauns, and Fairies.*

Seelie Court – the home of the light or good fairies.

Sgian dubh [skeen duve] – a small, single-edged blade.

Sorcha – a woman Chris meets in a pub, and proceeds to have a relationship with.

Tantallon Castle – a semi-ruined mid-14th-century fortress in East Lothian, Scotland. It sits atop a promontory opposite the Bass Rock, looking out onto the Firth of Forth.

<u>Teind</u> [tend] – a tribute due to be paid by the fairies to the devil every seven years.

<u>Transmutation Regulations</u> – regulation passed during the Industrial Revolution limiting the practice of alchemy in the US.

<u>Wight</u> [wahyt] – a small, winged fairy commonly found in gardens.

ALSO BY JENNIFER ALLIS PROVOST

The Chronicles of Parthalan, a six volume epic fantasy (and one short story collection)

Heir to the Sun

The Virgin Queen

Rise of the Deva'shi

Pieces of Parthalan: Six All-New Stories From The Land Of Parthalan

Golem

Elfsong

Sunfall

The Copper Legacy, a four book urban fantasy

Copper Girl

Copper Ravens

Copper Veins

Copper Princess

A duology based in the Copper world:

Redemption

Salvation

Poison Garden, an urban fantasy filled with seers, witches, and one seriously hot detective:

Belladonna

Oleander

Bleeding Hearts

Thornapple

Wolfsbane

Mistletoe

Mandrake

Gallowglass, an urban fantasy set in Scotland and New York

Gallowglass

Walker

Homecoming

Winter's Queen, an urban fantasy set in Scotland and Elphame

Touch of Frost

Giant's Daughter

Elphame's Queen

Merrowkin, an urban fantasy set in Ireland above and below

Merrowkin

Death's Door

Manannán's Pearl

Changes, a contemporary romance

Changing Teams

Changing Scenes

Changing Fate

Changing Dates

About the Author

Jennifer Allis Provost is a native New Englander who lives in a sprawling colonial along with her beautiful and precocious twins, a dog that thinks she's a kangaroo, a parrot, a junkyard cat, and a wonderful husband who never forgets to buy ice cream. As a child, she read anything and everything she could get her hands on, including a set of encyclopedias, but fantasy was always her favorite. She spends her days drinking vast amounts of coffee, arguing with her computer, and avoiding any and all domestic behavior.

Find Jenn on the web here: http://authorjenniferallisprovost.com/

For up to the minute sale notifications, follow her on Bookbub here: https://www.bookbub.com/profile/jennifer-allis-provost
    For exclusive content, follow her on Patreon: https://www.patreon.com/jenniferallisprovost/
    Friend her on Facebook: http://www.facebook.com/jennallis
    Follow her on Instagram: @jenniferaprovost
    Happy reading!